"What if it wasn't a lie.

Thom spoke before his rational brain could kick in and stop him. "What if...say, you went out with me a few times, we got to know each other and at the wedding we could say that we were casually dating?"

"What?" Jill blinked at him.

"You need a date to your sister's wedding," he said. "I'm saying, what if it wasn't a lie?"

"Are you willing to do that?" she asked.

"Oh, you mean the misery of taking you out a few times?" he asked with a laugh.

"No, well...maybe." Jill cocked her head to one side, seeming to evaluate him.

"That was a joke," he said. "It wouldn't be misery. I've got Miss Belinda's cabinets to install, but other than that, I have my evenings free."

"I do, too." She smiled then, her face lighting up.

"Look, it's a Valentine's Day wedding," he said. "Miss Belinda is right—I'm painfully single right now. I wouldn't mind something to do to pass the dreaded V-Day."

Dear Reader,

There is something about Amish stories that appeals to me. I like a tight-knit rural community that takes care of each other, people with strong moral fiber and all that amazing food! I make myself hungry when I write, and if I give you a craving for cherry pie, I feel like my work here is done.

If you enjoy this story, I hope you'll leave a review on Amazon, BookBub, Goodreads or wherever you bought the book. I'm incredibly grateful for each and every honest review that my readers leave because it helps me to sell more books and keep these stories coming your way. You're also helping other readers to discover great fiction—and that's a good deed!

If you'd like to see more of me, come by my website at patriciajohns.com and sign up for my monthly newsletter. You can also find me on Facebook, Twitter and Instagram. I love connecting with my readers, and it would be a pleasure to hear from you.

Patricia

HEARTWARMING

Her Amish Country Valentine

———

Patricia Johns

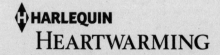

HARLEQUIN
HEARTWARMING

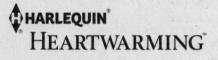

HARLEQUIN®
HEARTWARMING™

ISBN-13: 978-1-335-58490-8

Her Amish Country Valentine

Copyright © 2023 by Patricia Johns

Recycling programs
for this product may
not exist in your area.

For questions and comments about the quality of this book,
please contact us at CustomerService@Harlequin.com.

Harlequin Enterprises ULC
22 Adelaide St. West, 41st Floor
Toronto, Ontario M5H 4E3, Canada
www.Harlequin.com

Printed in U.S.A.

Patricia Johns is a *Publishers Weekly* bestselling author who writes from Alberta, Canada, where she lives with her husband and son. She writes Amish romances that will leave you yearning for a simpler life. You can find her at patriciajohns.com and on social media, where she loves to connect with her readers. Drop by her website and you might find your next read!

Books by Patricia Johns

Harlequin Heartwarming

Amish Country Haven

A Deputy in Amish Country
A Cowboy in Amish Country

The Second Chance Club

Their Mountain Reunion
Mountain Mistletoe Christmas
Rocky Mountain Baby
Snowbound with Her Mountain Cowboy

Home to Eagle's Rest

Her Lawman Protector
Falling for the Cowboy Dad
The Lawman's Baby
Her Triplets' Mistletoe Dad

Love Inspired

Amish Country Matches

The Amish Matchmaking Dilemma

Visit the Author Profile page
at Harlequin.com for more titles.

This book is for my very own valentine. I love you! You're still the best choice I ever made.

CHAPTER ONE

JILL WICKEY WAS looking forward to her sister's Valentine's Day wedding—but she was dreading it in equal measure, too. After two years of planning, it was finally happening.

Jill's sister Elsa and her fiancé Sean had picked Jill up from the airport, and her sister had chattered the entire drive about wedding details. It shouldn't bother her. It *didn't* bother her, she told herself. Her sister was excited about her own wedding—that was both natural and good—and Jill couldn't blame her own irritable mood on her only sister's happiness.

Soon, they arrived at their great-aunt Belinda's place, the *Butternut Amish Bed and Breakfast.* She'd be staying here for the next week and a half. Jill carried her bags up the wooden steps, recently shoveled clear of snow. The bed-and-breakfast was a two-story house, capped with a mantle of snow, a broad, cheery veranda around the front and side, and an attached stable. This was the kind of place that should show well with some nice glossy photos in a brochure, but convincing her Amish great-aunt to do something that splashy would be next to impossible.

The door bounced open before Jill could knock, and their elderly aunt beamed at them from the doorway. She was plump, with pink cheeks and blue eyes that glittered from behind a pair of rimless glasses. Her white hair was pulled back under her white *kapp*, an Amish head covering that sat over a woman's bun. She wore a blue cape dress with a white apron on top, and a brilliant smile to match it all. They stepped into the mudroom—a white room with a sink, some shelves on the wall for boots and shoes, and a short, low bench. The side door sported a paned window that let in a flood of natural light.

"Jill!" Belinda pulled her into a hug that smelled of fresh baking. Then she released her and did the same for Elsa and Sean.

"Thank you for letting me stay with you, Aunty," Jill said.

"As if I'd let you stay anywhere else, dear girl," Belinda said, shutting the door behind them all. "I'm so happy we'll have the time together. I know that Elsa and Sean will be incredibly busy, and you and me can keep each other company and catch up properly."

Jill shot her aunt a smile. Aunt Belinda was a down-to-earth woman who would make this family wedding easier to bear. In a few days, Jill and Elsa's parents would be joining them here, but Belinda was right—for a few days, it would be just the two of them.

"You know, Aunty, I always think the same thing when I see your sign out front," Jill said. "You named the place such a cute, homey name, and we could build on that. Butternut Amish Bed and Breakfast would be a great draw for a lot of people in Philadelphia who just want to get away from the city a bit. My coworkers would flock to a place like this."

"That's my sister for you," Elsa joked. "Always working. I think if she ever actually unplugged, she'd melt."

"Har, har," Jill said, casting her sister a bland smile over her shoulder. "Why shouldn't our aunt benefit from my experience? I certainly benefit from hers."

"Well, your work friends had better not flock," Belinda said. "I only have the three bedrooms. Besides, the house is on Butternut Drive. That's where the name comes from. So you might be giving me a little more credit than my due."

"Very practical." Jill shot her great-aunt a

grin. "But you should make use of my expertise, Aunt Belinda. Advertising is my job."

Advertising was her life lately, truth be told, and it felt like her job followed her everywhere she went. Even her sister's wedding. She'd discovered that a potential client was going to be at this wedding, and she was hoping to use the opportunity to convince Kent Osborne that she was the right one for the job. This was a family affair, but that didn't mean she couldn't give her career a boost at the same time, did it? Mr. Osborne would be out in Danke, and she did happen to have a few mock-ups with her for his campaign...maybe she could sway him in her favor.

"I'm not sure I'd have what your city people want—not really. I don't have electricity," Belinda said, squinting. "And I don't have TV, or radio, or...whatever it is you *Englishers* like so much. Wi-Fi. That's the computer thing, right?"

"Yes, the computer thing." Jill stepped aside, and her sister and Sean went into the kitchen ahead of her. "But if we spin it right—a getaway from the busyness of the city and slipping into a simpler world—there could be big interest in a place like this. A few nicely placed ads in some travel magazines, and—"

"You're here for your sister's wedding, not to work," Belinda replied, moving ahead of her through the mudroom and into the kitchen. "Come on in where it's warm. And don't mind the mess—I'm doing some renovating."

The sound of splintering wood met them, along with a loud *thunk*. Jill rushed forward, her bags still clutched in her hands, and she found her aunt standing by the black wood-stove, and Elsa and Sean by the table, side by side. A tall, tanned man stood next to an old kitchen cupboard on the floor with a crow-bar in his hands. He looked to be in his thir-ties, with dark, curly hair and a fringe of dark lashes that gave his gaze a more direct look than he might intend. He nodded at Jill, then hoisted the broken wood over to a pile in the corner.

A makeshift shelf stood against one wall, the dishes piled there.

"You're renovating?" Jill asked. "Now?"

With a Valentine's Day wedding coming up?

Belinda said, "Thom's putting in new kitchen cupboards for me. He was supposed to come in the spring, but he had an opening early, and I thought the sooner, the better, with those old kitchen cabinets. There was a big storm and my old roof didn't hold up to the leaks, so it has to be done. I've got a flooring man coming in to do the last bedroom in a couple of weeks, too. What can you do when nature has its way?"

"Thom's the best," Sean said. "I'm glad you took my recommendation, Aunt Belinda."

"That would be your truck out front," Jill said, looking back toward the carpenter.

"That's mine." He pressed his lips together in a friendly enough way without actually smiling. "I'm Thom Miller. Miller Carpentry."

"Hi. Jill Wickey."

"I'm using the summer stove on the back porch for now," Belinda continued, "and most of my dishes—except for the few necessities you and I will need—are down in the basement. But I think we'll be fine, Jill. We can sort it out together."

"Oh, someone came by while you were out," Thom said, turning to Belinda and pulling a scrap of paper out of his pocket. "A Nellie King? She said you were helping her with something."

"Yes, Nellie!" Belinda nodded with a smile. "I'm her matchmaker, actually. Her father is looking to pass the farm on to the younger generation, and if Nellie can find a nice farmer to marry who can run the place, her father will leave it to her. Otherwise, he'll leave it to her younger sister who is already married."

Jill and Elsa exchanged a look. Their great-aunt's matchmaking had always been a constant source of interest for them. Amish ways were just different, and in a lot of ways staying at the B&B was like stepping into another world.

"A younger sister jumping the line to inherit because she got married?" Elsa sounded just the tiniest bit smug.

"Hardly fair," Jill replied. "She could run that farm with a band of girlfriends, if she really wanted to. I don't see how a husband makes the farm any more profitable."

"A husband means children, and children inherit that land after her," Belinda said. "Profitability matters, but inheritances are a higher priority still. Her father is trying to keep that land in the family."

It irritated Jill all the same, but arguing Amish ways with her great-aunt wasn't going to change how things worked here. And maybe the Amish had a more practical solution to these things.

"You're a matchmaker, Miss Belinda?" Thom spoke up.

"Just Belinda, Thom."

"Sorry, ma'am, I don't think I can do that," Thom said with a small smile. "If I can't call you Mrs. Wickey, then it's going to be Miss Belinda. I just can't do differently. My own elders would roll in their graves."

"Oh, Thom," Belinda said with a chuckle. The Amish didn't use the terms Mr. and Mrs., but Jill understood the discomfort there. It was one of the culture clashes between the Amish and *Englishers*—or the English-speaking Americans who surrounded them.

"I didn't know you were a matchmaker," he said, and he glanced at Sean and Elsa. "You didn't mention that."

"Well, if you aren't Amish, it won't do much for you," Elsa said with a chuckle. "Amish women marry Amish men, period. But I could set you up, Thom."

"No, no," Thom said with a laugh. "I'm fine. Thanks, though."

"I have been a matchmaker for decades," Belinda said. "It's not the sort of thing we advertise, though. The people who need to know, know."

"That's Amish advertising for you," Jill joked.

"You don't exactly put out a sign for services like mine," Belinda said. "'Quality Amish Matchmaking. Apply within.'"

Jill laughed. "You have a point, Aunty."

"If Jill here would come to the Amish, I could have her married in a month," Belinda added.

"I'm a bigger pain in the neck than you think," Jill joked back. "I wouldn't count on it."

"Neither would I," Elsa laughed. "She's known about this wedding for two years and hasn't filled out her RSVP card yet. I still don't know if she's got a plus-one."

Jill shot her sister an annoyed look. Elsa knew there was no *plus-one*. Everyone knew it. She'd been incredibly single ever since her sister announced her engagement.

"I already have someone in mind for Jill," Belinda said with a wink.

"Oh?" Jill said with a wry smile.

"We'll get to that later. All in good time." It was Belinda's turn to look smug.

"So you're going to…arrange a marriage for this woman?" Thom interjected, not to be derailed from his original curiosity.

"If all goes well, yes." Belinda took off her thick shawl and headed back to the mudroom to hang it up.

"You know how I was talking about the monogrammed handkerchiefs for the groomsmen?" Elsa said, turning to Jill.

"Uh-huh."

"I picked them up before we went to the airport, and they're perfect! They're just gorgeous. Men like that sort of thing, don't they?"

"Sure." Did they? Jill looked over at Sean and Thom. They were the experts here.

"Yeah, sure," Sean said, and Thom nodded along, although more noncommittal. It didn't matter at this point. The gifts were purchased.

Elsa was the perfectly domestic sister—the one who knitted her own scarves and mittens and looked like a cute little chipmunk when wearing them. She cooked like a pro, found places that would embroider handkerchiefs at short notice, and she was the first one to get married—which counted for a whole lot with their mother.

"I got one made for Sean as well. Instead of his initials, I put The Dube. It's our little joke," Elsa said with a laugh. Her fiancé's last name was Dubencheski. "Right, honey?"

"Yeah, sure is." Sean looked down at Elsa fondly.

"He thinks it's adorable when I imitate his friends," Elsa said, seeming determined to explain her cleverness here. Then she looked up at Sean and gave a cute little wince. "Oh, we should nail down those plus-ones..."

Jill glanced between her sister and Sean.

Sean was the one who knew Kent Osborne—his father's friend, or something like that. It had occurred to her to ask Sean to speak up on her behalf, but that plan ran the risk of undermining her even more. Her work should speak for itself.

"I know you're always so busy with work," Elsa said, turning back to Jill, "and way back when I first sent out the Save the Dates, you said you might bring someone, but it's been months since then, and I thought maybe you had someone special, and…well, I thought I'd check."

Right. Except that Jill was the workaholic who never had time for love—at least that was the way Elsa saw her.

"And I should say I'm going to be downright offended if this is how I find out about some boyfriend!" Elsa said, and she laughed. She turned to Sean and Thom. "The backstory here is that Jill is ridiculously private. Either she never has a man in her life, or she's hiding him. And honestly, I have no idea which way it goes!"

"Hilarious," Jill said. "I'm a busy woman, Elsa." The last serious boyfriend Jill had she'd kept private…and then they'd broken up for some very good reasons before she'd ever told anyone he existed. So in her sister's defense, she certainly appeared to be chronically single. Everyone had their roles here, and they'd be playing them for an audience.

"There's always time for love," Elsa said with a beaming smile. "I made time, didn't I?"

And she'd done it first. Elsa was the success in her personal life, and Jill was the success in her professional life, which was generally thought to be not as important.

"So a plus-one?" Elsa prodded. "Yes? No?"

The assumption was that Jill would come to Elsa's wedding, smile for the pictures, cut a rug with whatever single uncle needed a partner on the dance floor and go home early. And that mental image of how the wedding would very likely go irritated Jill.

"Elsa, not now," Sean murmured, shooting Jill an apologetic look.

What if she did have a date? What if her focus on her career wasn't a detriment to her social life? What if her financial success wasn't a sign of romantic failure like everyone seemed to assume? It was possible for a woman to be both successful in her career and have a romantic life.

"You have those colleagues who could come," Elsa said to her fiancé. "It's important for your work schmoozing. If Jill doesn't have a date—"

Work schmoozing, indeed. As if Jill didn't have her own to do. The mature thing would be to tell the truth and let her sister think whatever she wanted, but somehow when Jill opened her mouth, what came out was, "I do have a date, actually."

"What?" Elsa's smooth, cheery voice was gone, and in its place was surprise. "Seriously?"

"Yes," Jill said. "Thanks for checking in about that."

"Oh. Great. Um, that's really nice," Elsa said. "Who?"

"It's just a casual thing—" Jill inwardly winced. This was a new low. It was a blatant lie, and Jill wasn't the lying kind.

"Oh." Elsa nodded a couple of times. "Seriously? I find out like this?"

"I have a date, not a marriage proposal. I'll tell you stuff when you need to know, kiddo," Jill said, shooting her sister a smile. "Enjoy your wedding prep. You only do this once, right?"

Elsa hated when Jill called her *kiddo*, and Jill knew it. She also didn't care at this point. Her lie was embarrassing, and Jill had only made this worse for herself.

"We should get going," Sean said, slipping a hand around Elsa's waist and tugging her toward the door. "We've got that meeting with the caterer, right?"

"Right." Elsa's earlier cuteness was gone, but she followed her fiancé to the door. "I'll see you later, Jill. Bye for now, Aunt Belinda."

"Goodbye, dear," Belinda said.

"And take good care of my great-aunt's kitchen!" Elsa added, casting Thom a smile.

"Will do." Thom's tone was flat, though, and Jill hated that this whole scene had played out in front of a stranger—a stranger to her, at least.

Jill's gaze slid out the big window toward the road as an Amish buggy passed by, the horse trotting cheerily in the chilly air, breath billowing out in front of it.

As Elsa and Sean left, Jill wondered what it would be like if finding someone to spend her life with was as simple as sitting down with a local matchmaker. But life and love were not that simple. Jill wasn't Amish, and if she were, she wouldn't have the freedom to pursue the career she loved, either. There was always a price to pay, wasn't there?

Belinda came back into the kitchen. "You two girls always seem like you're in a battle."

"Because we are," Jill said.

Thom turned back to his work, and Jill was glad to be ignored.

"You're sisters," Belinda said, mild reproval in her voice.

"She doesn't care one bit about those extra spots for Sean's colleagues, you know. She just wants to rub in my single status."

"But you have a date," Belinda said, frowning.

"No, I don't," Jill said, keeping her voice low. "I...lied."

"Jill..."

"I know! I feel ridiculous. But I lied. I just wanted to shock her for once." She sighed. "Look, I'm not normally this petty. I'm a bit sensitive about the whole thing. Besides, there's a potential client who's going to be at the wedding, and I've been rather focused on how to try and land his campaign, and that would only strengthen Elsa's view of me."

"Why not take Thom?" Belinda asked.

"What?" Jill asked in surprise.

"Thom, why don't you go with Jill to her sister's wedding?" Belinda said, raising her voice to include him in their conversation.

"That would work nicely. She just told her sister she's got a casual boyfriend who's her date, and it was a bit of a fib, and she needs someone to fill in."

So much for discreetly keeping the cute carpenter out of this.

"Aunty!" Jill said, her cheeks now flaming hot. "Just because he's here and he's male?"

"And because he's very decent, and I like him a lot," Belinda replied. "You want to land that client, you said, right? And if you just come at him at the reception, it will come off wrong. He'll likely think you're romantically interested in him. In this situation having a date would be helpful, would it not?"

"It would be…" she admitted. But her aunt's ability to think through this level of deception was a surprise.

"Thom has a good reputation around Danke with the Amish and English alike. Plus, he's a handsome enough young man, isn't he?" Belinda smiled sweetly in Thom's direction. "What do you say, Thom? You're single, aren't you? Are you free this Valentine's Day Sunday for a wedding?"

THOM CHUCKLED NERVOUSLY. The older woman peered at him expectantly while her niece's face bloomed pink. Sean and Elsa had already driven away. He knew Sean from their school days, and now he knew Elsa through Sean. But he'd never seen Elsa quite like this… Obviously, Elsa and her pretty sister from the city didn't get along so well. Wow.

Thom took his crowbar to the next cabinet and wiggled it underneath the cracking wood. He levered the nails out of the wall one by one with a *creak*, trying to buy himself some time. He hadn't expected this, and he wasn't sure how serious the old woman was. He had his own reasons for being cautious, though.

"Is this you matchmaking, Miss Belinda?" Thom asked, attempting a joke.

"What?" Belinda rolled her eyes. "This is me solving a problem. I'm a problem solver, Thom. I understand a complicated relationship between sisters. I had a sister who drove me crazy for years. She competed with me in baking pies, in knitting blankets, and the only thing that helped us was when she and her husband moved to Florida. So I understand the situation. That's all."

"What's this about her needing a man on her arm?" He couldn't help but chuckle at that one.

"It's a bit complicated," Jill said. "And not your problem. Don't worry about it."

"I'm curious," he said.

"I want to land a client for the advertising agency where I work. It would help me to get a foot up in competing for partner. If I go and make a pitch to the guy at the wedding, it's going to look like I'm stalking him. And as my aunt pointed out, he might think I'm trying to hit on him. But with a date on my arm, I come off as less terrifying." She cast him a wry smile. "But again, this is not your problem."

Thom grimaced as he popped the last of the nails out, then caught the falling cabinet with one hand, swinging it to the ground before it could fall. He put the crowbar down on the counter and turned back to Belinda.

"Of course it isn't his problem," Belinda said. "But a nice meal, a pretty date, dressing up... It might be an enjoyable evening for you, Thom."

"And you want me to—" Thom spread his hands, and when Belinda didn't answer, he continued "—pretend to be her boyfriend for a day? Are you asking me to lie?"

That should put an end to it—the Amish were nothing if not honest. And he was the wrong choice if they wanted a man to play a part. He wasn't capable of it.

"I'm not asking you to do anything!" Jill interjected. "Is anyone listening to me?"

"I'm just asking for a favor, Thom," Belinda said quietly, completely ignoring Jill's interjection.

Oh, she was good! He started to smile, but Belinda met his gaze earnestly. This wasn't a joke. The old woman really did want him to step in and take her rather attractive greatniece to the wedding. And it appeared that neither of them realized he was already invited.

"I'm not good with this sort of thing," he said. "I think that walking into a wedding with a woman and pretending that you are something that you're not is asking for trouble. I'm a simple guy. I believe in telling the truth."

"I like your strong sense of personal ethics," Belinda said thoughtfully. "And I'd never ask you to lie. I was hoping you could just quietly sit next to her... If you were Amish, I'd have you engaged within a month, too, you know."

"Miss Belinda, you're a handful," he said with a chuckle, and he turned toward the next cabinet, but as he did, he caught a glimpse of Jill Wickey standing there, her cheeks ablaze, her brown gaze cast down. She was embarrassed now, and he hadn't liked the way her sister had been needling her. That had been rude and uncalled for.

"It's fine, Aunt Belinda," Jill was saying.

"I'll tell Elsa the next time I talk to her. And maybe it'll be good for me to let go of some pride and let my little sister see that I've got my own vulnerabilities, too. Right? They can use that extra plate for Sean's colleague. He's weirdly connected."

Belinda shook her head. "If you gave me some time, I could introduce you to a local foot doctor who I think you'd like a lot."

"I'm here to support my sister." Jill sounded tired, and she pulled her shoulder-length mahogany hair away from her face. Her phone pinged, and Jill looked down at it. "It's work. Give me a second, okay?"

Thom watched her wander toward the sitting room. Belinda came closer to him.

"I don't mean to put you on the spot," Belinda said. "I apologize if I went too far. But Jill is such a wonderful woman, and her sister does rub her single status in her face rather obnoxiously. Elsa is a sweetheart, but she and Jill have been such opposites all their lives, and truth be told, Elsa has always been a little jealous of Jill's success. Sisterly dynamics can be prickly."

This sounded like a whole lot of family drama that wasn't his business, but all the same, the situation was familiar to him.

"It's okay," Thom said. "Don't worry about it." He moved to the next set of cabinets and wedged his crowbar under the wood.

"Jill is smart," Belinda said softly. "Really smart, you know? She's climbed in her career in advertising because she has a brain that can work wonders. I don't really understand everything that she does, but I'm so proud of her. I hate to see her feeling like this."

"Does she visit often?" Thom asked.

"Once every year or two, I suppose," Belinda said. "She writes me lovely letters, though. She sends me greeting cards that pop up. They're quite something. Let me find one…" Belinda pulled open a kitchen drawer filled with scraps of paper, some pens. She hadn't emptied any of this out yet? He felt a tickle of worry.

Belinda emerged with a card that she opened to reveal a pop-up flower garden. He could see neat handwriting on the bottom. *To Aunt Belinda. Thinking of you, as always! Love, Jill.*

She was intelligent, successful and had a soft spot for her aged great-aunt. And here she was out in Amish Country, about to be embarrassed by her soon-to-be-married younger sister and doing her best to get that new client. Dang. He was starting to wish he could help. But maybe he should think twice before he launched himself into the middle of this.

"Miss Belinda, I'll need you to empty out these drawers in the next day or so," he said. "All of this—" he gestured to the countertop "—is coming out."

"Of course!" she replied. "I'll do it this evening."

He hoped she would. Just then, Jill came back into the kitchen, still typing into her phone, then she pocketed it and looked up.

"Sorry about that," Jill said. "That's the client who we're trying to land. I've got a couple of mock-ups to give to him to hopefully sway him in our direction. I've just let him know that I'm in the area."

Thom leaned against the counter and eyed her for a moment. Her dark hair contrasted with creamy skin, and she had a very coordinated way of dressing. Her plum-colored woolen pants fit perfectly over her slim hips, and the sweater that looked soft enough to touch was lighter, pinker, and somehow pulled it all together. She was intimidating, in a way.

"Are you meeting up with him?" Belinda asked.

"He'll come by here tomorrow and grab the mock-ups I've prepared."

"I'm sure he'll be properly impressed," Belinda said.

But there was tension in Jill's face. There was a crack in the confidence. She needed help.

"What if it wasn't a lie?" Thom said before his rational brain could kick in and stop him. "What if…say, you went out with me a few times, we got to know each other, and when we got to the wedding we could say that we were casually dating?"

"What?" Jill blinked at him.

"You need a date to your sister's wedding," he said. "I'm saying, what if it wasn't a lie?"

"Are you willing to do that?" she asked.

"Oh, you mean the misery of taking you out a few times?" he asked with a laugh.

"No, well…maybe." Jill tucked her fingers into her pocket, then cocked her head to one side, seeming to evaluate him.

"That was a joke," he said. "It wouldn't be misery. I've got Miss Belinda's cabinets to install, but other than that, I do have my evenings free."

"I do, too." She smiled then, her face lighting up.

"Look, it's a Valentine's Day wedding," he said. "Miss Belinda is right—I'm painfully single right now. I wouldn't mind something to do to pass the dreaded V-Day, too."

"And you'd be willing to be my plus-one to the wedding?" she asked.

"Yeah, sure," he said. "But I don't want to walk into that wedding and make a fool of myself in front of your family, either. I live around here. And I'm a stickler for the truth. So let's get to know each other, go out and have a good time, and then if I act as your plus-one, at least we won't be lying to everyone in that room."

"I'd be okay with that. I wouldn't ask you to lie. I have that business connection I want to speak with when I see him. If you'd be willing to stand there and smile, and maybe make yourself scarce if we start talking business…"

"I'd be your little trophy on your arm?" he joked.

"I know how offensive this sounds…"

"No, no, it's fine. How many men have used the right woman on their arm to do the exact same thing?"

"Elsa and Sean will have to believe we're something more," Jill said. "Sean knows this guy."

"You think Sean would ruin this for you?" Thom asked.

"I don't know." She shook her head. "Is this too much to ask?"

Yes, it absolutely was. But what else did he have to do with his Valentine's Day weekend? He might as well overcomplicate his life and distract himself from his own mildly depressing reality.

"It's fine," he said. "Are you free tonight?"

"I am." She met his gaze. "What did you have in mind?"

"I can show you the skating pond, if you like that kind of thing."

"I don't have any skates," she said.

"I have several pairs that I lend to my guests," Belinda said. "I'm sure I have some to fit you. You should get out and have some fun, Jill. A good rest will help your productivity later at work, too. Exercise and fresh air is good for the brain."

Jill cast her aunt a smile. "Getting rid of me?"

"Only for a couple of hours," Belinda said, batting her hand.

"Well…then, yes," Jill said, her warm gaze swinging back to meet his. "That sounds fun."

"Great."

He was on the hook now, and he was feeling a sudden rush of misgiving.

"I shouldn't keep you from your work," Jill said. "It's nice to meet you, Thom."

"See you later on," he said, and he forced a smile. Yes, this was rash, but it was a distraction from Valentine's Day and all the hopes it contained for people already settled into nice, sensible couples.

Jill and Belinda went up the creaking stairs, each carrying one of Jill's bags, their soft voices filtering back to him.

It looked like he had a date for Valentine's Day. Imagine that.

CHAPTER TWO

JILL LOOKED INTO the neat bedroom at the top of the stairs. Inside the attractive little room was a queen-size bed with a big, downy wedding ring-patterned quilt. The theme was certainly appropriate for the upcoming weekend. A white dresser stood against one wall, and a padded armchair was angled up beside the window. Everything smelled faintly of cloves and cinnamon—a cozy scent that had a way of sparking an appetite.

There was a portable battery sitting on the top of the dresser, and Jill was glad to see it. She needed to stay in contact with the office this week.

"For your cell phone charging," Belinda said.

"Very nice addition, Aunt Belinda," Jill said. "How do you charge the charger when it's dead?"

"An *Englisher* neighbor helps me," Belinda said. "It's all completely aboveboard. The bishop has approved it all."

"You think he'd approve Wi-Fi?" Jill joked.

"No." Belinda didn't even crack a smile.

Jill peered out the paned window at Belinda's property and the Amish farm next door. Outside her aunt's stable, she saw an old draft horse and a new addition—a long-eared, rather short, donkey. Or maybe he just looked short next to the draft horse.

"You got a donkey?" Jill said.

"Oh, that's Eeyore," Belinda replied. "An *Englisher* family paid me to board their donkey, and then they realized he was more work than they could handle. So they gave him to me. And now he's mine."

"Eeyore?" Jill asked with a smile. "From *Winnie-the-Pooh*?"

"What?" Belinda frowned. "I don't know what that is, dear. I tried changing his name to Gus, and he refused to respond to a new name. So Eeyore he shall stay. He's a sweet fellow, and he keeps the horse company."

Jill's gaze slid over to the farm next door.

"Do the same old men live next door?" Jill asked. "They were brothers, right?"

"*Yah*, they were brothers. Eli is still there. Josiah passed away last year," Belinda said. "Eli hasn't been the same since."

"Oh, really?" Jill cast her aunt a sympathetic look. "What's he like now?"

"Bothersome," Belinda said, rolling her eyes. "Those two brothers were confirmed bachelors. They had no ability to speak to a woman when they were young enough to attract wives, and they didn't improve with age. Josiah passed away, and Eli—being lonely, I suppose—has been pestering me something fierce."

"Pestering you how?" Jill asked.

"Oh, asking me to mend his shirts, or just coming by to ask about the local gossip." Belinda sighed. "I sewed and darned and mended until my fingers ached in my younger years, and now that I'm old, I have no desire to do that work for my bachelor neighbor. He can learn to sew up his own shirts."

Jill laughed. "So he does it himself now?"

"Well, I've been teaching him how. He brings his shirts over here, and he plunks himself down at my kitchen table and I show him the basics. How that man survived as long as he did without a wife, I'll never know. Josiah must have been the handy one."

"Is he…interested in you, Aunt Belinda?" Jill asked.

"What?" Belinda shook her head. "Hardly. He wants me to take care of him, that's what.

He sees a cook and a seamstress and a maid. And like I said, I'm not interested in that. Not one bit."

"Fair enough," Jill replied.

Outside the window, she saw a small herd of cows munching on a large round bale of hay, and an old Amish man hobbling in their direction with a bucket in one hand. He wore a black felt hat and a dark green coat.

"I'm glad you have a friend next door, all the same," Jill said.

"*Friend* is a stretch," Belinda said with a low laugh. "I have a neighbor I feel obliged to be kind to. That's what I have."

Jill turned to look at her aunt and laughed. "Doesn't he at least keep your life interesting?"

"If you were thinking that somehow he'll make me feel young, you're wrong," Belinda said. "He annoys me."

A buggy turned in the drive, and Jill leaned toward the window to get a better view. A pie-bald horse pulled the black covered buggy, and from what Jill could see, there was a young woman at the reins.

"You've got company," Jill said.

Her aunt joined her at the window. "Oh, Nellie's back. I'm glad. I'm sure I'll find her a good husband. I have a good feeling about this one."

"How will you do that? Do you just tell men that she's got a farm coming to her?" Jill asked.

Belinda looked over at Jill with an amused smile. "What? No, that would be crass. I mean, I do mention it, because time is of the essence, but a marriage is about far more than property. I have to find the right man to run that farm with her. They have to have a spark, a connection. He has to see more than land when he looks at Nellie King, because land isn't going to keep a man warm at night, is it? That's harder."

"You don't think this is wrong? She shouldn't be able to inherit without a husband?" Jill asked.

"What if she wants a husband?" Belinda asked, raising her eyebrows. "Ever consider that?"

Jill nodded. "Good point. I'm all for helping women live their best lives."

Jill wasn't single by choice. She wanted a lifelong partner, it just hadn't happened yet, and she resented being judged for something outside her control, just as much as any other woman would.

Belinda patted Jill's arm affectionately. "Get settled in, dear. I'll be downstairs with Nellie for a few minutes."

Jill turned to unpacking her bags and putting her clothes into the chest of drawers. She hung the dress she intended to wear to the wedding in the closet. It was a simple black dress, meant to avoid notice. Let Elsa have her day, and let Jill melt into the background if at all possible. And if she was lucky, it'd also make her look competent and professional at the same time.

Jill picked up her cell phone and glanced at a few new texts. Two were from work—a meeting had changed locations, and another executive was wondering about a meet and greet that Jill would miss while she was here. And the second text was about Mr. Osborne's ad campaign. They were worried that another firm was going to sign him. He'd been seen having a lunch meeting with their competition. She spent a couple of minutes chatting with the senior partner about their approach, and they finally decided that her being at the wedding was as far as they dared to go. When that was finished, she flicked to the last text waiting.

It was from her mother.

Hi, Jilly. Are you at your great-aunt's place now? Your sister is in a flurry about her bridesmaid outfits—something about one bridesmaid who refuses to wear the right shoes? I don't know.

I was hoping you could check in with her. She needs family support, and I hate that I won't be there until just before the wedding.

Jill sighed and rubbed a hand over her eyes. Shoes? She was in a flurry about shoes? This was why her sister drove her crazy. She texted back: I just saw her and Sean. They were going to see a caterer or something. She seems fine to me!

Her mother replied almost instantaneously: Every wedding needs someone willing to be the toughie and get things done. You know how Elsa is. She can't stand up to this bridesmaid.

That was the way things had always been—Elsa was the gentle one who cooked and baked and did yoga and was forever afraid of making anyone not like her. Jill was the strong one who took care of business. Jill had a hide like a rhino, people said, which hadn't been true, but next to Elsa, she probably looked that way.

I'm not being the toughie this time, Jill texted back. I'm on vacation.

And while she wasn't willing to get into it with her mother, she had bigger problems to worry about. She pocketed her phone. Maybe it was time Elsa learned how to fight a few of her own battles…or just let go of her perfect wedding fantasy. Jill didn't care which one her sister chose, so long as she left Jill out of it.

Downstairs she heard Nellie's and Belinda's voices in the sitting room, right beneath Jill's bedroom. Jill looked outside again, and she saw the horse, still hitched to the wagon, but now with a blanket over his back and a pile of fresh hay in front of him.

Jill did know a little bit of Pennsylvania Dutch. Her grandfather had been Amish, after all, and Jill had always had an affinity for languages. She paused, listening to the voices downstairs.

"You need to know what you want, Nellie," Belinda was saying in English. "This farm is going to make you very popular for a little while, and I think you'd better know exactly what you're looking for so you get the kind of husband you want. Now…what is your wish list in a man?"

"Oh, I don't know…" Nellie said in Pennsylvania Dutch. "Just a nice man."

"Come now," Belinda said, and the rest was a mix between the two languages. "More than that, I'm sure. There are some very nice men who look like goats, or who are old enough to be your father. This is the time to say very clearly what you want."

"I wanted to be chosen by a nice man who wanted to marry me without a farm attached," Nellie said, and Jill's heart went out to the young woman. This farm would draw in some interest, but would it be the right interest?

"Yah, yah." Belinda's tone softened. "I know it's hard for a nice Amish girl like you to do the choosing, but you're in a position to do just that. So let's be practical, shall we? How old is too old?"

In the Amish world, they needed some tough women, too, who were willing to say things like they were. They needed someone who'd defend the plight of young women with property coming to them, and they needed neighbors who refused to do the "women's work" for the man next door. Female strength and fortitude mattered everywhere, and kept the world spinning.

Jill didn't want to listen in any longer as they switched to Pennsylvania Dutch again. It was harder for Jill to follow, muffled through floorboards, and she trusted in Aunt Belinda to fill her in on the details later on. Nellie King's need for a husband pronto was probably the most exciting thing happening around here.

Jill made her way down the stairs, each step creaking in that old familiar way. Thom wasn't in the kitchen. She saw him out the side window, piling broken wood into the back of his truck. Belinda poked her head out of the sitting room.

"Jill, would you come in here a minute?" Belinda asked.

"Um…yeah. Sure."

Nellie King sat, straight-backed and motionless in a rocking chair, her hands clasped in her lap.

"Come in," Belinda said. "Nellie finds herself in a situation she doesn't know how to deal with, and I think a nice, modern *Englisher* young woman like you might have some insights."

Nellie looked, wide-eyed, at Belinda, her gaze pleading for this to stop.

"I don't come from the same background, though," Jill said. "I understand if Nellie would rather stick to Amish advice."

"Some things, like men, are universal," Belinda replied. "Now, you're single, too, Jill. And you've lived long enough to know what you want and what you don't, am I right?"

"I'm thirty this year," Jill said with a smile. "I've come to a few conclusions."

And she'd learned a few lessons the hard way.

"Good." Belinda sat down on the couch and motioned for Jill to join her. "Now, if you were looking for a husband, what would you be looking for?"

"Someone kind," Jill said. "Someone who'd put our relationship ahead of his friends, or his family. Family drama can be just miserable."

"Hmm, yes," Belinda said. "Go on."

"Well…for me, I'm working in advertising, and I'd want someone who valued what I do for a living." Jill noticed Nellie squirming slightly in her seat. None of this applied to this young woman's situation. "And I suppose I'd want someone I thought was handsome."

"Looks aren't the most important thing," Nellie said. "Character is what is supposed to matter."

"Nellie," Jill said, leaning forward. "This is the man you're going to kiss good morning for the rest of your life. He's the one you're going to crawl into bed next to. I agree that he doesn't have to be a GQ model, but you need to at least want that kiss, you know?"

Nellie's cheeks blushed pink. "We don't talk about that."

"But I did notice that you mentioned character," Belinda cut in. "So that's something you want in a man—someone you can trust to be good based on his own determination to be so."

"Yah." Nellie nodded. "Of course. That matters the most. A woman can't follow her husband around to make sure he behaves well. It's got to be part of who he is."

Belinda smiled at Nellie. "Good. We're getting there."

"And he should be a farmer," Nellie went on, seeming to have gathered some bravery now. "Obviously. I also think it's important that he's a kind farmer—that he cares about his animals. And that he likes children."

"Very good!" Belinda's smile broadened.

"And he should…he should…" Nellie glanced toward Jill uncertainly. "He should find me moderately attractive."

"Moderately?" Jill said. "How about, he should find you stunning?"

"Oh, I'm not stunning," Nellie said with a quick shake of her head. "I require a farm to get a man to marry me, so I know exactly how attractive I am on the outside. But I'm a hard worker, and I'm a good cook and I can get a stain out of just about anything. So I have that in my favor."

Jill and Belinda exchanged a look. Nellie didn't see her own beauty. Sometimes the world could be a cruel place, and many a beautiful girl was kept in the dark about her own good looks.

"How come you aren't married?" Nellie asked, turning to Jill. "Thirty is pretty old."

Jill winced. "Ouch."

"Sorry…"

"It's okay. It's not that old for us. But I've been busy, I suppose," Jill said. "And I haven't found the right man yet. It's not quite so easy… is it?"

"And you're very pretty," Nellie said with a sigh. "If you can't find someone, then a girl like me has less hope. You even have a matchmaker in your family."

"But I don't have a farm," Jill said, and reached out and squeezed Nellie's hand. "Besides, I think you're gorgeous. And don't you dare hand that land over to a man who thinks anything less. You've got a choice of cooking for a husband who thinks he's the luckiest man on earth, or for one who takes you for granted. I don't know about you, but I'd choose the first kind."

A smile flickered at Nellie's lips, and she brushed an errant strand of pale blond hair off her forehead. The side door banged, and Jill heard a man's footsteps coming into the house. She guessed it was Thom.

"And don't worry about our Jill," Belinda said. "She does have a matchmaker as her great-aunt, and I've got something in the works for her already."

"You were serious about that?" Jill chuckled.

"The man I'm thinking of is a young foot doctor here in town. He's a few inches shorter than you, but he's got a wonderful practice, and he lives with his mother on the other side of town." Belinda gave her a meaningful nod.

"No, Aunty."

Belinda shrugged innocently. "We'll see how it goes…won't we? If you happened to meet him—say at a family wedding—you could tell me how you like him."

"But Thom is going to be my plus-one," she said.

"Yes, yes, but Thom is just a stand-in. Besides, sometimes men like a bit of competition," Belinda said. "Men, as I keep telling you, are universal." Belinda winked. "Now, Nellie, back to you. I have a few ideas of some good Amish farmers' sons you could meet. There's one particular man from Indiana I'm thinking of…"

At the very least, Jill had a plus-one for the

wedding who could help her sidestep her great-aunt's well-intentioned matchmaking. And when Elsa's wedding was past, Jill was going to breathe a big sigh of relief.

BY THE TIME Thom finished work for the day at the bed-and-breakfast, the sun hung low in the sky. He rolled his tight shoulders and gathered up his tools. He could hear the *clank* of pots and the *thunk* of knives against cutting boards from the summer porch where Belinda and Jill were cooking. Amish women who used wood-stoves had two of them—one inside, and one on the summer cooking porch. No one wanted to be cooking at a woodstove inside in July.

"Thom?" Belinda called from the back porch as Thom pushed open the screen door and stepped outside. He had to walk around the house to see her. The back porch was partially walled in around the stove, and the rest was covered only by screen. The women wore coats, but they seemed warm enough next to the stove where they worked.

"I'm done for the day," Thom said.

"Will you still stay for dinner?" Belinda asked.

"Thanks for the offer, Miss Belinda," Thom said. "But I've got some things to do at home, too. Plus, I don't have my skates with me. I'll be back in an hour or two."

"That makes sense," Belinda replied. "We'll see you later."

Thom looked toward Jill. She was dressed in a pair of jeans now, and she'd pulled her hair back in a ponytail. She still had that city look about her, even with her more casual attire. She didn't fit in here, and he had to wonder how she'd survive a week of outdoor cooking with her aunt while he replaced cabinets. Would she abandon the bed-and-breakfast and head to a hotel? He'd give her another day or two of country living reality—Amish to boot!—and she'd very likely head out to something more comfortable.

"I'll see you in a while," he said.

"You know where to find me." She cast him a smile, and he found himself looking down at his own boots. Darn—she was definitely pretty.

"Well…see you."

Thom tossed his tool bag onto the back of his truck, and then hopped up into the driver's seat. How much trouble had he gotten himself into here? He pulled out of the drive and headed down Butternut Drive toward the main paved road that led back to town. He flicked on the radio, heard someone dedicating a song to his girlfriend, and flicked it back off again. It wasn't that he begrudged anyone their happiness. He was attending Sean and Elsa's wedding, wasn't he? But it was tough when he was settling back into single life again, getting used to being on his own and having the constant reminders of how cozy it was to be in a couple.

He pushed those thoughts aside, and determined to just enjoy the drive. He loved the way the seasons eased past out here in Amish Country, how a sunset could make a simple day of working with his hands feel like fate, and the way the Amish horses trotted down the roads pulling their buggies, reminding him that there was a whole other way to live that just slowed down.

His tools rattled in the back of his pickup truck, and he slowed as he came up behind a black buggy. He signaled, gave it lots of space as he eased around it. He leaned forward to nod at the driver, and the bearded man nodded back and touched the rim of his black felt hat.

This was the kind of life that had settled into his heart—a slower pace, more time to appreciate the nuances, and with any luck at all, a family of his own one of these days. Miss Belinda set up marriages for the Amish folks around here, and while he didn't like the idea of arranged marriages—a woman with land and a farmer to farm it—he did wonder if he was missing some detail about how a guy found the right woman and settled down. He was thirty-two and still hadn't gotten it right. Yet, he had a stubborn streak that balked at the thought of just picking someone and making it official. If there was one thing he'd learned, it was that relationships weren't that easy. They took work, and they required two people who both thought it was worth it—even when it was really hard.

Thom lived in a little bungalow that had been built in the fifties. He'd fixed it up himself, redoing everything from the studs on up, and he was happy with the result. It was small and cozy, but just to his liking with sliding barn doors, open spaces and hardwood floors that he'd polished to a deep cherry glow. He'd gotten a lot of decor ideas from the Amish homes he worked in. He liked their simplicity and how a well-made piece of furniture could become the heart of a whole room.

He parked outside his garage—a separate building, as they'd built them in the fifties— since he wouldn't be home for too long. He grabbed his tool bag out of the back of his vehicle and let himself into the side door of his house. He flicked on the lights as he went inside and deposited his tools on a bench beside the door.

He washed his hands and face and changed his clothes. There was leftover lasagna from last night, and he dished himself up a big square of it to microwave. He was looking forward to tonight. He hadn't been to the skating pond in years, but somehow it had popped into his mind when talking to Jill about exploring the area.

His cell phone rang, and he picked up the call. It was Sean.

"Hey, man," Thom said. "Good to see you today. How's the wedding planning going?"

"Good, good," Sean replied. "Elsa has a list of things for me to finish up, so I'm scrambling. We didn't really get a chance to talk over at Aunt Belinda's. How are you doing?"

"Pretty good. You know me—always working."

"Look, we were talking about it over there, but we really need to solidify the guest numbers for the reception," Sean said. "I've got a couple of managers from work that it might be good for me to invite, you know? I didn't even think of it until now, but there are a few people whose plus-ones have fallen through, and we figured we could use those for those work connections. We've got you down for you and Natasha. I'm pretty sure that's changed, though, right?"

"Yes, yes, that's changed," Thom said. "Sorry about that. I should have told you today. Yeah, it's just me."

"Don't let me guilt you out of using your plus-one, though," Sean said. "If you've got someone you want to bring, it's yours. Friends matter more than schmoozing, right?"

"Of course," Thom said with a laugh. "Understood. But I won't need mine, so feel free to use it on someone else."

They were worried about numbers, not who was accompanying whom. They already knew Jill was attending, so his plus-one might as well be put to good use.

"So…how are you doing since the breakup?" Sean asked.

"Not half as well as you're doing," Thom said, attempting to joke. "Don't worry about me. You should be fully focused on your own happiness right now. It's perfectly okay to be selfish when you're staring down the barrel of your own wedding."

"Yeah, yeah," Sean chuckled. "You know,

I've got a few single cousins who will be at the wedding. I can introduce you. Plus, there's Mae—you know her. I should have linked you two up a long time ago."

"Not necessary," Thom said. "I'm sure I'll stumble across them during the wedding. Again, focus on yourselves, not me! I'm golden, man. Seriously."

"All right. Well, you take care. I'll just update the list to you coming alone, right?"

"Perfect. I'll be there. Looking forward to it."

As Thom hung up, the microwave beeped, and he pulled out his hot plate of lasagna. This was the part that was awkward after a breakup—the pity, and the attempts to throw literally any single woman in his direction. Like Mae, one of Sean's good friends who'd been nursing a crush on the man for as long as Sean had been with Elsa. But they meant well, and Thom knew it. At least he'd have Jill there, and they could endure all that happiness and joy together.

Thom put the kettle on to get some hot chocolate ready in a thermos. It would be cold out there tonight, and he figured she'd like something hot to drink.

He sat down to eat his lasagna, and as he ate,

he opened his laptop and checked his emails. He saw one from his dad.

Hi Thomas, Dad here. Just wanted to say hello. Thought you'd like this funny cat photo thing. It was great to have you home at Christmas, and your mother wants to know if you'll be coming back for Easter. You're getting an Easter basket, either in person, or in the mail. Be warned. I told her that you're a grown man and grown men don't need Easter eggs, but she's feeling nostalgic. She's worried about the quality of your Valentine's Day, too. I told her that grown men didn't get bent out of shape over card company holidays, either.

Anyway, call your mother. She misses you.
Dad

Thom chuckled. True to form, his father had included a forward of a cat meme. His parents were only now discovering the joys of internet cats that couldn't spell. He'd answer his father later on…and then call his mom.

Thom liked his mom's care packages. A few times a year he'd get a recycled Amazon box in the mail from his mother, and it would be filled with little sweet treats, an item or two she'd dug up from the basement from his school days and a little note in his mother's neat handwriting saying she loved him and she hoped he was eating enough.

The truth of the matter was he wanted the kind of romance his parents had. They'd met in high school, were married at nineteen and had proceeded to have four kids pretty much right away. Thom was the youngest. His dad worked in a lumber mill, and his mom was an elementary school teacher, and they'd just gone about the business of loving each other for the next forty years. They'd gotten through a cancer diagnosis for his mom, and a few layoffs for his dad and all the other little ups and downs that came with a life together. And through it all, his mom and dad were a unit. They worked together. They supported each other, and his dad still winked at his mom and insisted on carrying the heavy groceries. His mom still woke up early to make sure she made breakfast just the way her husband liked it. They were happy.

But Thom hadn't met the right woman in high school, and he hadn't been able to just get on with the business of loving someone. The template that his parents' marriage had set up for him was growing more out of reach with every passing year. It got harder as he got older. There was more to lose, and he and whoever he dated were more stuck in their ways. They'd never be "just a couple of kids starting out." That ship had sailed.

Thom glanced at the time on his laptop. He needed to get back to Miss Belinda's place and pick up Jill. He polished off the last of his meal just as the kettle turned off, and he set about doctoring up some powdered hot chocolate mix with extra cream. He rummaged around in his closet until he found his skates, grabbed his coat and a pair of gloves.

Tonight wasn't about figuring out his life. It was about getting some distraction and getting past dreaded Valentine's Day so he could look forward to seeing his family at Easter. Life marched on. He'd figure something out eventually, and maybe he'd even ask Miss Belinda for a tip or two if he got really desperate. But if he wanted to be set up with someone random and available, his friends had proven that they could take care of that easily enough.

Thom flicked off the lights as he headed back to the side door, then he paused and pulled out his phone. Mom was "feeling nostalgic" according to Dad, and he didn't want to leave her hanging. He typed in a quick text: Hi Mom. Just wanted to say hi. I'll call tomorrow. Love you.

It would have to do. He pocketed his phone and headed out the door toward his truck. Time to show Jill some of this Amish Country magic.

CHAPTER THREE

JILL HOPPED UP into the warm truck and stashed her borrowed skates by her feet. Heat pumped into the cab, and it smelled ever so faintly of musk and wood shavings. Thom sat in the driver's seat wearing a winter coat that was half-unzipped, and she could make out a shadow of whiskers across his chin.

"Thanks for doing this," she said, casting Thom a smile. She adjusted the white knitted headband across her head so it covered her ears properly. It was a cold night, and would be colder still out there on the pond.

"My pleasure," he replied.

She buckled up as Thom put the truck into Reverse and pulled around to drive back up to the road.

"So how was your evening so far?" he asked.

"My aunt is determined to set me up with a podiatrist here in town," she said.

"Yeah, she mentioned that," he said with a short laugh.

"She doesn't see the same warning signs I do. He lives with his mother. For the Amish, that would be perfectly normal for an unmarried guy, even at our age. For the rest of us… well, you get it."

"Is she talking about Dr. Evan Gregorson?" Thom asked.

"You know him?"

"Yeah, I did some work in his office when he opened it," Thom replied with a teasing grin. "He's nice enough… You saying you aren't interested? He's a doctor, after all."

That was Aunt Belinda's argument, too. Dr. G, as she called him, was single for the time being, and someone had to marry him.

"I'm here for a wedding, I'm spending a few days with family and then I'm going back. I know Aunt Belinda means well, but I don't always have to be set up, you know?"

"She can't be as bad as Sean and Elsa," he said with a low laugh, and there was something very familiar in the way he said the names.

"Do you know them well?" Jill asked.

Some color tinged his cheeks, and he sighed. "Yeah, I should probably fess up. I was already invited to the wedding. Sean called me tonight to see if I had a date coming with me. Last we discussed it, I still had a girlfriend."

"Oh…" Jill's heartbeat sped up. "Wait, so… you know my sister?"

"Well, I know Sean mostly," he replied. "We grew up in the same town—Morris, about fifty miles from here. Somehow we both ended up out here, and reconnected. I know your sister through him."

"I probably look pretty foolish right about now," she said, her stomach sinking.

"Why?" He looked over at her.

"I'm the bride's sister, trying to avoid telling her that I'm still single," she said. "That's a story that'll be told later."

"Well, you have the added bonus of having a potential client you want to wrangle in at the same time," he said with a grin. "That's kind of juicy, too."

She grimaced.

"Look, I'm a friend of the groom trying to dodge him setting me up with his single cousins," he said, casting her a smile. "Same boat. I'll keep your secrets if you keep mine."

"If you wanted to be set up with one of those single cousins—" she started.

"No." He shook his head. "I don't. There comes a point when people just heave anyone single in your direction, you know? No thought about what you might have in common, or if they're even your type. Besides, Sean is just feeling that blissfully happy, about-to-get-married guilt about his single buddies. It happens to the best of them—they start trying to make everyone connected to them as happy as they are."

"So are we going to be able to pull this off?" she asked. "Walking into that wedding together, I mean. Since they know both of us…"

"I was wondering the same thing, but you know…they'll all be too busy to ask too many questions, so I don't see why not," he said. "We aren't trying to fool anyone long-term, right? We just want to get through one wedding without all the outpouring of pity over our singleness. You need to sign your client. After which, you can probably dodge all personal questions and focus on your job. And for me, after the wedding I can say that we had a good time and that was the end of it."

"True," she said.

They were heading down the road, past some Amish farms. Cattle stood close to feeders, and a full moon spilled silvery light over the patchwork fields, connected by barbed wire fences that ran like neat stitches across the land. It was like a painting—idyllic, beautiful. The Amish farmhouses were lit up with that soft yellow kerosene light, but they were so far from each other. If someone shouted for help, would their neighbors even hear? If someone decided to start robbing Amish homes, who would stop them? There were no phones in the houses to call for help. There were no security systems to blare out a warning. All the silence and solitude could be dangerous, too.

Thom slowed and made another turn onto a road that had two buggies ahead of them, their reflectors shining in the truck's headlights.

"It's going to be busy at the skating pond," Thom said. "A nice night like this, the Amish young people come out in droves."

Thom stayed behind the buggies and slowed to a crawl. Jill could see the pond ahead—the expanse of white ice, some lanterns set up on stumps around the edge, and when they got past a copse of snow-covered firs, she spotted the skaters. Two young Amish men were pushing snow shovels across the surface, and some Amish women in dresses skated together holding hands. One fell and her laugh surfed the winter air. The skaters circled back around and picked her up. Jill leaned forward, looking a little more closely. The one who fell— was that Nellie?

The two buggies ahead of them pulled into a parking area in front of the pond, and then Thom pulled in to the side, the big truck tires crunching over snow until he came to a stop a respectful distance from the horses.

"It's like a Norman Rockwell painting, isn't it?" she said.

"Yeah, a bit," he agreed. "It's a nice life out here."

"I meant...it's idyllic on the surface," she said. "Country living is more work than most city dwellers realize."

"Yeah," he agreed. "But it's worth it."

"It's a great vacation spot, that's for sure," she murmured.

He gave her a veiled look, then pushed open his door. "Let's get our skates on."

Jill got out of the truck and grabbed her skates. She slammed the door behind her and followed Thom out to a bench. She saw several pairs of black boots lined up behind the bench as she took a seat next to Thom. She pulled out her cell phone and looked to see if she had service out here. She did. She had two bars—that was something. She pocketed it again.

"When's the last time you skated?" Thom asked.

"It's been a few years," she said. She stepped

out of her first boot and into the skate. "But I can hold my own. I'm Pennsylvania born and raised, after all."

"Did you grow up around here, near your aunt?" he asked.

"Great-aunt. My dad's side of the family, and no, I was raised in Pittsburgh," she said. "My branch of the family tree left the Amish life. My grandfather on my dad's side, Aunt Belinda's brother, left for the city when he was a young man. But he kept in contact with his family. He wasn't baptized yet when he left, so he was able to do that. Aunt Belinda was my dad's favorite aunt, and I used to write letters to her as a little girl. We've stayed close."

"How did Sean meet your sister?" he asked.

"Online." She grinned. "The modern matchmaker."

That was a possible direction to take for the Osborne campaign for their online dating site—matchmaking with an almost human touch. She could work with that.

"It's a little different for the Amish woman with the farm, though, isn't it?" he said. "Don't get me wrong. I'm not against people using whatever they can to find love, but a woman marrying a guy to inherit land? And that guy marrying her in order to get a farm? That feels…like taking advantage somewhere. It's too much about money."

"I know." She shrugged. "But my aunt pointed out that Nellie wants to get married. And she wants her family farm. What should she do, not even try?"

"Maybe I'm saying Nellie should be incredibly careful. I mean, there are bad men out there who'd do a lot to get their hands on a fully paid farm. That's worth a lot, you know. Especially out here where farmland isn't so readily available anymore."

Jill stood up on her skates, the blades buried in the snow to keep her stable. "True, but they're Amish. Nellie will know all these potential suitors…or they will be known in their communities. That's where Aunt Belinda comes in. She's the one to make sure the guy is on the up and up."

Thom finished tying his laces and rose to his feet next to her. "Amish people aren't immune to human foibles, though. It's risky."

They made their way toward the ice. Thom wasn't wrong, and she had the same sense of misgiving when it came to a rather sheltered woman looking for an arranged marriage. Jill had encountered one unprincipled man in her romantic life. It had a way of crushing a woman's spirit, even though she knew he was the one in the wrong.

"I talked with Nellie and my aunt, and I think her confidence has taken a hit somewhere, because she's incredibly shy and was afraid to ask for anything in a husband. That's kind of dangerous."

"Incredibly," he said.

"I told her to find a guy who thinks he's the luckiest man in the world to be with her."

"And if that gem of a guy isn't presently available?" Thom met her gaze.

Jill sucked in a breath. "Let's hope he is. But Aunt Belinda isn't selling her off. Nellie is the one with all the power here. She gets to be picky. Here's hoping she figures out how to do that."

They made their way down to the pond's edge to a snow-dusted space with skate marks gauged into the ice. Jill took her first step past the marked ice and pushed off onto the glistening surface. Beyond her the Amish women were laughing and skating fast in a circle around the pond. The two young men seemed to know Thom, because they waved at him. Jill circled around as Thom came onto the ice. He skated up to her and swished to a stop at her side.

"You know them?" she asked.

"Yeah, we worked a job together a couple of years ago," he said.

"What kind of job?" she asked.

"Rebuilding a farmhouse that burned down. The whole town pulled together." He started to skate and looked over his shoulder, waiting for her to catch up. He seemed like a really decent man, she had to admit.

"Have you been out here before?" Thom asked as she reached his side.

"Not for skating," she said. "I used to visit Aunt Belinda during the summer. I did come out here to fish with her once."

"Then you've missed out." He held out a gloved hand, and she hesitated a moment, then reached for it. He took her hand in his, and with a powerful push, they were off. Cold wind whisked past her face, and she caught up to him with a few strokes of her own. As they came around the edge of the smooth ice, she looked out at the snow-covered trees beyond them, glistening in moonlight. Kerosene lamplight shone warmly from the far edge of the pond as she and Thom whisked past the two young men with the snow shovels.

"Hello!" Thom called to them on his way

past, and Jill looked back to see them leaning on their shovels.

The women ahead of them slowed down and glided out of the way as Jill and Thom skated past. Nellie looked up, spotted Jill and smiled. But then they were past and making another loop of the pond in the brisk night air.

Another buggy had pulled up to the parking area, and Jill could hear the chatter of children's voices before she spotted them running to the bench, skates bouncing over their shoulders. Jill and Thom came around the pond again, swooping in closer to the shore as an Amish woman came after the children, a thick shawl wrapped around her. She was calling out instructions to the children in Pennsylvania Dutch, but all that Jill could make out from the rapid speech was "Hurry up, come on! Hurry up!"

As they swept past, Jill looked over her shoulder to see a tall, thin man kneeling down in front of the first child to help him tie his skates while the mother bustled about arranging the boots, shaking out the snow that had gotten inside, still talking in the motherly tone of voice that didn't need translation.

Thom slowed then, and Jill fell in next to him, slowing them down farther. She felt the urge to watch this family from across the pond—the obvious love between them evident in simple gestures.

"That's what everyone's aiming for," Thom said, his voice quiet and deep.

She looked up at him in surprise. "Six kids?"

He grinned, then laughed softly. "Maybe not six, but the family. The kids. The unity... It's what people are trying to buy when they pick up Amish-made goods. It's like some ideal life from the past where hard work honed character at the same time as providing a good life. They want to enjoy a time when a handshake meant something, and homes lasted. They want a taste of that."

"I think you're right," she said. "You should work in marketing with an instinct like that."

"In a boardroom, with flip charts and suits?" he asked, humor in his tone.

"That's where the magic happens," she replied with a laugh. "I have my own little office with a view of the city streets below. It's not like the movies, but I do like the view. The coffee in that conference room is notoriously bad, but there is an undeniable thrill about pulling an advertising plan together and knowing that it'll work."

The next step up was creative director, and

Leila James would be retiring in the next couple of years. A spot would be opening for her to step up into both partner and creative director in one step, and Jill was the most qualified one in the firm right now. It was a good plan.

"You really like it," he said.

"I love it," she replied.

"I like it out here where I can watch all this wholesomeness firsthand," he said. "This is where the real magic is."

"You said everyone wants this kind of family life. Do you, too?" she asked.

Thom looked away then, his gaze moving out across the pond once more. "Of course."

"Should be easy enough to find a local woman who wants what you do," she said.

"You'd think."

He didn't elaborate, and she was afraid to look up at him. Her gloved hand was still in his, and she could feel the strength of his grip. Then Thom gave her a tug and they started skating again, and as the brisk wind blew back her hair, her heart fluttered with the pure joy of whisking across an open pond.

If only this feeling of freedom and hope combined with winter wind and smooth ice could be bottled...or captured in a thirty-second TV commercial slot. Because she needed a way to think about all of this that kept her from feeling too much. Thom was a little too good-looking, and those strong hands of his made her stomach flip. She needed to keep her perspective here, and her professional lens was the only way she knew of doing that.

So Jill wouldn't think of his laughing eyes or the way he drew her over the ice with the powerful strokes of his skates. Instead, she'd think of advertising campaigns—she was good at those, and this time would not be wasted. Jill had one week until her sister's wedding, and she'd best keep her feet—with skates on them or otherwise—firmly on the ground.

THOM DIDN'T HAVE to hold Jill's hand out there on the ice, but he wanted to. They were supposed to be casually dating for a week—holding her hand wasn't too far over the line, was it? But skating with Jill's hand in his was an unexpected pleasure, and they stayed out on the ice another half hour until Thom's feet were numb and his fingertips were chilled through his gloves. Jill's cheeks were cold-reddened, and her eyes sparkled with laughter as he swung her around on the frozen pond, and he delayed going back for hot chocolate longer than he would have if it wasn't for that laugh.

The Amish family with the six kids got onto the pond after a long time of negotiating skates. But once they got onto the ice, even the littlest one who couldn't have been more than three or four was skating around and keeping upright as he clung to his mother's hand. The father started a snap the whip game with the older kids, and he gave Thom a friendly nod as he skated past.

The ice was getting busy now, and when Jill started to slow down and breathe hard, Thom nodded toward the bench.

"You ready for something hot to drink?" he asked.

"That would be great."

He let go of her hand then, and they skated side by side toward the edge of the pond. They reached the bumpy ice by the shore, and Jill slipped. Instinctively, Thom grabbed her, catching her arm and waist. For a moment Jill stayed in his arms as she regained her balance. She felt nice so close to him, smelling faintly of perfume.

He released her once she had her balance again. He had to stop that. She was beautiful and intriguing, but she didn't belong in Danke. That always had been his problem, hadn't it? Not steering clear of obvious red flags. He'd done that with Natasha, and he'd promised himself he'd never do it again.

"Thanks," Jill breathed and sidestepped up the incline toward the bench. Thom sat down on the wooden bench next to her and bent to untie his skates. They both worked on their laces in silence for a moment.

"So what's your story?" Jill asked, slanting a look at him from the corner of her eye as she took off her first skate.

"What do you mean?" he asked.

"You're single, everyone is trying to set you up, you want a family and kids—which pretty much makes you catnip to ninety percent of the single women. But you're on your own. I'm thinking you've got a fresh breakup."

"Okay, you're pretty good at this," he said with a low laugh.

"What happened?" She pulled off her second skate and put her foot into her boot.

Thom pulled off his first skate. How much did he want to say? "Her name is Natasha. We had an immediate chemistry, and we dated for two years. I was serious about her, and I thought she felt the same way, but we wanted different things."

"What things?" Her voice was quiet.

"She was a city girl at heart." He raised his

gaze to meet hers. "She wanted to move to Pittsburgh and live a life out there. I wanted this life—right here. I wanted small community and deep relationships."

"So you broke up?"

He was silent for a moment. "Yeah." There was more to it, but that would suffice.

"I'm sorry," she said.

"It's okay. Breakups happen. But that's why I'm painfully single right now and everyone is feeling sorry for me." He pulled off his second skate and slipped his socked foot into his cold boot. "And the pity can be stifling."

"So you don't want mine added to the mix," she said with a rueful smile.

"I'm drowning in pity," he said with a short laugh. "I don't need more."

"Got it."

Just then, Nellie came up, still in her skates. Her face was cold-reddened, and she rubbed her gloved hands together.

"Hi, Jill," Nellie said with a smile. She looked at Thom from the corner of her eye, but didn't say anything to him. She wouldn't—he was an *Englisher* man, and the fact she'd approach Jill was surprising enough. Amish social circles could be hard to break into, and he'd only managed his own forays into their world because of his expertise in carpentry, and an extra carpenter was never wasted around here.

Thom got up to give Nellie space to sit.

"Want me to take your skates?" he asked Jill.

"Thanks." She passed them over, and he took a minute to get a good grip on the laces before he headed back to the truck, leaving Jill and Nellie to chat without his intrusion.

"Hi, Thom!" one of the Amish men called. It was Mark Yoder, a man in his twenties. He was of middle height, pretty slim, and he had his boots back on, too, skates in one hand.

"Nice night," Thom said.

"*Yah*. Really nice." Mark caught up to him. "I'm just putting my skates back. My feet are freezing."

"Yeah, me, too," Thom said.

Mark fell in beside him and Thom put his skates into the back of the truck and grabbed the thermos of hot chocolate and two plastic travel cups. He turned back to Mark, who still had his skates over his shoulder, and nodded in the direction of the bench. Jill was sitting with Nellie, her white knitted headband glowing in the lamplight. Their heads were tipped together in conversation as the other women skated past. The other young men had joined the skaters, and were skating backward in front of the women, showing off.

"Who is that *Englisher* woman?" Mark asked. "The one Nellie's talking to."

"Her name is Jill Wickey—Belinda Wickey's great-niece," Thom replied. "I'm doing some work in Belinda's kitchen for the next week or so."

"Belinda's great-niece—" Mark nodded a couple of times, and his jaw tensed. "She's a matchmaker. Did you know that?"

"Miss Belinda?" Thom nodded. "Yeah, I just found out. Are you thinking of using her to find a wife, Mark?" He was joking around, but Mark didn't respond like it was a joke. His expression stayed serious.

"No, not me. So you're around the Wickey place, then?"

"Yeah," Thom said, sobering, too.

Mark was coming around to something, but he was having trouble doing it. The younger man chewed on the inside of his cheek.

"Nellie's going to get married one of these days soon," Mark said at last, "and I would never ask you who you saw there talking to Belinda Wickey. That would be an invasion of privacy. But someone's going to marry Nellie. I just wish I knew who."

Mark's gaze moved back toward that bench, and this time Thom recognized the miserable look in the young man's eyes.

"You know, you could put your hat in the ring," Thom said. "So to speak."

"Me?" Mark shook his head. "Nope, I'm not a farmer. I'm a plumber."

"Right. And she needs a farmer. I'm sorry. Maybe you could learn to farm, though."

Mark shot Thom an annoyed look. "I'm not a farmer," he repeated pointedly.

"I know, but if you like Nellie a lot, and—" Thom stopped when Mark looked away. Some *Englisher* guy arguing for it wasn't going to change facts.

"I was working myself up to ask her home from singing," Mark said quietly. That was how the Amish young people dated—went to a social event and then the young men would drive young ladies home.

"Why didn't you do it?" Thom asked.

"I'm two years younger than her. I went to school with her little sister, and I don't think she ever quite saw me as a man, you know?" Mark sighed. "Whatever. It doesn't matter, I guess. She needs a farmer."

"Do you want me to mention anything to

Miss Belinda?" Thom asked. "That's her specialty, right?"

"No!" Mark looked over his shoulder at the other Amish people a few yards off and lowered his voice further. "Don't mention it. I shouldn't have said anything, anyway. Nellie's got a chance to get a farm. She'd be crazy to let that pass. Don't say anything. Please."

"Okay," Thom said.

"I'll see you around," Mark said. They exchanged a nod, and Mark headed over to his buggy where he tossed his skates into the back and then made his way over toward the Amish young people.

Thom rejoined Jill at the bench, and when Nellie saw him, she took her leave, picking her way over the snowy bank to go back out to skate again. Thom sat down on the bench next to Jill and handed her a plastic cup.

"What's going on?" Thom asked.

"Just girl talk." She cast him a mysterious smile as he filled first her cup and then his with steaming hot chocolate.

"Any luck finding herself a farmer?" Thom asked.

"Aunt Belinda will figure something out," she replied, taking a sip. "I think Nellie is scared she'll end up with someone who's a virtual stranger."

He took a sip of hot chocolate. "Yeah, that would be bad."

"It's her chance at getting married and starting that part of her life, though," Jill said. "For Amish girls, they're raised to be wives and mothers, so this is a really big deal for her. It's her chance."

"I'm glad we don't have those kinds of pressures," he said quietly.

"Don't we?" Jill sipped her hot chocolate. "My little sister is getting married, and trust me. I'll have my parents, my uncles and aunts and every other well-meaning relative asking about when I'm going to find someone, too. As if I have control over when that happens, you know? We don't have the same weight put onto our shoulders, but it's still there. For women, at least. You're a man. It's probably easier for you."

"I just had my first single Christmas in a long time," he said. "Couples everywhere. Mistletoe, advertisements to pressure guys into proposing over the holidays... 'All I Want for Christmas is You' playing in every single store imaginable..."

"Right?" Jill looked over at him, a smile

coming to her face. "I love that song when I've got someone, but when I'm single, it stabs, you know?"

"It does." He met her smile. "The holidays are misery when you're single, and every year they seem to start earlier. So I think I can sympathize with Nellie's situation a bit. The world is set up for couples."

"Yeah…" Her voice was soft, and she took another sip of hot chocolate. "Here's hoping she finds someone who really cares for her, though. Because the rest of your life is a long time to live with the wrong person."

"You see that guy over there?" Thom leaned forward and nodded in the direction of Mark, who was sitting on a stump, watching the others skate.

"Yeah?"

"He's in love with her," he said.

"What?" Jill looked over him, eyes wide.

"Be cooler than that!" he said with a laugh. "We're trying to be discreet here. But yeah, he's in love with her. He's two years younger, and he doesn't think she sees him as on her level— like maturity-wise. And he's not a farmer. So he can't help her run that farm."

"What does he do?" she asked.

"He's a plumber. He lives just outside of town. His father owns the dry goods store."

"An Amish plumber?"

"The Amish have pipes," he said. "And he has a wagon that carries all his tools and stuff, and he mostly serves the Amish community, although I have seen his wagon in front of a house or two in town."

"Huh." Jill's gaze moved out to the ice again, and a strand of hair blew in front of her eyes and caught in her long lashes. She brushed it aside, then drained the last of her hot chocolate. "This is really good. What's your secret?"

"Extra cream," he said. "Not milk—cream."

"Decadent," she said with an approving smile. "It's delicious."

"You ready to head back?" he asked.

"Yeah." She handed him the cup. "I should tell my aunt about the plumber."

"Oh—" Thom winced. "I told Mark I wouldn't tell Miss Belinda. So you'll have to be sworn to secrecy."

"What?" She stood up and laughed. "Are you serious?"

"Completely." He waited until she stood, too, and they started back toward the truck together. When they'd gotten far enough away from people, he said, "Sometimes people want a matchmaker, and sometimes they don't. You've got to respect their wishes."

"And if I tell her anyway?" she asked with a teasing sparkle in her eye.

They stopped at the passenger-side door of his vehicle.

"Then you're out of the circle of trust," he said with a laugh. "But seriously, he doesn't want any meddling. If he wants to marry Nellie, let him go talk to her himself. He'll have to convince her to see him as more than a younger guy, and that'll have to be done personally. I think it's more powerful that way, anyway."

"When a man looks a woman in the eye and says he's smitten?" she asked with a small smile.

A chill wind whisked her hair away from her face, and he stifled the urge to tug her in closer. She was the kind of woman who sparked a chemical reaction in him. That wasn't always safe.

"Yeah," he said. "Something like that. It takes a lot more bravery than you think to put yourself out there, lay your heart in front of her and see what she does with it."

"I'm not meaning to minimize that courage," she said, and she looked toward the pond again. "I'm deflecting. Who doesn't want a heart at her feet?"

Whose heart was Jill thinking about now—Mark's on the line with Nellie, or some guy in her own life? Thom watched her for a moment, then pulled open the truck door. She smiled her thanks, and then climbed up into the cab and he firmly closed it behind her. The horses that stood hitched up to the buggies stamped in the cold air. Thom listened to the laughter of the skating children for a moment.

Who didn't want love, indeed? But getting his heart mangled when the woman he loved had to marry someone else... Thom didn't envy poor Mark. He wondered if Mark would put his heart out there, anyway.

That was what men did, even when it was utterly hopeless.

Poor guy.

CHAPTER FOUR

Jill rubbed her hands together in front of the heat vent as the truck rumbled away from the pond. It had been a pleasant evening, she thought as she leaned back in her seat. The laughter and Pennsylvania Dutch chatter was left behind them, but Thom had turned out to be more interesting than she'd expected. He had made a place for himself here in Danke, something that wasn't always easy to do in a place with its own culture.

"So you have quite a few Amish friends," Jill said.

Thom stopped for an intersection and signaled a turn. "Yeah, well, you live somewhere long enough, you get to know people."

"They trust you, though," she said. "It's hard to gain Amish trust. They tend to stick to themselves, unless they're offering a service. That young man—Mark?—he really trusted you with his personal stuff."

"You've got extended family out here," he said. "You're very close to your great-aunt."

"I have more than one great-aunt." She shot him a meaningful look. She had cousins by the wagonload out here, but not many whom she knew personally.

"Oh... Right."

"I'm just saying that really says something about you that the community here trusts you like that," she said.

"So what about the rest of the family?" Thom asked.

"I have cousins—quite a few—but nothing in common with them, you know? And there are aunts and uncles, but our line of the family left the Amish life. It's called going English. Anyway, for the most part, they're polite, but they don't really open up. Not like Aunt Belinda. She's...special."

Aunt Belinda had been the Amish family member who lived an authentic Amish life, but who never had minded the differences of Jill and Elsa's branch of the family. Maybe it was her personality, or that she worked so much with the public, but she'd simply opened her home and her heart, and welcomed Jill and Elsa right in. The Amish family didn't seem keen to get to know Jill, but Elsa had made a bit of headway with them, and it made Jill wonder if she could do the same. Family was family, right?

"Miss Belinda really is special," he agreed.

"As for me, I'm a city girl," she went on. "I work in a big office building. My job consists of social media campaigns, print advertising and TV commercials. I embody everything the Amish world tries to avoid."

"They know what you do in your job?" he asked, glancing at her.

"I don't think so, but I give off the big-city vibe." She smiled faintly.

"Yeah, you do."

What did he see when he looked at her, exactly? She knew she stood out here. She'd grown up cut off from a large section of her father's side of the family, and she and Elsa had felt the disconnect. She knew she had cousins out here that she'd never met, and likely never would unless she pushed the issue. It hadn't seemed worth it before.

Jill shrugged. "It's who I am. It's what I have to offer. I have some great ideas to help grow Aunt Belinda's business. She doesn't want the help, though. Truth is, she doesn't need it. But I still try and offer what I'm good at, anyway."

"Sign of a true workaholic," he said with a teasing grin.

"You might have a point." She leaned back in the seat, enjoying the truck's warmth.

"So what would you do to market the bed-and-breakfast?" he asked. "It doesn't have Wi-Fi. That's a tough sell."

"It's all in how you spin it," she replied. "People hunger for what they don't have. In a busy city, they long for quiet, solitude, some salt of the earth, you know? People in the country long for..." She eyed him. "You live out here. What do you long for?"

"Nothing." He shot her a rueful grin, but she didn't believe him for a second.

"That can't be true."

"I love this life. I have everything I need."

"Everything?" She nudged his arm. "There isn't some picture in your head that you're striving toward? Something, that when you reach it, you'll have arrived?"

He didn't answer, but everyone had something.

"See, that image that you won't speak of right now?" she said. "That's what advertising wants to bottle for you. We try to tap into people's deepest desires."

"That sounds deceptive," he said. "Manip-
ulative."

"It can be," she agreed. "But I do have personal integrity when it comes to my work.
For example, I can see exactly what my aunt's
bed-and-breakfast offers, and I can see how
to portray that to people in the city. It's not a
lie—Butternut Bed and Breakfast does provide an idyllic Amish experience. From the
woodstove to the homemade meals and des-
serts, it's like slipping into the past. And for a
long weekend, it would let busy desk workers
get an actual break. That lack of Wi-Fi can be
seen as the key to a proper rest."

"You need the break, don't you?" he said.

"How did this become about me?" she asked
with a chuckle. "I might, though. I work incredibly hard. I can get work emails at seven
in the morning on a weekend. It never stops."

Not that she really wanted it to. It filled her
downtime. It made those Saturday morning
breakfasts feel less alone when she was kept
company by emails and pleas for her help.

"You're replaceable, you know," he said.

"Is that supposed to comfort me?" She arched
an eyebrow.

"No, I mean, you're dedicating your life—

every spare minute—to a job that can replace you. That's risky."

"Technically," she said quietly, "unless I climb high enough, and then I'm the one calling the shots."

"How close are you to that?" he asked.

She held up a thumb and forefinger half an inch apart.

"Yeah?" He smiled.

"Yeah. It's close. The next promotion will set me up in a very comfortable position. I've worked for this. I wouldn't have worked this hard if it weren't worth it in the end."

"I hope so," he said quietly. "For your sake."

She eyed him silently.

"I'm not criticizing," he added.

Wasn't he, though?

"I get it," she said. "My family sees me the same way. I'm the heartless, ice-blooded career woman. I'm the one who prioritizes all the wrong things. But guess who they come to when they need something fixed? Right here."

"I didn't say that," he replied, softening his tone. "The thing is, I was replaced pretty easily not so long ago. Natasha went out to a job in the city and left me behind. And I'm just as single as you are, so I'm not pointing fingers, I promise."

"She just left?"

"Not exactly. But she applied for the job, interviewed for it and then got it before she told me anything. She wanted me to go with her. She begged me to go with her... And I loved her, but I just couldn't make that leap for her. And she couldn't stay here for me."

"So you broke up," she said.

"Yep."

She sighed. "I'm sorry about Natasha."

He didn't answer right away, and as Jill's gaze trailed out the window, she spotted the green reflection of a deer's eyes in the tree line. The animal didn't move as they swept on past.

"What does your family want you to fix?" Thom asked.

"Right now?" They were passing some Amish acreages, signs standing out front, shining in the moonlight to advertise what the different families sold. Eggs. Milk. Crafts. Honey... "My sister had a bridesmaid who is thwarting her wishes in something. I'm supposed to march in there and put her in her place."

"Why you?" he asked.

"I'm tough and cold, remember?" She looked over at him. "My sister is a people pleaser. My role in the family is the opposite."

"Ah." He nodded. "So what will you do? Go tell the bridesmaid to cooperate?"

"Nope." Jill shrugged. "I'm doing absolutely nothing."

"Really?"

"Really. I think it's high time that Elsa stood up for herself... Either that or let go of her fantasy of the perfect wedding. She likes things just so. Her proposal had to be Instagram worthy. She knew it was coming. Sean gave her a heads-up so she could get her nails and hair done. There was a photographer present to capture her fake surprise."

"Have you been engaged before?" he asked. She shook her head.

"When it happens, you don't want pictures of it?" he asked.

"I won't need pictures of it," she replied. "I'd want the moment to be private and stay that way. Not that it matters. It's not my relationship. It's hers, and she and Sean are really happy together. It doesn't matter if I would do things differently."

She was preaching to herself right now, because it was easy to judge her sister. That had been their problem for years—judging each other for different choices, different paths.

"She drives you crazy," Thom said.

"Yeah." Jill sighed. "And I feel bad about that. She's my sister. I honestly don't begrudge her this happiness. You know her—everyone loves her! She's adorable, sweet, funny..."

He nodded. "Yep."

"So you get it," she said. "It just frustrates me when she can't see me any differently than she always has. I'm not a full person to the family—I'm a role."

"Aren't we all," he said.

They slowed at Butternut Drive and he made the turn.

"Thom, can I ask you something?" she asked.

He slowed again as they approached the snowcapped sign for Butternut Bed and Breakfast. "Sure."

"Why didn't you go with your girlfriend to the city?" she asked.

"We never could agree on it," he replied. "I like a life where I know everyone, and everyone knows me. I like having a business where it's just me—not a whole team. I don't want to manage other carpenters. I want to do the work myself. I liked staying small. And she longed for bigger things than I could offer."

He turned into the drive and pulled up to the house. The golden glow of kerosene light emanated from the kitchen window. A whisper of smoke was visible in the night sky, rising up from the chimney.

"Some people grow in different directions," Thom went on, his voice soft. "Like you and your sister, like me and my brother, like me and Natasha... I've learned that I grow deep, wide. I want to understand myself. I want to understand others, too. I feel happiest and most secure on the ground level, shoulder to shoulder with the likes of Mark Yoder during a barn raising, or chatting with Miss Belinda while I work on her kitchen cabinets. Keep me close to the earth."

And Jill felt most at home on the fifteenth floor of an office building, looking out the window over the traffic below... It was safer up there. It would be safer still when she had that corner office.

"Your perspective would be worth your weight in gold to the advertising community," she said quietly.

"My perspective is not for sale." He met her gaze, and a smile softened the words.

"The best ones aren't." She reached for the door handle.

"Can I ask you something?" he asked.

"Sure."

"What draws you to the city when you could have all this?" he asked.

She glanced around—not much to see past the light from the truck and the house. "Some people feel safer farther from the city. I've got friends who feel like miles from society, they've got less to worry about. And then there are people who feel safer with a crowd on a city street—humanity around them, someone who'd hear them if they yelled for help. I'm the second one."

"You don't worry that the teaming mass of humanity might be the danger?" he asked.

"Not as much as I worry about having no one to help me," she replied.

He nodded. "That's fair."

"Did Natasha ever regret leaving?" she asked.

"Nope."

Jill could see the hurt in his eyes. That woman had done a number on him. But Natasha had asked him to go with her—as a woman Jill could sympathize there. She hadn't just disappeared; he hadn't wanted to go with her.

Jill looked back toward the house again. It was late, and she shouldn't be monopolizing so much of Thom's time. This wasn't a real relationship, after all.

"Well, that's probably enough deep revelations for one night," she said, forcing a smile and hoping to dispel the heavy mood.

"Sure," he said, and there was a smile in his voice.

She'd probably shared too much, and asked him too many questions, too. They were just going to sit together at a wedding, dance a little, smile like they belonged together. They didn't need to understand each other this well, did they?

"Thank you for the evening out," she said. "It was fun...and cold."

"My pleasure," he said. "Go on inside and warm up."

Jill pushed the door open and hopped down. As she shut the door solidly behind her, she glanced back at Thom. He met her gaze through the glass—serious, direct—and she felt her stomach flutter in spite of herself. Was it just a quiet night, some moonlight and a handsome man?

Probably. It was also an upcoming wedding, and while Jill tried to convince herself that she was just fine as she was, she envied her sister's happiness. Elsa had done the impossible—planted herself right in the middle of the Amish family's turf and made a place for herself. She'd done it on her own terms, too, and Jill had to respect that.

Jill headed toward the side door of the house, and it wasn't until she opened the door that the truck started to reverse.

Dang, he was a gentleman, too.

As Jill went into the house, she spotted a pair of men's boots on the mat, and a black felt hat and a woolen winter coat hanging on the peg above them. Her aunt's voice and the deeper, gravelly tones of her visitor stopped as Jill shut the door. Her aunt appeared in the mudroom door.

"How did it go?" Belinda asked.

"It was great. Thanks for letting me borrow the skates." She accepted a rag from her aunt, dried the skate blades and then put them into a cubby above the shoe rack. "You have a guest?"

"Yes, Eli popped by." Belinda widened her eyes slightly as she said it and Jill smiled ruefully in response. Yes, Eli, the neighbor who drove Belinda nuts. Once Jill was out of her own boots and coat, she followed her aunt into the kitchen.

An older man sat at the table, a rumpled pair of pants in front of him and a threaded needle in one hand. He had grizzled gray hair and a shaven face to show the Amish community that he'd never been married, although there was about two days of growth there. And he sported a generous bald spot on the top of his head.

"Hello," Jill said. "I'm Jill Wickey, Belinda's great-niece."

"*Yah, yah*, she was talking about you." He gave her a nod and saluted with the needle. "I'm Eli Lapp."

"Nice to meet you," Jill said. "Doing some mending?"

"*Yah*, a task goes by faster with a bit of company," Eli said, bending to the work again.

"And it's your task to do, Eli, not mine," Belinda said meaningfully.

"Of course." Eli looked up with exaggerated innocence. "By the way, I can oil up your tack in the stable, if you like. I took a peek inside on my way over, and it's looking a little too dry for my liking."

"I can do that myself," Belinda said. "I'm perfectly capable."

Eli shrugged. "Just pointing it out."

Jill couldn't help but smile, and she went to the counter to get herself a muffin from a Tupperware container sitting there. Eli turned his attention back to the pants, and he winced, then sucked on his thumb.

"Use the thimble, Eli," Belinda said.

"It doesn't fit over my thumb!" he retorted. "And the fabric is too thick. I need something to push it."

"Use this—" Belinda handed him a thick piece of leather.

"Ah. Smart." Eli continued his work.

"You really won't help him, huh?" Jill said with a short laugh.

"I am helping him," Belinda replied. "You teach a man to fish, and he can feed himself for life."

"I don't have that much life left on this end of it," Eli said.

"What's left will be lived with dignity, Eli," Belinda said. "You're doing just fine. You're much improved since last time."

Belinda crossed her arms and cocked her head to one side as she looked over Eli's shoulder.

"How long have you been neighbors?" Jill asked.

"Oh, for what…fifty years?" Belinda said.

"Longer," he said. "Fifty-five, I think."

"Yah, yah…" Belinda nodded. "Ernie and I moved here when we got married, and you

and Josiah inherited the farm about three years after."

Jill listened as they discussed years and did the math for how long they'd actually been neighbors.

"Fifty-six years," Belinda concluded.

"Fifty-six…" Eli nodded.

"And you never married, Eli?" Jill asked.

"Nope," he replied with a shrug. "Never did."

"So who did your mending before this?" Jill asked.

"My brother was handier with a needle than I was," Eli replied. "And we had a cousin who used to help us with our mending and things until more recently. Then she moved to Florida to be with her daughter after Josiah passed…"

"And just left you on your own?" Jill asked sympathetically.

"She advised me to marry." Eli didn't raise his eyes, and Belinda pressed her lips together into a thin line.

"Well, Aunt Belinda is a matchmaker," Jill said. "Is she helping you? There must be some widows who would be glad of some companionship."

Eli shrugged. "No luck yet, I'm afraid."

Jill cast her aunt a curious look. How hard had Belinda tried to find a match for old Eli?

He had a farm of his own. There might be a widow with a grown son to help him run it. Belinda tapped Eli's shoulder.

"That should do it. Tie off your thread now."

Eli did as he was told, clipped the thread and then gave his pants a tug, testing his handiwork.

"Good. Thank you, Belinda," he said.

"You're welcome." Belinda headed over to the cupboard and pulled down a couple of plates. "I'll give you some pie before you head back, if you want it."

"I wouldn't turn it down," he replied.

"You should learn to make pie, too, Eli."

"Now, that is where I draw the line, woman!" he quipped. "I will mend my own clothes, cook my own meals and clean up after myself. But I will not ever in my lifetime bake myself a pie! That's a step too far."

Jill chuckled. "Belinda makes wonderful pie."

"*Yah*, she does." He accepted a plate with a slice of apple pie on it from Belinda with a nod of thanks. "Do you have any milk to go with it, by any chance?"

Jill sat down next to the old man and eyed him curiously. "How come you never married?"

"Oh, it happens," Eli replied. "There was a

girl I liked a whole lot. But she married someone else. And over the years there were others
I liked, but for some reason or other it didn't
happen. Then the longer you spend alone, the
more set in your ways you get. My brother and
I sorted out our lives pretty well between us."

"They had a whole litter of piglets in the
house one winter," Belinda said. "And then
there was a calf they kept inside the next winter. The entire place smelled like a barn!"

"It was a short-term solution," Eli said
mildly, taking a big bite of pie.

"They made a whole batch of thistle jam
as a joke and sold it to *Englishers* at a road-
side stand," Belinda added. "And gave us all
a bad name for years! It caused horrible stomach upset."

"Josiah read it was good for arthritis," Eli replied. "And we had so many thistles. It seemed
like a good idea at the time."

"If it wasn't one thing, it was another," Belinda said. "And that is why they never married. No sane woman wanted to take them on!"

"A man gets bored after a while," Eli replied quietly.

"Bored! Bored!" Belinda threw her hands
up. "I did find a match for Josiah one year.
The woman took one look inside that house

and walked away. There was plenty you could have done with your time, Eli. Like clean!"

Eli looked up meekly and took another jaw-cracking bite of pie. "I'm a changed man now," he said, his mouth full. "If you came over to my place for a tea one evening, you'd see for yourself."

"I'm doing nothing of the sort, Eli Lapp," Belinda retorted. "Until I see a pile of garbage as high as your stable outside of your house, it will be nowhere near clean, and I'm not going to mince words with you. What animals do you have in the house now?"

"Three hens," he replied.

"Hens! That isn't sanitary!"

"They're good layers," he replied. "And it's been a cold winter. I lost a hen to the cold last year, and I don't want to do it again."

Belinda smoothed her hands over her apron and sighed. "That is why you're a confirmed bachelor, Eli. You insist upon doing things your own way instead of being normal like everybody else. No woman is ever going to take on a house that's never been properly cleaned and has barnyard animals living inside of it. Mark my words. As a matchmaker, I have to deal with both the ones who are hopeful for a marriage as well as those who are not ready for the blessed union. And you, Eli, are still not ready. Unless you clean yourself up and change your ways."

"I'm seventy-eight," he said. "Is there more pie, Belinda? It is awfully good."

Belinda muttered something under her breath, snatched his plate and stalked back across the kitchen to get him another slice. Eli winked at Jill.

"She likes me," he whispered. "This is just the way she shows it."

"Do you want pie, too, Jill?" Belinda asked, softening her tone. "I'm sorry, dear. I'm not normally this scatterbrained."

"Oh, I'm fine," Jill said. "I have a muffin."

"So what brings you to Danke?" Eli asked as Belinda handed him a plate with another generous slice of pie.

"A wedding," Jill said. "My sister is getting married."

"Oh, how nice!" Eli beamed in Belinda's direction. "I do enjoy weddings. Are you going, Belinda?"

"Of course I'm going," Belinda said. "And it's not an Amish wedding, so there's no room for extras."

"Hmm. So I'm not invited," he replied. "That's

okay. Weddings are very nice, though. I've always enjoyed them."

"You like to eat," Belinda said.

"Of course!" he replied. "Don't you? There's no shame in enjoying wedding food. It's the best cooking I get in a year, unless it's from your table, Belinda."

"I'm going to teach you to bake a pie one of these days, Eli," Belinda said, shaking a finger at him. "If you choose a single existence, then you can very well learn to feed yourself the food you like. No one should feel one bit sorry for you."

"Oh, I do all right," Eli said, and he shot Belinda a smile. "Now, I'm going to take some of your tack home tonight with me, and I'm going to oil it up for you. And I don't want any sass out of you, Belinda. It needs to be done, and I've eaten your pie. So the payment has been had before the work done."

"Sass?" Belinda's eyebrows went up. "Sass?"

"You heard me!" he said, rising to his feet. "I'm going to oil that tack, and that's final."

Belinda pressed her lips together again and glared at Eli as he made his way, sock footed, over to the mudroom. There was the sound of grunting and stamping, and then the old man poked his head back into the kitchen, his coat and hat on.

"As always, it was a pleasure, Belinda. Remind me to tell you about Rebecca Lehmann's second oldest son when I see you next." He cast Jill a sweet smile. "And very nice to meet you... Jill, is it?"

"Yes, Jill. The pleasure was mine, Eli."

He put a hand over his heart, winked and then disappeared again. The door banged shut as he left, and Belinda shook her head.

"Don't encourage him, Jill," Belinda said. "He'll get ideas."

"It's not me he's sweet on, Aunt Belinda," she replied. "He likes you."

"He likes the prospect of a woman to take care of him," Belinda said. "The man is utterly impossible, and I would know. He's been my neighbor for what did we say? Fifty-six years. He's always been a stubborn fool, and now he's a stubborn old fool who's lonely and wants the benefit of a wife after all these long years of hardly caring if he had one. Mark my words—he'd marry any woman who'd take him now, in a heartbeat. And the women in our community know better."

"How hard did you try to match him?" Jill asked.

Belinda's cheeks pinked. "Not as hard as I could have, I admit. The problem is I have to be able to vouch for a bachelor—tell a woman that he'll make an excellent husband. I couldn't do that for Eli. I know him too well, unfortunately. If he wanted a wife, truly, he'd have mended his ways long ago. He's lived his life. He's made his choices. And this is the consequence. I can't change that."

Jill nodded. "I get it."

"How did you enjoy your evening?" Belinda asked, deliberately changing the subject.

"It was fun. I saw Nellie."

"Oh?" Belinda perked up.

"We chatted a little bit."

Belinda nodded. "Now, I am working very hard to find our Nellie King a good match. She's a sweet young woman, and she deserves everything good."

"Being a matchmaker is harder than it looks, isn't it?" Jill asked.

"Definitely," Belinda replied. "It takes a spine of steel to be able to match the wayward hearts of our community. People think it's just introductions, but it's so much more than that. It's a stern lecture when necessary, and it's having the ability to spot a lie when it's told. A good matchmaker is like the mother of her entire community. And sometimes, a mother has to slap some fingers in the process."

Jill smiled. "It's neat to see you in action."

"I do my best, dear," Belinda said.

Jill yawned. "I think I'm going to take a bath and turn in, Aunty."

"You do that," Belinda said with a kind smile. "I'll warm up some milk for you, if you like. You'll sleep like a baby."

Belinda was like a mother…but also a whole lot like a cattle wrangler. Because when Jill saw Aunt Belinda in action, she reminded her of a cowboy at a rodeo, grabbing a steer by the horns. Elsa didn't need Jill to go sort out her bridesmaid. She needed Aunt Belinda!

As Jill made her way up the stairs, she thought of holding Thom's hand as they skated on that frozen pond, and she closed her fingers into a fist, as if she could somehow hold on to the moment. He was handsome, sweet and knew exactly what he wanted. Jill had a pretty good idea of what was good for her, too.

But some people stayed single, not because they'd chosen to be difficult, but because love was difficult. That romantic connection wasn't something that sprang up so easily, and sometimes years could slip by before a person noticed that they'd gotten stuck in their ways.

Sometimes holding out for exactly what you wanted could leave you absolutely sure about yourself, and absolutely solitary, too.

It happened to the best of them.

Maybe that Amish matchmaking—the arrangement of sensible marriages that Thom disliked so much—was worth more than they tended to think. Because finding that kind of relationship on her own hadn't proven easy.

CHAPTER FIVE

THOM'S DRIVE HOME was a thoughtful one. He'd known it would be nice to spend some time with Jill, but he hadn't expected to feel quite so happy after this evening. It had felt a little too much like a first date with a woman he really liked. Like a beginning.

"Don't do that," he muttered to himself.

This was not a date. It was an arrangement to get the two of them through a romantic Valentine's Day wedding when their personal lives were anything but. This was a new friendship, not a new romance. A useful one, too, because everyone had been so bent on feeling sorry for him after his breakup with Natasha that having a date at this wedding would be a relief. They'd both benefit from this.

When Thom got home, he called his mother while he tossed a load of dirty clothes into the washing machine.

She was happy to hear from him, chatted about extended family gossip, including his brother Mike's life at Penn State as the machine sloshed away.

"Mike is working on his book about some mythological brothers," she said. "He's very excited about it. I understood about five minutes of what he was talking about."

Brothers—that was ironic. He and Mike hadn't had a real conversation in about five years.

"What's it about?" Thom asked, suddenly feeling tired.

"They're brothers in Greek and Roman mythology," she said. "Apparently, it depends on who wrote about them, but the story Mike is looking at, there is one brother who is the god who distributes wealth to humanity. That's his gift to people. But he's blind and can't pick and choose who gets it. And the other brother— also a Greek god—is very poor, but his brother doesn't give him any wealth. I suppose because he's blind and can't see who gets it. Anyway, the poor brother works hard and invents the plow to hook up to oxen. So his gift to humanity is one that allows people to make their living. It's interesting, actually."

Brothers at odds—the rich one and the blue-collar worker. It was a tale as old as time, apparently. This was the sort of thing Mike didn't tell Thom about. The last time they'd talked, Mike told him about stocks that were doing well and then had to go after ten minutes.

"And Mike's writing a book about this?" Thom asked.

"Yes, he's just started. There's another professor at the university who's a specialist in African folktales, and apparently, there's some great connections between stories," she said. "They have a publisher already interested in their work. Once it's done, of course."

"You see the irony, don't you?" Thom asked. "Two classes of brothers…"

"Each providing something important," his mother concluded. "Thom, don't you think it's high time you and Mike sat down and sorted this out?"

"Sorted out what, exactly?" Thom asked. "That's the problem! Nothing happened to make this divide. He's disappointed in me. I run my own business, own my own home and that's disappointing to our Ph.D in the family. I'm sick of it. I've got a good life I'm proud of. If he can only hobnob with other academics, then so be it. I'm done trying, Mom."

"He's your brother," she said.

"This is a lecture you should be giving him,

not me. But I don't think it would make much difference."

"Well…" His mother sighed audibly.

"How're Janelle and the kids?" he asked, changing the subject.

"They're fine! The kids are enjoying school. Janelle is really involved in the PTA," his mother replied. "But enough of Mike and Janelle. I was worried about you."

"I'm fine," he said. "I'm working on a kitchen reno right now, so it's keeping me busy and fed."

"You're so good with that, son," his mother said, a smile in her voice. "You have such a sense of how to make things beautiful."

"Thanks, Mom." He chuckled. "You're biased."

"I don't mind if I am," she replied. "But with Valentine's Day coming up, I know you had plans to take Natasha on a trip, and… Sweetie, I just wanted to make sure you're doing okay."

"I'm fine," he repeated.

"Are you?" she pressed. "Natasha called me a few days ago, you know."

He froze. "What? Why?"

"To say hello. I mean, we knew her rather well, and we'd gotten attached to her. And I suppose she felt the same way. She just wanted to say hello. In fact, I wondered if the two of you might be patching things up."

"No, Mom. Sorry. It's been six months," he said. "I'm getting over her."

His mother was silent for a moment. "Okay. I just wondered... Listen, there's a really nice young woman at our church. She's very pretty, and she sings like an angel—"

"Mom!" he laughed. "Stop trying to set me up! I'm fine. I'll figure this out. And don't encourage Natasha, either. That's over. She and I wanted different things, and she found it pretty easy to plan her whole life and not let me in on the details. That was eye opening. Just... let me lick my wounds."

"Sometimes the best way to get over heartbreak is to find love again," she said.

He shut his eyes for a moment. Was it time to pull out his pity-busting news? "Look, Sean Dubencheski is getting married, right? I'm going to be at his wedding. And I've got a date."

"Oh!" His mother's tone brightened. "Who?"

"The bride's sister, actually."

"Well, now...what's her name? What does she do?"

"Never mind all that," he said. "It's very casual. It's just two people going to a wedding together."

"There's nothing casual about going to a wedding with someone!" his mother said. "It's incredibly romantic. Trust me—no woman walks into a wedding with a man without a few designs of her own."

Jill did have designs—just not the kind his mother was thinking of.

"Mom, trust me. This isn't serious, but it is a step in the right direction, okay? I'm fine. I'm taking care of myself. I've even got a date for Valentine's weekend to the wedding. So you can stop worrying about me."

"You do seem to have it in hand," she conceded. "I'm glad to hear it. You remember how much you have to offer, Thomas. You're handsome, kind, hardworking and you're an absolute catch. Don't you sell yourself short."

"You've told me that since I was a teenager," he said.

"It's been true the whole time," she retorted. "Now, I mailed you and your brother each a box today. Yours should get there tomorrow or the day after. I thought you could use something special."

"You're the best, Mom," he said with a smile.

"I love you, Thomas. And your brother says hi."

"Does he really?" he asked.

"Yes, he does really," she said. "I'm serious—you two need to patch this up."

"Hi back to Mike," he replied. "I'll talk to you later."

There was the murmur of his father's voice in the background.

"Oh!" she interjected. "And your father says to check your furnace filter. That's his way of saying he loves you, too."

Thom chuckled. "I'll talk to you guys later."

He hung up the phone and looked down at it for a moment, processing. So Natasha missed his family, at the very least. He shook his head. He'd wondered what he'd say if she ever asked to get back together, but he knew now that he'd never be able to do it. What they'd had was in the past, and he was moving forward. She should do the same.

Ironically, Natasha was the one life choice Mike had fully supported. Mike liked her. Natasha had been like a bridge between the two brothers. But she'd never been one hundred percent on Thom's side. Mike had agreed with Natasha that they should settle in the city.

Thom wondered how that mythological story ended with the brother who invented the plow. What kind of life did he get? A good one? Did the brothers ever unite on anything? He probably shouldn't Google that. He knew enough to know that classical mythology wasn't filled with happy family dynamics.

THE NEXT MORNING was cold and bright, cheery sunlight reflecting off the snow. Aunt Belinda had made a delicious breakfast that included sausages, eggs and a potato casserole that Jill had never had before, but was absolutely delicious.

Thom arrived after the table was cleared, and he waited while Jill and Belinda did the dishes before he took over in the kitchen again. He smiled at Jill as he stepped past her, and she found herself remembering what it felt like to be holding his hand out on the ice.

He was far too good-looking.

"This sink is coming out soon," Thom warned.

"We'll be fine," Belinda said. "Do what you must, Thom."

Things moved at a more leisurely pace out

here, and it was hard for Jill to slow her mind down. Thom got to work in the kitchen, and she answered emails, texted with Leila about the ad campaign for Kent Osborne and still, Jill couldn't quite calm her own nerves.

She even did a little mindfulness exercise on her smart watch, and while she did a few breathing exercises, her mind drove forward without her.

Elsa texted about some seating kerfuffle. Would Jill mind if she and her "secret date" were seated with a different table of family members… Jill didn't care either way.

And then Kent texted to say he was five minutes away. It was the text she'd been waiting for.

"Good," she said.

"What's good?"

She only realized then that she'd spoken aloud, and she smiled sheepishly.

"Remember the client we're trying to land? He'll be here in five minutes for me to give him my mock-ups. I'll feel better once I've had a chance to gauge where he's at, you know?"

Thom nodded. "The one that will make you a shoo-in for the higher position?"

"The very one." She eyed Thom for a moment. "This might be too much to ask, but since you're already signed up to be my fake date, what would you think about making a brief appearance for this? It might make me seem less aggressive. Just me and my boyfriend at a bed-and-breakfast... That's relatable."

"What do you want me to do?" He squinted at her.

"Just wait five minutes, come to the door and wave at me. Stand with me on the step while he pulls out."

"Very Norman Rockwell." He shot her a grin.

She chuckled. "Maybe. I have a feeling it'll soften him up. You have a very wholesome look about you."

"Do I?" He looked down at himself. "Okay, sure. I can stand on the step and act all manly and committed."

"Thanks." She shot him a smile. "I had no idea how much I was missing out on with having a husband or boyfriend on my arm. I should have done this sooner."

"Or you could get a real one." But his tone was joking.

If only it was that easy.

When Jill saw a conservative, tan-colored Mercedes pull into the drive, she put on her woolen coat, picked up her leather art satchel and headed outside into the cold. The car stopped a couple of yards from the step.

"Good morning!" Kent called as he pushed open the driver's-side door. "I'm sorry to intrude on your vacation time."

"No worries," she said. "I'm just glad to have a chance to show you what we're thinking of. I can take you inside, but there are some renovations going on. Or I can just show you out here. Up to you."

She opened her bag and pulled out a folder.

"No, no, I won't take up your time," Kent said. "I'll take a look at these later when I can give them my full attention."

Shoot. That wasn't ideal. She'd hoped to give him a short presentation, but she understood. She handed over the folder and he peeked inside, nodded and tossed it into the car.

"I don't know about you, but I always enjoy a wedding," Kent said. "This is neat that we're connected to the same couple. Small world, isn't it?"

"It really is," she agreed.

"My wife always loves an excuse to get out here to Amish Country, too. Do you come often?"

"As often as I can manage," she said. "This

is my aunt's B&B. So I've got a few connections."

"That's nice. I'll have to bring my wife by here."

The door opened and when Jill turned, it wasn't Thom on the step, but Belinda. Belinda wore a pair of rubber boots, and her shawl was tugged close around her shoulders. She marched out toward the stable, frowning.

"That's my aunt," Jill said.

"Eeyore!" Belinda called. "Eeyore!"

The donkey? Jill turned and looked around. There was no sign of the animal, but the horse was in the corral, munching at a feeder. Thom appeared on the step then, his tool belt gone. He raised one hand in a wave.

"That's Thom," she added.

"Oh. That's great." Kent nodded a couple of times and waved back. "Look, I won't hold you up any longer, but really nice to see you out here in the wild instead of in the office."

"Likewise." She smiled. "I'm sure we'll see you at the wedding."

Kent got back into his car, and Jill went up to the steps and stood next to Thom. He slid an arm around her waist, and her heart skipped a beat at the intimacy of the gesture. She smiled and waved as Kent pulled the car around and headed back up the drive.

"Nicely done," she said when the car disappeared.

"Glad to help." He dropped his hand. "How'd you explain me?"

"I just said you were Thom," she said.

"No juicy backstory?" he joked. "I could be the college sweetheart you reunited with. I could be a blind date that went well. I could be some guy your aunt set you up with! That's almost true…"

"Oh, cut it out," she laughed. "I didn't need to explain anything. You standing there was enough."

For now. Thankfully. It was a good start. Leila, the creative director, would be thrilled.

"So…was that successful?" he asked.

She nodded. "Yes, not too bad. I had hoped to show him the plans myself, but if he looks at them later when he's relaxed, that might be better, anyway."

Jill looked toward the road where the car had disappeared. If they didn't land this client, at least she'd know she did everything she possibly could. Besides, all she needed was to get him to look at her plans. Her mock-ups would speak for themselves.

"WHAT'S HAPPENING OVER THERE?" Thom asked. He watched the old man from next door come out of the stable toward Belinda. Her hands were on her hips, and from her posture, she looked upset. Eli looked defensive. Something seemed to be up.

Jill shrugged. "No idea. Should we go see?"

They headed back down the steps in the direction of the stable, a cold February wind whisking past Thom's shirt. He wished he'd grabbed a coat, but he'd survive.

"I locked up!" Eli was saying. "Do you think I'm new to farmwork?"

"You can say that you made a mistake, Eli," Belinda said. "I can forgive an honest mistake. You know me better than that, after all these years."

Eli shook his head irritably. "I would admit to it if I had. That donkey is smart. I think he let himself out. I didn't let him out last time, and I didn't let him out this time. When he decides to go for a wander, he finds a way."

Thom stopped next to Jill by the wooden fence. There was no reason to put his arm around her again, but he had to admit, he'd enjoyed playing the part of her supportive boyfriend in the background. It was a role he could get used to, if he wasn't careful.

"So the donkey does this from time to time?" Thom asked, raising his voice so that Belinda and Eli could hear him.

"Oh, *yah*," Eli replied. "He escapes every few months. He heads up that mountain." He turned back to Belinda. "I'll go after him, but it would be nice if you stopped blaming me every time this donkey goes for a wander."

"You were in the stable getting the tack to oil, is all," Belinda said.

"And I closed everything up tight behind me," he replied. "I know my work."

Thom let his gaze move over the rocky incline, dotted with evergreen trees and sparse grass. There were a few spots that looked like they might be dense enough to hide a donkey.

"I'll go myself," Belinda said tersely. "He's my donkey, and he comes when I call him."

So now two old people were going to argue about who was going to climb a steep hill in search of a runaway donkey? Yeah, he wasn't going to let that happen.

"I'll go after the donkey," Thom said.

"I'll go with you," Jill said, and she put a hand on Thom's arm. "Thom and I will go after him. I really don't think it's a good idea to send either of you up that hill."

Belinda and Eli looked over at them in surprise.

"We aren't that old," Belinda said, sounding mildly hurt. "I've fetched Eeyore before, and I'm sure I'll do it again."

"I run a full farm, if you're suddenly worrying about my abilities," Eli said. "I'm not exactly in a *dawdie* house yet!"

A *dawdie* house was an in-law suite built onto the side of an Amish house, or set back on the property a little ways to allow the old people to retire. Thom had done the kitchen installation and other indoor cabinetry in several *dawdie* houses over the years.

"Of course, but—" Jill looked back at Thom. "We want to. Don't we, Thom?"

And with those brown eyes fixed on him almost pleadingly, he couldn't deny that it was an appealing prospect.

"Yeah," he said quickly. "It's why I suggested it. If you don't mind me taking a bit of time off the cabinets, Miss Belinda. I'm more than happy to go get Eeyore."

Something crossed Belinda's face—an almost pleased look—and she shrugged. "Well, if you want to. Eli, I'll make coffee for when you're done with your chores. I'm sorry that I blamed you."

Belinda gave Eli a conciliatory smile.

"I can get the donkey," Eli said irritably, not so easily won over after Belinda's tongue-lashing.

"Let them do it." Belinda's tone softened further. "They're young, Eli. They're *young*."

Eli met Belinda's gaze, then looked over at Thom and Jill in faint surprise. He nodded a couple of times and gave Thom a meaningful look. "Right. *Yah*. Of course. Enjoy yourselves."

It was a none-too-subtle assumption that something romantic was going on between him and Jill, but he'd let the rumors fly if it meant keeping an elderly couple from that rocky hike.

"Good," Thom said, and he shot Jill a relieved look. "Let's get moving."

"I'll go get some carrots," Belinda said, turning toward the house. "Eeyore loves carrots."

JILL ACCEPTED A plastic bag of carrots from Aunt Belinda, and she followed the old woman's pointing finger with her gaze up the steep, rocky slope. Bare patches of stony ground stood out against snowy patches, and the hill almost seemed to blend into the cloudy sky behind it.

"He always heads up that way," Belinda

said. "If you get just over the crest of the hill, you can normally see where he's at. It's pretty steep, though, and be careful on the rocks—they can slide out from under you if you aren't careful."

All the more reason for the older people to be staying safely below.

"Okay, we'll figure it out," Jill said.

"He's sensitive," Belinda added. "He likes to be called a pretty donkey, and you have to watch your tone with him."

"My tone?" Jill squinted at her aunt.

"You have to sound sincere. Not like you're trying to lure him. You have to sound like you've simply come to see him, and then he'll come for the carrots."

Jill glanced over at Thom. His breath hung in the cold air, and he shrugged. "Donkeys are emotionally complicated."

"Sounds like it," she murmured, and cast her aunt a smile. "We'll go find him."

"And take these," Belinda added, handing a halter and lead rope over to Thom. "Good luck out there."

Thom went inside for his coat, and he came back out a minute later, zipping it up. As Jill and Thom trudged off across the yard, their boots crunched across the well-trampled snow.

She could see a few fresh hoofprints, although most of them hadn't left much of a mark behind.

"Thank you for standing in as my fake boyfriend back there," she said. "I know it seems silly, but it will help…so long as you don't tell the hilarious story to Sean anytime soon."

"I won't do that," he said. "I'll save it for a couple of years until it doesn't matter anymore."

It would have to do—all the complications that came with a ruse like this one… She should have thought further ahead. Jill glanced over her shoulder to find Belinda and Eli standing shoulder to shoulder, watching them. They turned when she spotted them and headed toward the house.

"What do you make of those two?" Thom asked.

"You mean, are *they* romantically involved?" Jill asked.

"Yeah." He glanced down at her, his gaze warming.

"You're as bad as Aunt Belinda," she said with a laugh. "They're just friends. From what I can gather, they've been neighbors for almost as long as Aunt Belinda has lived there, and she and my great-uncle moved there when they got married. So they know each other very well."

"You think that's it?" Thom asked. "Just old friends?"

"I know that's it," she replied. "I mean, it's clear that he has feelings for her, but Eli drives her right up the wall. He refuses to do anything the proper way, and apparently has a real penchant for keeping farm animals in his house with him."

"Oh." Thom frowned. "Huh. So he's a bit of an oddball?"

"But a really sweet oddball," Jill said, remembering the old man with a hand over his heart as he said his farewell. "I think he's good for Aunt Belinda—he keeps her on her toes."

When they got to the edge of the property, Jill spotted a break in the brush. There were some hoofprints in the snow leading up to rockier ground. It would be a long walk up that hill. They headed past the back of the property and toward a well-worn path that led up the hill. Belinda was right—it was a steep climb, and loose rocks tumbled behind her as she made her way up, half a step behind Thom.

"They think they're setting us up to climb this hill and fall in love with each other, you know," Thom said, glancing over his shoulder.

"Yeah, I got that feeling," Jill said with a rueful smile. "Single people make them feel unsettled."

"They're as single as we are," he pointed out.

"But they're old enough to think it's different." She grinned. "Look at us wondering if they're more than just neighbors…it makes us feel unsettled, too, doesn't it? We want to see them in a lasting relationship that we can quantify. We're no better."

"As if old friends and lifelong neighbors isn't good enough?" he asked.

She waggled a gloved finger at him. "Exactly."

"But who finds a match for the matchmaker?" he asked, and this time he didn't look back.

"Are you teasing?" she asked.

"Yep," he replied with a laugh.

But he had a point—did Aunt Belinda need a bit of a nudge to get her to see more in Eli? Because while he definitely drove Belinda crazy, he was endearing, too.

Jill found herself breathing hard after about five minutes of climbing. She stopped and put her hands on her hips.

"Yoga didn't prepare me for this," she said. "How come this is so easy for you?"

"My legs are longer than yours," he said with

a grin. "You probably spend too much time at your desk."

"That is not true," she said, then shook her head. "Okay, I probably do. But I go to a yoga class twice a week, and that's something."

"Yep, sure is."

She caught his eye and grinned. "I should do more hiking in my spare time."

"It would prepare for you chasing donkeys. Come on." He held his hand out. She took it and he tugged her up the incline to his side, and they continued forward.

"So what's your experience with donkeys?" she asked.

"I've known a few people who've had them. They're great guardians for a flock in a field."

"You said they're emotionally complicated?" she said.

"Oh, yeah. Definitely. They've got their own ideas, and you have to respect that or you get absolutely nowhere with them."

She waited for a "just like women" joke to drop, but it didn't. She smiled faintly. Good for him. It made her like him more. Since Thom wasn't as winded as she was, she held out the bag of carrots for him to take from her.

"You carry that, would you?" she said.

Thom took the bag and held his hand out

again. "You can go back down, if you want. I can find Eeyore alone."

"Nope, I'm coming." She caught his hand again and used him as leverage to pull herself up even with him. This time he didn't let go, and they carried on hand in hand.

"I'm going to let those two bicker without me to bother them," she said breathlessly.

They crested the top of the hill, and she loosened her scarf as she looked around them. Hills rolled over the landscape unbroken toward the horizon, and she could see the neatly fenced-off farms and fields. A buggy drawn by two horses crept down a winding road, and some cattle wandered by a large round bale of hay in a feeder. Some Amish children were sledding down a hill, their faint shrieks of laughter reaching Jill on the winter air, and farther away there was a break in the clouds and golden sun rays shot through, warming up the scene. From up here, the farms didn't look as far apart as they did from the road. It was oddly comforting.

"Wow," she murmured.

"It's unspoiled," Thom said.

"How well do you really know your neighbors out here?" she asked.

"Pretty well. Come here." He tugged her over so that she stood in front of him, his broad chest right behind her shoulders. She could feel his warm breath against her ear, and Thom pointed out across the landscape. "You see that Amish farm over there with the red chicken coop?"

"Yeah."

He put his hands on her shoulders. "I built that coop. It's a special one because the owner's daughter is in a wheelchair and she likes to take care of the chickens." He shifted, keeping a hand on her shoulder, holding her in place, so close she could feel his breath against her cheek. "You see that winding creek? Just past it there's that little mobile home—"

She nodded.

"They're building a house next spring, and they've already got me scheduled to put in their kitchen. They've been married for a couple of years and they want a baby really badly. It hasn't happened yet." He shifted again. "And those kids sledding?"

"Yeah..."

"They're cousins. The Amish couple who owns that land had a few kids of their own, and then adopted their nieces and nephews after their parents died in a house fire."

"Oh... I didn't know."

"You get to know people over time. You hear

their stories. They hear yours," he said. "And you see past the highway, the hill with all the trees and snow?"

"Uh-huh…"

"That's where my place is. I bought it a few years ago. It was a mess, but the price was right, and I've been doing the work on it myself ever since." He dropped his hands. "I know this area…the people here, the community. When I look around here, I see…" He sighed, going silent for a beat. Then he said, "I see home. Do you know any of your neighbors?"

"I live in an apartment downtown," she said.

"Does that mean no?"

She could see his argument. Human connection was good. Isolation was bad. But the reality was more complicated in a way she wouldn't apologize for.

"Look, in an apartment building, you live so close to other people that you don't get a lot of privacy. So we all kind of…agree to ignore each other. It's the polite thing to do."

"It sounds lonely to me," he replied.

"When people are so close they can overhear private conversations, or they see you when you're heartbroken, or they hear a slammed door when a couple fights…you need some space. Physical space isn't possible. So people give it in other ways."

"And that's the problem with the city. A bunch of strangers living squashed together. It's good to know people. It's healthy."

He was a whole lot like her Amish family—his opinions were deeply rooted. From the outside, their immovability was reassuring. But the closer she got to them, the more frustrating it became. They wouldn't change their views for anything or anyone.

"I agree," she said. "I've been burned by not knowing enough. Trust me. But… I still like my privacy in the city. It's healthy in its own way."

"But the Amish life still draws a lot of city people because they're missing something that we have out here," he said.

He wasn't wrong. How many of Jill's colleagues did just that? Including Kent, apparently. Jill looked back out over the hills, and as her gaze slid past the trees and rocks, she spotted the gray hindquarters of a donkey.

"You know," she said quietly, "this Amish world might seem perfect from the outside, but my family was torn apart by it. My grandfather left the Amish life, and my dad still relates stories that his father told him about what it was like to be cut off from everyone he knew or loved. They started avoiding him, and it really hurt. They were so upset he didn't stay Amish. There was no recovering their relationship after that."

Thom swallowed. "That sounds awful."

"Our family was forever changed by that," she said. "There was us and them. We knew we weren't wanted, because if we ever visited the Amish side of my dad's family, they were polite but distant. We were a threat. They wanted things to stay the same—and when you let people into your life in a real way, things change. And they certainly never reached out to visit us."

There had been a few years as a teen when Jill had identified with her Amish ancestry and tried to write some letters to cousins. Only one answered, and the replies had dwindled away. Maybe that was why she'd built her life the way she had around the job that welcomed her. To simply be accepted and valued was a powerful need fulfilled.

"Your sister made a life here," Thom said.

"True," Jill agreed. "And from what I understand, she's managed to bond with a couple of Amish cousins. That's more than I managed. I still feel very much on the outside."

Thom's expression softened. "And I'm getting protective of my home, too."

"You are."

"I'm not trying to push you away, Jill."

"No?" Because it sure felt that way to her. Jill pointed down the incline. "There's Eeyore."

Thom followed her gaze and nodded. "Good. Now, watch your attitude."

She laughed incredulously. "Come on, Thom… Are we fighting right now? Because it kind of feels that way."

Thom looked back toward her again, and she saw the suppressed irritation in his gaze. She drove him a little bit nuts, didn't she? She wasn't even sure what this was about. Maybe they were just so different. But she'd lived with the burden of being "too much" all her life. She'd had too much personality, too much intelligence, too much ambition. She'd found one place where all of those things came together into success—and that was the business world.

But not out here, apparently. Danke was the kind of place where Elsa could thrive with her chirpy personality, her desire to build a traditional life and her penchant for people-pleasing. But Jill couldn't.

"We're different people," Thom said. "I'm

sorry. I don't mean to get testy. I'm glad you come out here for your aunt."

"Okay." Jill met his gaze. "Good. I'm glad we're not fighting, then. But we should probably get the donkey."

It was why they were up here. It was safer to keep to facts…at least when it came to this.

CHAPTER SIX

THOM DIDN'T KNOW what he was hoping Jill would see up here. This probably wasn't even about her...it was about Natasha, who'd never been able to see what he could. Why was he starting to hope that Jill would understand him on a deeper level?

Because you're a glutton for punishment, he told himself.

He ambled toward Eeyore where he was sure the donkey could see him. He slowed his pace when the animal shuffled his feet, tucked his tail and took a step back.

"Hey, buddy," Thom said, keeping his voice conversational. "We wondered where you'd got to. Miss Belinda's laying into Eli something fierce, you know."

The donkey looked up when he heard the hollow crack of carrot being bitten into behind him. Jill was slowly chewing, all of her attention focused on a carrot she held in one hand. Eeyore watched her.

Jill wiped something off the carrot with one gloved hand and took another bite. Eeyore took a step toward them, and Jill utterly ignored the animal—if she noticed his interest, she didn't let on. She swallowed and took another cracking bite.

Eeyore trotted toward her, and only then did Jill's gaze flicker in the animal's direction. She waited until he came all the way up to her, then offered him the last half of her carrot. Eeyore took it happily.

Thom used the opportunity to slip the halter over Eeyore's nose and buckled it. He shot Jill a grin.

"Nicely done."

"Hey, I work in corporate America," she said, breaking another carrot in half for the donkey and offering it on the flat of her palm. "If I know nothing else, I can play it cool."

They started up the incline again, Eeyore now plodding along cooperatively.

"For the record," she said, "I do agree that not knowing people very well can be a big problem. Out here you've got people who know each other. They can give you a heads-up if there's something you should know."

Thom walked beside her and noticed she was breathing hard again by the time they got to the top. The winter wind ruffled Jill's hair, and he realized that her hair wasn't quite so smooth this morning as it had been before. No electricity for women's hair tools…that must be it. Somehow, even with less makeup and her hair going back to nature, she had a certain authority about her, like she was used to being obeyed.

Eeyore followed along easily enough, and he started back down the hill toward home without any urging.

"Sounds like you have some personal experience there," he said, matching her stride.

She looked uncertain if she'd answer him or not.

"Hey, you know my romantic baggage. Fair is fair."

Jill smiled faintly. "All right. But no one out here knows this, so I'd appreciate some discretion."

"Of course." He wasn't about to betray her confidences.

"Two years ago I was dating a guy I really cared about. I thought he was the one. I hadn't told my family about him yet. I was going to bring him home for Christmas."

"Yeah?" he said.

"He agreed to the visit, went shopping with

me for gifts for the family, was completely invested—or so it seemed. And then just before we were set to leave, he started acting cagey, and when I called him on it, he told me he couldn't come. He had other plans…with his wife and kids. He was married, and I had no clue." She shook her head. "I didn't see it coming. I broke it off, obviously, but that kind of thing tends to leave a woman angry."

"Yeah, no doubt," he replied. A married guy leading her on. That rankled a protective part of him deep inside. "Where'd you meet him?"

"Work." She cast him a sidelong look. "I learned a lot from that experience. I'm not the kind of woman who dates a man who is taken."

"I believe you."

"Good. Because that qualification matters. But I might have a few personal issues, too."

Jill turned sideways to ease her way down a steep stretch, and he caught her hand again to help her. Eeyore went nimbly down the rocky slope.

"Did you date anyone after him?" Thom asked.

"Nope. I haven't come across anyone worth the effort, I suppose," she said. "Plus, like you say, it is difficult to really trust someone when you don't have a community to let you know if they're decent or not. I have to say, having someone like Aunt Belinda vet a match for me would be mighty helpful."

But Miss Belinda had spoken for him, hadn't she? He felt a mild sense of accomplishment there. Miss Belinda was a good judge of character, and she approved of him.

Jill turned sideways again to go down the next steep but slippery spot, and when she got to the bottom where it was easier going, she released his hand. Thom led Eeyore toward the stable, and Jill jogged ahead to open the door. Eeyore trotted inside and allowed Thom to lead him into an empty stall with fresh hay waiting. Thom shut the stall door and made sure it was secure.

He let out a slow breath, and when he looked over at Jill, her eyes shone in the low light.

"Full confession?" she said softly.

There was more? But when he looked at her, her defenses seemed to be down. She wasn't the secure executive looking up at him. This was the woman…possibly even a friend.

"Sure."

"I hadn't told anyone I was bringing that guy home with me for Christmas, and when I got home, ready to get some sympathy from my family, Elsa and Sean announced their engagement."

"Ouch," he murmured.

"Yeah… I didn't tell anyone anything. I let my sister have her moment."

"So this Valentine's Day, when she gets married—there's more riding on this than just a rocky relationship with your little sister. This isn't going to be an easy Valentine's Day…"

"I suppose not," she agreed. "My confidence took a real hit, and all the questions about my single status wouldn't help."

Jill, the one everyone expected to be so strong and competent, was capable of getting her heart crushed, too. And she'd shouldered all of that alone, while being happy for her younger sister's much less complicated happiness. That took guts and solid character, and he was more than impressed…

"We need a better story," Thom said quietly. "To tell at the wedding, I mean. We're going to have to really sell this."

"What?" A smile touched her lips.

"Don't you think?" he asked. "Let's make sure we give them something to talk about that doesn't revolve around your personal history. Or mine, for that matter."

Jill laughed softly. "What did you have in mind?"

Thom shrugged, catching her gaze and holding it. "We've met before. But where?"

"I was in Danke a couple of months ago. I was dropping off some wedding stuff for my sister. Maybe then?"

"Perfect," he said. "I took one look at you, and I was smitten. I mean, absolutely bowled over. We started talking, and I asked you to go with me to the wedding because I couldn't take my eyes off of you."

"Thom…"

"Unless you want to say that you were smitten with me…" A smile tickled his lips. "I wouldn't argue too much over that."

"Okay, you were smitten with me."

"That's not a stretch, you know," Thom said quietly. "You're a beautiful woman, and I did… notice."

"Really?" She sounded a little breathless.

"Yeah. That surprises you?"

"I just didn't realize…"

"And when we tell them a few weeks later that it didn't work out, we'll say something about how it burned too bright and hot to last, or something like that. I'll tell them you're the one who got away."

"You'll get sympathy again." A smile glittered in her eyes.

"Maybe I'll need it." He caught her hand.

"You're willing to do all that for me?"

"Yeah. I am." He moved closer and picked a stray piece of straw out of her hair. But the movement brought him so close that she had to tip her face up to meet his gaze, and he suddenly found himself looking at her plump lips, her hand in his.

His breath caught, and he waited for her to move back, to pull away, but while she looked as surprised as he was, she didn't move.

"I'm not your problem," she whispered.

True, but he hated the thought of that guy lying to her, embarrassing her, breaking her heart. He wasn't the only one who'd gotten his heart mangled, and maybe he was relieved at that, too.

"Sometimes a guy needs to be the hero… somehow," he murmured back.

He reached up and touched her jaw, and as he did it, he knew it was overstepping. But she didn't move back. This would all be a whole lot easier to brush off if she'd just step away. Or he could…

The stable door rattled from the outside and then opened. Thom exhaled a pent-up breath and took a step back as Eli came in. His heart hammered in his chest…but an interruption was probably for the best. Otherwise, he would have done something he'd regret.

"You found Eeyore!" Eli said jovially. "I'm glad. I do hate it when it looks like I've let Belinda down. I really did lock up. That donkey is too smart for his own good." Eli's gaze flickered between them, and color suddenly touched the old man's face. "Oh… I'm interrupting…"

Yeah, he was, but it was okay. Thom pressed his lips together, wondering how this looked. Would it get reported back to Miss Belinda?

"Nonsense," Jill replied, and suddenly, she was all cool confidence again. "We were just leaving." She brushed past Eli and disappeared out the stable door.

"Is it just me, or does she seem a lot like Belinda when she talks like that?" Eli said thoughtfully. *"Nonsense."* He mimicked her tone perfectly.

"Maybe a bit," Thom admitted with a wry smile. "They're strangely intimidating women, aren't they?"

"A fine horse takes more time to tame," Eli said.

"I don't think they'd appreciate being likened to horses," Thom said.

"Maybe not," Eli replied. "But Belinda doesn't appreciate a whole lot of things that I do. All the same, I know her better than anyone in this community. I'll win that fine woman yet."

And maybe Eli would. What did Thom know? Persistence sometimes paid off.

"I'd better get back inside," Thom said. "I've got a paying job to finish."

Eli nodded. "Thank you for fetching that donkey. I put up a good fight about what I can do still, but truth be told, that climb winds me pretty bad at my age."

"Not a problem," Thom replied. "I was happy to do it."

"I'd best get back to my own chores now, too," Eli said, and he turned toward the door. Thom followed. It looked like even in old age, a man had his pride.

And so did Thom... He was only realizing now how close he'd come to kissing Jill, and his pulse sped up in alarm. Good grief, he'd almost kissed her! He'd have to be a whole lot more careful if he wanted to keep this under control.

She wasn't what he'd expected, and she wasn't the only one with a heart worth protecting.

JILL STEPPED INTO the house and leaned against the door as she shut it behind her. For a moment she just stood there, her cheeks feeling hotter than they should. What had happened out there? She might be a little rusty at this, but it had certainly felt like Thom was about to kiss her...

And she'd been about to let him.

She pulled off her gloves, stuffed them in her pockets and hung her coat up. She rubbed her hands over her face and shut her eyes. Thom was more complicated than she'd given him credit for, and more tempting, too...as if she was the kind of woman who had weeklong flings. Because if she let herself go there, that was all this would be—a very short fling.

Jill was careful—at least now she was. Even when a guy turned out to be a complete cad, saying goodbye hurt, and she wasn't about to put herself through any more unnecessary heartbreak. Thom was one of the good ones... he was sweet, and wounded and a little bit bossy, to boot. If he lived in Pittsburgh, she'd be willing to take a chance, but he knew what he wanted—a life right here in Amish Country. Good for him.

"It's just the wedding..." Jill murmured. She wouldn't be this susceptible to Thom's sweet brand of empathy if it wasn't for her little sister's upcoming nuptials. If she was back in the city, safely ensconced in her life there, she'd feel more in control.

"You're back," Aunt Belinda said with a smile as Jill came into the kitchen. An Amish man sat at the table, his hat and steaming mug of coffee on the tabletop in front of him. For all the comforts provided, he looked uncomfortable. He had a full married beard with a few strands of gray already showing in it. His hairline was receding just a little, and his fingers were stained from outdoor work.

"Yeah, we found Eeyore," Jill said. "He's in the stable again."

"Thank you," Aunt Belinda said. "This is Morris Smucker. He's a widowed farmer from our area."

"Oh!" Jill nodded toward the stairs. "Of course. I'll give you some privacy."

"No, no, it's good that you're here," she said with a bat of her hand. "I'd like your opinion on a few things, as a completely outside observer. Plus, you've met Nellie, so you have a good sense of what she's looking for, too."

Morris regarded Jill uncertainly, but he didn't seem willing to cross Belinda outright.

"Hi," Jill said. "Sorry to intrude."

"Coffee?" Belinda asked brightly.

"Please," Jill replied, and her aunt brought a steaming mug to the table and put it in front of her.

Jill looked out the side window and saw his black buggy, still hitched, standing in the drive. She also spotted Thom striding through the snow toward his pickup truck. He glanced toward the house, but didn't seem to be able to see inside. She dropped her gaze.

"If we could continue in English," Belinda said. "Now, Morris, what are you looking for in a wife?"

"I…ah—" Morris looked over at Jill again uncomfortably. "I have five *kinner* who need a *mamm*. And I need a woman who will help me raise them, help me with the housework… I'm working a farm with my brother right now, but it's cramped."

"Do you want more children?" Jill asked.

"Yah, yah," Morris replied.

"How many were you hoping for?" Belinda asked.

"As many as Gott would provide," he replied.

Belinda nodded soberly. "And the ideal wife for you—what would she be like?"

"She'd be wise with money," Morris replied,

"and patient with *kinner*. She'd be a good cook, and she'd be good with a thread and needle. Like my late wife was."

"That's a job description," Jill observed. "What would she be like…as a wife and a companion to you, personally? The children will grow up, Morris. And then it'll be the two of you."

"Oh…" Morris shifted in his seat. "She'd be…kind to me, too. And maybe she'd like to hear me talk about my day. My wife…she used to like long walks, and I'd like to find that again. Someone who'd go walk the fields with me. My wife and I also used to play board games with our friends, and I'd like a woman who'd enjoy that again, too."

"What was your wife's name?" Jill asked softly.

"Johanna."

"That's pretty."

"*Yah.* She was…wonderful. I'm still close with her family, her brothers and their wives especially. So a new wife would have to be okay with that."

"Of course," Belinda murmured. "Do you have any questions about Nellie?"

Morris moved his mug in a small circle in front of him. "She's in her twenties, and I'm thirty-seven this year. I suppose I'd want to know if my age would be a disappointment to her."

"I don't think it would be, for the right match," Belinda said.

"What does she want?" Morris asked. "From a husband, I mean. What is she hoping for?"

"She wants to be loved," Jill said.

Morris looked surprised, then nodded. *"Yah, yah."* He sucked in a breath. "Well, I can run a farm. I've been married before, so I know how to be considerate of a woman. And as for the rest, it would have to be discussed between the two of us in private."

"That's fair," Belinda agreed. "I'll let you know if we'll move forward with that."

"Thank you, then," Morris said, pushing himself to his feet. "I'll be on my way."

Morris made his way to the door, and Jill heard Thom's voice as he opened it. The men politely greeted each other as Morris left, then Thom came inside with two bags of tools, one in each hand.

"Thank you for fetching the donkey, Thom," Belinda said. "It was kind of you."

"Not a problem." Thom glanced over at Jill, and a small smile turned up his lips. She felt her cheeks heat and to hide it, she picked up her coffee and took a sip. She hadn't added cream or sugar yet, and it was bitter—not the way she normally drank it. Thom crossed to the cabinets where his work awaited.

"You didn't want cream?" Belinda asked, nudging a little cream jug toward her.

"Oh…yes." Jill refused to look in Thom's direction again, and she doctored up her coffee.

"So," Belinda said, "what are your thoughts on Morris Smucker?"

"He seems decent," Jill said.

"*Yah*, very," Belinda agreed. "But for Nellie? He matches all the criteria that Nellie asks for, but…"

"He's in love with his first wife," Jill said. "And I don't blame him. She had his heart, and he lost her. But that man is looking for a replacement for Johanna, not a new woman."

"That was my sense, too," Belinda said with a sigh. "I'm not sure Nellie would notice, though."

"Maybe not, but I sure did," Jill replied.

"He can farm," Belinda said. "And he does need another wife. It would be good for Morris to find someone else to love, have another child…"

"If you set up a marriage between those two, Nellie will end up unhappy, missing out on something she can't quite identify, and she'll blame herself for it," Jill said.

Belinda pursed her lips thoughtfully. But Jill could see it in her mind's eye. Nellie would see an older man who was kind, considerate, never said anything terrible and who had certain expectations of how his home would run. And Nellie would do her best to give him what he wanted. But she'd never fully have his heart, and she'd probably only realize that on a subconscious level.

"She's sensitive, but she's also naive," Jill added. "She'll never quite feel satisfied with him, and she'll blame herself. That's my two cents."

"And it's appreciated," Belinda said. "That's my sense, too, but Nellie King needs a husband quick. I do have another couple of farmers to speak with who've expressed some interest."

"Expressed interest...how much interest?" Jill asked. "Are any of them properly smitten with her?"

"That's to be discovered when I speak with them." Belinda smiled.

"And what if there were a man who was interested in Nellie who wasn't a farmer?" Jill asked.

Thom cleared his throat loudly, but Jill ignored him, plunging on. "What if there were someone who really cared for her?"

"Those things can happen on their own," Belinda replied, standing up and going to the cupboard. "I've been asked to provide her with a farmer. And that's what I'll try to do. This is about a farm, and if she marries a man who can't run it, she won't inherit. That's what it comes down to."

Belinda took something out of a crinkly package and handed it to Thom. "For your throat, dear."

Jill looked over at him then and he met her gaze with a suppressed smile, and he obediently opened the cough lozenge and popped it into his mouth.

"Nellie is a sweet girl with a big heart," Belinda went on. "She's smart, kind and has a lot to offer. Without that farm, the likes of Morris Smucker wouldn't be looking her way, but that doesn't mean that one of these men won't have found a true gem and an ideal wife in the process. But I don't want to abandon Nellie to a life of being second in her husband's heart any more than you do."

"Morris Smucker is interested in Nellie?" Thom interjected.

"*Yah,*" Belinda replied. "You know him?"

"A little bit," Thom said. "More like, I know of him. He's got a drinking problem."

"What?" Belinda blinked. "You must be thinking of someone else."

"Morris—who just left," he said.

"Yah..." Belinda frowned.

"I worked with him at a construction site. He was taking on some extra work," Thom said. "He didn't arrive on time, and the foreman said he was ready to fire him. He said ever since his wife died, he'd been showing up late and smelling like booze when he arrived. They tried to cut him some slack considering his loss, but he didn't improve."

"How long ago was that?" Belinda asked.

"This past September," Thom replied.

So about five months ago. Jill exchanged a wide-eyed look with Belinda.

"And that, my dear girl," Belinda said quietly, "is why a wise matchmaker has her nose in everyone's business. Somehow, that detail missed me, but it's good to know. No, Morris won't do for Nellie at all."

Belinda grabbed her thick shawl and picked up a bucket of kindling. She headed out onto the porch for the stove outside, and Jill went to the window to see her bent over by the open stove door, pushing kindling inside to start a fire. Thom shot Jill a questioning look. He hadn't heard the last thing Belinda had said.

"Did I upset her?" he asked.

"No, you spared a sweet girl a very troubling future," Jill replied. "You're the good guy here."

It looked like Amish women had some near misses with the wrong men, too. The difference was that Nellie had a whole community looking out for her—people who didn't want to see her hurt. A community who paid attention could be incredibly helpful. But then, that same community could put on the pressure when a woman wasn't married yet, and they figured she should be. Jill was experiencing that pressure from her family these days.

Nellie was young and sheltered, and had a community looking out for her. While Jill had a little more life experience, she didn't have that same support to help her make her choices. She looked over to where Thom stood in the kitchen, a hammer in one hand and a couple of nails in the other. He seemed to feel her eyes on him, because he glanced over, a smile tugging at his lips.

Jill rubbed her arms to rid herself of a sudden rush of goose bumps. Yes, she would have to be careful, too.

CHAPTER SEVEN

THOM WORKED FOR the rest of the day, hauling out the last of the old, broken wood and repairing some damaged drywall. He tried to put his emotions into the job in front of him—it normally worked—but today that was proving difficult. Outside on the cooking porch, Miss Belinda and Jill were working on some muffins, and he paused for a moment to watch them.

Jill wore an apron tied on top of a thick Amish shawl, and she held a mixing bowl in one arm, a large whisk in the other hand. Her laugh at something her aunt said came filtering in through the closed window. That laugh—it had kept him out on the ice the other evening. He knew this was dangerous turf. Jill caught his eye then, and she looked surprised. He smiled sheepishly and turned away. No, he had to stop this.

He had to get back to work. This was why he was here—not for Miss Belinda's great-niece. He'd been eager to start on this job—not just for pay. Working on an Amish kitchen was a different kind of challenge. The hardwood cabinetry was made to last, and this hardwood setup seemed to be designed to outlast the actual kitchen, if it wasn't for the water-damaged surfaces. The cabinets were hard to pull apart.

The bottom cabinets had given him the most grief to remove. Whoever had built the house seventy or eighty years ago had nailed in the cabinets, glued the wood to the wall, added in some spacers that weren't quite the right size and done a few other things that made the work more complicated. Like how the kitchen was an odd size, and he'd had to build the cabinets both to fit the room and to give Belinda the kind of storage she'd requested. A half inch mistake would be a real headache.

But today, instead of focusing on not making those half inch mistakes, his mind kept wandering back to the moment in the stable with Jill's brown gaze fixed on his. Even the memory made his stomach float. The chemistry between them was undeniable...but he'd have to deny it. Opposites might attract, but they couldn't make a future. He had firsthand experience here.

Thom spent the next few minutes setting up the frame for half of the lower cabinets. It was a painstaking job, especially since one wall of the kitchen wasn't quite plumb, but he could work with that. The main problem was when he ran out of wood screws.

The side door opened, and he looked up to see Jill emerge from the mudroom.

"Aunt Belinda is one tough cookie. It's like the cold doesn't even touch her out there." She glanced around the kitchen as she untied her apron. "How's it going in here?"

"I've run out of wood screws. And I have a couple other things I should pick up. Other than that, it's coming together. What do you think?"

Jill scanned his work, cocked her head to one side. Why did he find himself wanting to impress her?

"Here—" He picked up a piece of sample wood and held it against the frame. "To help you imagine it."

"Very nice." She nodded. "This is going to look really good."

"It will, once I'm done," he agreed. "Admittedly, it's hard to tell now."

"I trust you."

"How busy are you?" he asked.

"Not terribly," she replied. "Aunt Belinda sent me in to warm up. I think she's used to cooking alone, and I'm getting in the way."

Thom looked out the window and saw Belinda bent in front of the oven again, poking inside with a long piece of wood.

"I've got to head into town and pick up those wood screws from the hardware store." He should say he'd be back later. Instead, he added, "Do you want to come along?"

"Sure." Jill shrugged out of the shawl. "Let me grab my coat and tell Aunt Belinda where we're going."

A few minutes later Thom and Jill were headed down the road in his pickup truck. Jill smelled faintly of wood fire and baking, and he noticed that she sniffed her coat, frowned and then sniffed a tendril of her hair.

"Yes, you smell like you've been cooking on an outdoor stove," he said with a grin.

She shook her head. "Sorry."

"Why apologize? I probably smell like wood dust."

"I'm used to a modern kitchen," she said. "In fact, you might laugh at me for this, but I get a box of grocery items delivered to me once every few days with the exact ingredients I'll need for some enclosed recipes."

"Are you serious?"

"Entirely. I'm a busy woman. I work long hours. I don't get a lot of time for wandering around grocery stores or cooking. It makes healthy meals cooked at home easier. I don't have a family member...or a roommate, or...a husband...to trade off with. So I make it easier for myself."

"That's fair," he said. "There are things that are simpler with a romantic partner. And ironically, eating is one of them."

"Also attending weddings."

"Yeah." He chuckled. "That, too." He was silent for a moment. "You know, I get why Eli has his heart set on Miss Belinda. It's tough enough being single. It would be harder still to be old and alone."

"His heart is set on her?"

"My words, not his," Thom replied. "But he said he was working on softening her up. He likened her to a fine horse—it was meant as a compliment."

Jill chuckled and shook her head. "You can tell he's never been married, can't you?"

"His compliments could use some work," he agreed.

"I was thinking about this morning..." Jill glanced at him from the corner of her eye. "In the stable... Look, I think we can just face it, right? There's attraction between us. I'm not saying you were even going to follow through on it, but there's something there."

"We're going to talk about this?" he asked hesitantly.

"We probably should," she said. "It'll take away the power of it."

"Okay…"

"We want different lives—that's a big deal," she said. "But we also seem to have some pretty natural chemistry."

"It's okay," he said. "I get it. And I fully agree. Yes, I'm attracted to you. I think you're trying to say that you feel it, too." He cast her a rueful smile. "And thank you for that, by the way. It means I'm not some jackass annoying a woman. But we wouldn't work as a couple, and it's better to just admit that and not get hurt."

"Yes." She let out a pent-up breath. "You said it better. And you aren't a jackass."

"Don't worry," he said, and he reached over and gave her hand a quick squeeze. "I'm capable of friendship. I'm not a Neanderthal."

"I didn't think you were," she said with a low laugh, and somehow, he was gratified to hear it.

"Good. And I mean…you…are capable of just being friends with *me*…right?" He was only joking, but the way her eyes snapped made him chuckle.

"Yeah, yeah, you're safe, big guy," she muttered.

"I mean, seriously, I'm a good-looking man," he said. "I get it if you'd have trouble with all of this sawdust and testosterone. I'm quite the tasty snack."

Jill burst out laughing. "Are you, now?"

"Hey, I'm just saying, if you struggle with keeping this strictly platonic, I get it. It's not your fault." He grinned over at her.

"I think I'll be just fine, Thom," she said, but she was laughing now.

"Well, that settles that," he said, dropping the joking tone. "Because I'd really like for us to be friends. You're interesting."

Her cheeks colored again and she nodded, not looking over at him. "Likewise, Thom."

The hardware store was located on Main Street in the town of Danke, and Thom pulled into an empty spot along the side of the street. Danke wasn't a huge tourist destination, but it did put out some effort to attract more than just the locals, and the downtown core was always seasonally decorated. For Valentine's Day, there were pink tinsel hearts that hung off the side of the light posts, and they lit up at night. Even the Amish enjoyed Valentine's Day around here.

Thom and Jill hopped out of the truck, and he circled around to meet her on the sidewalk.

"I'm just going into the bookstore while you get what you need in there," she said.

"Sure." He didn't expect her to follow him around everywhere, but he did glance over his shoulder once as he headed into the hardware store, and he saw her disappearing in the next-door shop.

Danke Hardware was a large shop, run by an Amish man with a mix of Amish and English employees. Thom noticed a display at the front of the shop with Valentine's cards. On his way by, Thom glanced at them. Some were packages for children, and others were cards for a significant other that had religious verses on the front. Most were in Pennsylvania Dutch. The card store carried the Valentine's Day card section for everyone else, but the Amish would come here. He was half tempted to pick up a children's card for Jill, but he'd probably pressed his limits as much as he dared, so he carried on past and went to the appropriate aisle for wood screws.

When he came back out of the shop with his little plastic bag in hand, he spotted Sean and

Elsa coming down the sidewalk toward him. This wasn't terrific timing, and Thom glanced furtively toward the bookstore. He could see the back of Jill's coat through the window as she browsed inside.

"Thom!" Elsa called, and a smile broke over her face. "How are you doing?"

"I'm great. Hi, you two," he replied.

Sean shook his hand with a grin.

"So the big day is coming right up," Thom said. "Getting excited?"

"There's so much to do," Elsa said. "You think you're done, and then you aren't. Right, Sean?"

"Yeah, for sure," Sean replied. "We both have big families, and both of our families have strong feelings about the weirdest things. Like…napkins, place settings…"

"Vegan options!" Elsa said, and she and Sean met each other's gaze and laughed. There was obviously a story there.

"Just save those vegan options for someone else," Thom replied with a laugh. "I want meat."

"You bet," Sean said. "So…how's the kitchen coming along?"

The door to the bookstore opened, a bell tinkling overhead, and Thom looked over to see Jill coming out of the shop. She froze, her gaze flicking from Thom to Sean and Elsa and back again. It took her a beat to gain her equilibrium before she headed over with a smile.

"Hi, Elsa! How's everything? Sean—great to see you. Fancy running into you two out here, huh?"

"Thom, since you're working on Aunt Belinda's kitchen, I'm sure you know my sister by now," Elsa said. "But you know what? If she didn't already have a date to the wedding, we would have set the two of you up. Wouldn't we, Sean?"

Sean shook his head. "Nah. They're city and country. It doesn't mix."

"Oh…right." Elsa wrinkled up her nose. "It's a good thing she brought her own date, then, because all the guys here are country to the core." Her smile was too bright.

"Right." Jill's tone seemed strained. "Good thing."

The tension here was so thick, he could have plucked it like a guitar string. Elsa had her intense happiness on display, but he could feel all the subtext just beneath.

"Jill's the family bulldog," Elsa said. "She should have been a lawyer. My goodness. You need something done—get Jill. She'll take a strip right off them and leave them cowering.

Except for me, of course. She won't interfere when it comes to my wedding."

Elsa laughed a bright little laugh that sounded like a peal of bells, and Thom looked over at Jill to see something new in her eyes. He'd understand irritation or even outright anger, but Jill wasn't mad. Her eyes were filled with… hurt.

Oh, dang. That does it.

Thom reached out and caught Jill's hand in his, tugging her against him. Elsa was lording her soon-to-be married status over her older sister, and that just wouldn't do. Jill looked up at Thom in surprise.

"I don't know," Thom said. "Bulldog? I haven't seen that side to Jill… She's more of a pussycat with me."

Jill looked up at him, wide-eyed, and before he could think better of it, he bent down and caught her lips in a brief kiss. Her lips were soft, and he found himself wishing he could draw it out a little bit, but he didn't. When he pulled back, Jill blinked up at him.

Elsa and Sean were silent, and Thom looked over at them.

"Wait—" Elsa's quick smile was forced now. "Are *you* her date to the wedding?"

"Yes," Jill said, and she squeezed Thom's

hand hard. "Thom and I have been getting to know each other."

"Rather well, it would seem," Elsa murmured. "When did this start?"

"A few weeks back?" Thom said, meeting Jill's gaze. He was honestly asking. What was their line again?

Jill didn't even need to answer him. The vanquished look on Elsa's face was gratifying to see. Thom would apologize for that kiss later, but he had a feeling that the ends justified the means—this once, at least.

JILL'S HEART PATTERED, and she sucked in what she hoped would be a calming breath. Thom wasn't supposed to just kiss her like that—hadn't they covered where they stood on the drive over?—but then, they hadn't expected to bump into Elsa and Sean in the street, either. And if she was going to be believably matched up for the sake of that client, then they'd better start now.

Her lips still felt a little moist from his kiss. Thom released her hand, and she squeezed her fingers into a fist. That kiss hadn't been entirely fair, and when she glanced up at him, he avoided her gaze.

"Jill, come here." Elsa grabbed her arm and

angled her a couple of yards away from the men. Here would come all the questions—and Jill was determined not to lie again. She might not tell all of the truth, but there would be no more fabricating.

"Well?" Jill asked brightly.

"This is very new, right?" Elsa asked, her voice low.

"Yes, definitely," Jill replied. "But I have to confess, it's not serious."

That would make it easier when they later told people that nothing had come of their "relationship."

"It's not?" Elsa sighed in obvious relief, her gaze flickering over to where the men stood. "Look, Jill, Thom is a sweet guy, and he just got his heart mangled by his ex. She was awful to him, and it really crushed him. It was about six months ago."

"Yeah, I know about that," Jill said.

"Good. So you can appreciate that he's probably pretty fragile right now," Elsa said.

"*Fragile* isn't exactly how I'd describe Thom." He was strong, set in his ways and the only man in a very long time who'd managed to make Jill blush.

"Then you don't know him as well as you should," her sister said flatly.

"What do you think I'm going to do to him?" Jill asked, attempting a laugh.

"Just...don't toy with his emotions," Elsa said. "You're very focused on your career and you're having a fling—I get it! I do. But Thom is special, and he deserves more than to be toyed with for a few weeks before you go back to your priorities."

What exactly did her sister think of her? That a good man wasn't safe in her company?

"I'm not toying with anyone," Jill said curtly. Far from it. They were both very clear on where things stood, and it was hardly romantic.

Jill met her sister's irritated gaze and felt the years dropping out from under her. Like they were teenagers again, always on the opposite end of any issue. Elsa's expression softened.

"Okay, I get how awful I'm sounding," Elsa said. "I don't mean to. It's just that you don't seem to date too often, and this stuff can be delicate. He's really good friends with Sean, and Sean had a bit of an inside view of everything Thom went through. It was really hard on him."

Her mind skipped over the implied insult that she was some clumsy, inexperienced girl when it came to romance, and landed on her sister's worry over Thom. Was there more to this than Thom had told her?

"What happened…exactly?" Jill asked.

"Thom really thought Natasha was the one," she said. "We all thought they were great together. Then Natasha got this job. She and Thom had been talking about moving in together, and he thought that meant they were stable. But she was looking for jobs in the city behind his back, and she sprung it on him when she got a job offer. She wanted him to move with her, but she gave him an ultimatum. Move with her, or they were done. I don't think she was ready for commitment. In a serious relationship, you make your decisions together. Natasha wasn't willing to give up anything for him, and she figured he'd just follow her, I guess. Regardless, it was serious. Serious enough that he'd started asking Sean about engagement rings until she announced her job in the city."

"A ring!"

"He hadn't bought one yet, but it was on his mind. Thom is pretty old-fashioned that way. That's why I say don't toy with him. He'll take this more seriously than you."

"Wow…"

"And I know you're incredibly focused on

your career... Are you considering slowing down a bit?"

"No, I'm not," Jill admitted.

"So be careful with him," Elsa said. "Under all those good looks, that man has a heart. I know it, because we watched it break."

And how could Jill answer that? Her sister was right, and those were the very reasons why she wouldn't be looking for anything deeper with Thom. Underneath all of her bravado, she had a heart, too. Ironic that Jill's heart hadn't been on Elsa's mind.

"I'll be careful," Jill replied.

"Thank you," Elsa said with a nod.

"So enough about me," Jill said, changing the subject. "How's the wedding planning?"

"I thought Mom told you," Elsa said. "One of my bridesmaids, Mae, is being really difficult."

"Yeah, Mom mentioned... So tell Mae to cut it out."

"She's not my friend. She's Sean's."

"So why is she your bridesmaid, then?"

"Because Sean wanted her in the wedding. He was best friends with her before he and I started dating, and I don't like to advertise this because it makes things look...more complicated than they really are. But I can't really deal with her the way I'd deal with one of my own friends. She's part of the wedding because Sean wants her here. And now she won't cooperate. She's got the dress that I bought for her, but she won't wear the shoes. She says she hates heels."

"Okay, so that's definitely more complicated than I thought, but maybe just don't make a big deal out of it. Who cares if she doesn't like to wear heels?" Jill said. "Maybe they hurt her feet. Maybe she can't walk in them. You don't know!"

"She's determined to wear UGG boots."

Jill blinked at her. "As in the suede, floppy winter ones?"

"Yes." Elsa ran a hand through her sandy-blond hair. "She said they matched with the dress."

"Tan UGG boots go with everything?" Jill suggested with a wry smile.

"This is not funny! Think of the pictures!"

"Are you sure she isn't joking?"

"A week before my wedding?" Elsa shook her head. "She's not joking. She told me that they were comfortable, warm and that fashion is getting more daring these days."

"This isn't a catwalk," Jill said.

"I know! So what do I do?" Elsa asked.

"Tell her that you'll make sure she sits next

to a heater at the reception, and maybe find a cute shawl to go with the dress if she's afraid of being cold, but that the boots are out."

"I told her she had to match with everyone else, and she's being willfully obtuse about this."

If this was one of Jill's employees, she'd bring her in for a meeting about insubordination. But that wasn't a great idea for a wedding party.

"This is a tough one," Jill admitted. "She's Sean's friend... Is he still close with her?"

"Certainly not as close," Elsa replied. "She's more friends with the two of us together now, but she's definitely his friend."

"Why is she doing this?" Jill asked.

"I don't know why." Tears rose in Elsa's eyes. "But I have a lot on my plate right now, and the last thing I need is Mae wearing UGG boots in my photos."

"Do you want Mae there at all?" Jill asked.

"Yes!" Elsa wiped a tear off her cheek with her palm. "I do want her there. I'm not some bridezilla who needs utter perfection, but if everyone could just wear dress shoes, I can be flexible on which ones they choose—even the color if that's what it comes down to. But this is my wedding, Jill. I've been planning it for two years!"

"I know." Jill cast her sister an apologetic smile. "Mom suggested that I talk to her."

"Would you?" Elsa asked hopefully.

"Tell you what," Jill said. "Give it a couple of days. Maybe talk to her once more. She might have something else going on. And if you can talk to her, you two can bond, and she'll cooperate. That's a much better outcome than her being told off by me, right? The goal is to not cause big dramatic fights just before your wedding."

"True." Elsa nodded. "Okay, that's smart. I'll try."

"Your wedding is just one day, Elsa," Jill said. "Keep that in perspective. After this you and Sean will be married. This is going to be a watershed moment. Relationships will change...all of them! So maybe just be patient."

"I'm trying," her sister replied.

They headed back toward the men, and Jill noticed the grim look on Thom's face before he turned toward her.

"Ready to go?" he asked brusquely.

"Yeah...sure." She looked over at Sean and he shrugged sheepishly.

"I really thought you knew, man," Sean said. "I'm sorry."

"Don't worry about it," Thom said. "I'm always the last to know. This is par for the course."

Thom moved toward the truck, and Jill looked back at Sean and Elsa. Elsa looked as confused as Jill felt, but Sean gave her an apologetic look.

"Take care," Jill said. "Elsa, call me and tell me how things shake out with Mae, okay?"

"Of course," Elsa said.

Thom was waiting by the passenger side of the truck, the door open. He gave her a hand up—for the benefit of Elsa and Sean?—and then headed around to the driver's side. She was still buckling up when Thom pulled out of their parking space.

"What was that?" Jill asked.

Thom didn't look inclined to answer. He signaled a turn, taking them around town to head back toward the country once more. He seemed to be driving mechanically, his mind elsewhere and his jaw clenched. She sighed and leaned back in the seat.

As they came out of town and headed onto open road, Thom's grip on the steering wheel relaxed and he glanced over at Jill.

"Well?" she said.

"Apparently, there's some news about my brother Mike," he said.

"Oh? Is he okay?"

"He's fine," Thom replied. "He's moving to Georgia."

"What?"

"Sean has a younger cousin who was in my brother's Greek Philosophy class, and apparently, he announced it at the end of his class—that he'd accepted a teaching position in Georgia."

"And you had no idea," she surmised.

"Not a clue. I wonder if my parents know. Last I talked to Mom she was telling me about a book my brother was writing with a colleague."

"So you two aren't close…"

"No."

"And you think…maybe he wouldn't have told you at all?" she guessed.

"I don't know." He clenched his jaw again. "Maybe. Eventually. I'm a little offended to have to find out through local gossip."

"What happened between you?"

"We're just different," he replied. "He's got his Ph.D in Classics, and I'm a carpenter. We're opposites, and he doesn't respect what I do. He figures I'm one of the unwashed masses."

"Nice," she muttered.

"Yeah, it gets old, I can tell you that much."

"Do you want a better relationship with him?" she asked.

"It's hard to get when he thinks he's above everyone." They drove for a bit, then he said, "The answer is yes, I do want a better relationship with him. We've just never…improved things."

"You think it might be time?" she asked.

"Yeah, maybe." She saw the conflicted look in his eye, and she thought she understood it. She had a sibling who was her polar opposite as well, and she knew just how much they both had to swallow their pride these days.

But Jill was no better than Thom was in this area. She'd told her sister she had a plus-one, just to make a point. Family could bring out both the best and the worst in everyone.

Heaven help them at this wedding!

CHAPTER EIGHT

THOM CARRIED SOME broken wood out to his truck as Miss Belinda hitched up her buggy that afternoon. The day was sunny and cold, wind whisking eddies of dry snow around the yard. The old woman was hard at work buckling straps. She had more muscle than he'd given her credit for.

"Are you sure I can't help you with that?" Thom called.

"Oh, *dumhayda*, Thom," Belinda said with a wave of her hand. "I can hitch my own buggy. When I can no longer do this myself is when I have to move in with family."

So that was the litmus test, was it?

"What does *dumhayda* mean?" Thom asked Jill.

"It means nonsense," Jill replied. "She's calling you silly. I tried to help, too. She literally slapped my fingers."

"Oh." He smiled at the image. He should mention that kiss from this morning, and he fished around inside himself for the words to express himself. Thom had only meant to give Jill the leg up for a change, but he'd definitely crossed a line. He probably owed her an apology, but he wasn't feeling terribly apologetic.

Belinda tightened the last strap, and it looked like the job was done. She stopped to pet the horse's nose and spoke quietly to the animal for a moment.

"So you're going to see family, are you?" Thom asked, looking down at Jill. "Some of those cousins who were so cool to you before?"

"The very ones." She let out a slow breath. "I'm a bit nervous, but this is a good step forward. Aunt Belinda has been working behind the scenes to change some biases, I think."

"I'm glad you're getting this chance," he said.

"So am I. Family is important."

Thom watched as Belinda climbed up into the buggy and Jill cast him a smile and then followed her. The women settled in, and then the quarter horse started forward, clopping down the snowy drive.

Jill was getting a chance to connect with people she'd always longed to belong to, and he was glad she had Belinda to help bridge those gaps. As for him, he wasn't sure what it would take to repair a relationship with his brother that had been in decline since they were teenagers. It was ironic that for all his appreciation of a tight-knit community, it was Jill who was reaching out to the difficult family. Maybe he should take a note from her.

The bed-and-breakfast was quiet, and Thom worked alone until he had finished as much as he could reasonably do. The batteries in the portable lights he'd set up were running low, anyway. So he locked up the house with the spare key Miss Belinda left him.

As Thom drove down the highway toward his own house, he wished he'd said something to Jill about that kiss. He raked his fingers through his curls. He didn't want Jill to think he was taking advantage of her. This fake boyfriend thing was going to be more complicated than simply looking believable.

He'd talk to her tomorrow—that was the reasonable thing to do, anyway. They weren't a real couple, but kissing her today on that snowy sidewalk had certainly felt real. Pulling her close, holding her hand, that united front…they were playacting. This wasn't supposed to spark genuine feelings in him! But that kiss had changed something. He was feeling protective, even a little territorial when it came to her.

Once he got home, he attempted to distract himself with basic chores. He started the dishwasher even though it was only half-full, ran the vacuum, reheated some leftover pizza for supper. When all that was done, he finally caved in and picked up his phone.

If Jill could bridge the divide with her Amish family, maybe he could do the same with his brother. He dialed Mike's number and waited.

"Thom?" Mike said, picking up.

"Yeah, hi. How's it going over there?"

"Pretty good. You?"

"Yeah, not too bad. Working hard as usual."

"That's good. Glad to hear it."

This conversation was identical to every other conversation they'd had in the past decade. Chitchat, polite questions, no real information traded. But tonight was going to be different. Jill was right—it was time to get to the bottom of this mess.

"So I heard something today," Thom said.

"Oh?" His brother's tone turned cautious.

"That you're moving to Georgia," Thom said. "Something about taking a teaching position down there."

"Yeah. That." Mike sighed. "I just got off the

phone with Mom. So she would have told you about it soon enough. I accepted a position in the Classics department in University of Georgia."

"You were counting on Mom filling me in?" he asked.

"Uh—yeah. I guess. Look, I would have told you, but I figured Mom would probably get to it first. How did you find out, anyway?"

"Sean Dubencheski has a cousin in one of your classes."

"Greek Philosophy 330," he said.

"You know who she is?" Thom asked.

"No, it's the class I announced it to. Stupid of me. I shouldn't have said anything, but I'd just signed the papers, and I'd given my resignation and I guess I was high on the excitement."

"How does Janelle feel about it?" Thom asked.

"She's happy." But Mike sounded tense. "It's a step up. It comes with a better title. I'd be an associate professor."

"And the kids?" he asked.

"They'll like Georgia. They've got beautiful weather. No more wet, snowy Pennsylvania winters for us. Why, are you going to miss us?"

Thom chewed the side of his cheek for a

moment. "I don't actually see you, Mike. Not often enough for it to make much of a difference what state you live in. I guess finding out you were moving the way I did made me realize just how distanced we've become. You could have moved, and I wouldn't have even known."

"Come on, I'd give you my address," his brother replied.

"Maybe I want more than your address," Thom said. "Starting with your basic respect."

"So what, you called to fight with me?" Mike snapped.

"You realize that we're brothers, right?" Thom said. Maybe he *had* called to start a fight. "As in, if you needed a kidney, you'd be coming to me. I might not be the brother you wanted, but I'm the one you've got."

"Look, I'm sorry I didn't tell you sooner, Thom. That doesn't mean you aren't my brother. I don't know what else to say."

This wasn't going anywhere. It was the same old conversation—Mike willfully obtuse, and Thom frustrated with the state of their family dynamic. This wasn't really about his brother's move—it was deeper. But Thom wasn't sure how to even articulate it in a way his brother would understand. He wanted Mike's respect, his friendship. He wanted to actually matter in Mike's life instead of being an afterthought. But those things either existed, or they didn't.

"Just make sure I have your new address," Thom said.

"Of course."

When they said goodbye and hung up, Thom felt mildly foolish. What he wanted was to get back to the last time when they'd been buddies, walking to and from school together, talking about the drama from the day. It had been grade eight, the year after his brother's brush with death. What he wanted was to look his brother in the face and see that Mike actually liked him again. But that was so far in the past, it would likely never resurface.

THE NEXT MORNING Thom headed back to Butternut B&B, and when he pulled into the drive, he saw old Eli, ax in hand, standing next to the woodpile. He set up a piece of wood on the block and swung. The wood split with a crack that carried through the winter air.

Thom hopped out of his truck and grabbed his tool bag from the seat beside him, then headed over to where the old man was working.

"Morning," Thom said.

"Morning," Eli replied. *Crack*. Another

piece of wood split in half. Beyond, in the field, the horse and the donkey were munching from a pile of fresh hay.

"This is nice of you to help out Miss Belinda," Thom said.

"Normally, she's got boys in the family who come chop for her," Eli said. "But she's getting low in wood, and she's not feeling too well."

"Oh?" Yesterday she'd been pretty spry.

"*Yah*, she's got a cold. That woman is strong and healthy, but when a cold gets through, she lands hard." Eli grabbed another piece of wood and set it up on the block.

"How did you know she was sick?" Thom asked.

"I stopped to say hello when she came to let the animals out," he replied. "I ordered her right back inside again."

"Ordered, huh?" Thom chuckled. "How'd she take that?"

"She did as I told her, and that's how I knew she was sick," Eli replied seriously. "If she were any less than seriously ill, she'd have lectured me on the spot about having some respect. I said I'd take care of things out here, and she agreed. And went back in. That should prove to you she's not well."

"Yeah, I hear you," Thom said. "I could take

over for you, if you want. I'm sure you've got work of your own to do."

Eli glared. "I told Belinda that I'd do it, not that I'd get some younger man to take care of it for me."

Thom smiled and put his hands up. "Okay, fair enough."

"Jill is out there in the summer kitchen, attempting to whip up some breakfast," Eli said. "And I have to tell you, if I were some forty years younger, I'd be courting that one myself."

Thom chuckled. "Age doesn't slow you down, does it?"

"Not much," Eli replied. "But I have a piece of advice for you."

"Yeah?"

"Whatever monstrosity she pulls off that stove—burned black or raw as JELL-O—you eat it and smile."

Thom laughed out loud. "I've had breakfast."

"And Belinda said you were the one who knew how to act around ladies," Eli scoffed. "Well, suit yourself, then."

Eli swung the ax and it dug into the piece of wood. Then he lifted the ax and the wood together, and brought them down hard with another resounding *crack*. Eli glanced at the upstairs window, and Thom followed his gaze, but he couldn't see anything.

"I'm being noisy, so that she knows how hard I'm working," Eli said with a wink.

Thom shook his head, laughing to himself as he headed to the house. Taking advice from a confirmed bachelor who drove Miss Belinda absolutely crazy didn't seem like a great idea. Besides, he wasn't chasing Jill—even if it might look that way to old Eli.

He knocked twice, then opened the door and let himself in.

"Hello!" he called. "It's Thom! I'm getting back to work!"

From upstairs, he heard Miss Belinda's voice filter down. "Thank you, Thom!"

Crack. Another piece of wood split outside as he shut the door behind him. The far door that led to the porch with the summer stove opened and Jill came back inside. She was carrying a plate filled with some rather blackened-looking pancakes. She looked down at them dubiously.

"It's harder to cook on a woodstove than you'd think," Jill said with a wry smile. "These are garbage."

She shook her head, and came past Thom toward the trash can. There was something different in her eyes—she'd lost her sparkle. What had happened with the cousins last night? Thom caught her arm, and when she looked up in surprise, he plucked that top burned pancake from the pile.

"Just a bit browned," he said, and he folded it over and ate half of it in one bite. It was definitely burned, but Jill looked so pleasantly surprised that he didn't even mind. He ate the last of the pancake and carried his tool bag over to his work area.

"Add some syrup," Thom said. "They're not bad."

"Really?" She looked at the plate suspiciously, then changed course and put it on the table.

Yeah, he might regret this, because before the morning was done, he was going to eat his fair share of those charred pancakes, but maybe old Eli had a point about eating what a woman cooked. Sometimes it was just the decent thing to do.

JILL PUT DOWN two plates, forks and knives, and Thom joined her at the table. She looked at the pile of pancakes. Were they not as bad as she thought?

"Aunt Belinda had tea and toast this morning already," Jill said. "She's not feeling too well, so she went back upstairs to rest."

"Yeah, Eli mentioned."

Jill placed a bottle of syrup in the center of the table, labeled with an Amish farm's sticker on the front, and dished a pancake onto her plate.

"How did it go with your cousins?" he asked.

"Not as well as I'd hoped," she said. "We had dinner, played some board games and everyone was very nice and polite, but..." She shook her head. "There's a distance that I just can't seem to close with them. They know Elsa is getting married, and a couple of them are even attending. The others had excuses, but they were polite about it. Maybe I'm just being overly sensitive."

"You have a pretty accurate gut instinct in everything else, though, don't you?" he asked.

Jill looked up. "Yeah, I seem to."

"Then why are you questioning yourself?" he asked.

"Because the reality hurts," she said. "This is my family—we're blood relatives. I grew up with this deep respect for Amish ways. I knew what they stood for, why they did what they did. So here I am with a respect for their way of life, and I don't get that in return."

"Do they really disrespect your life that much?"

Jill took her first bite and found that Thom was right. The pancakes weren't actually so bad with enough syrup.

"They're scared of me," Jill replied. "That's what Aunt Belinda told me, at least. They don't know what to make of an *Englisher* cousin who works in advertising and lives so differently. It's so far outside of their experience that it freaks them out a bit."

"That sounds about right," Thom said. "My experience of the Amish is similar. Except, they understand my job—a lot of Amish work in carpentry. So my work is the bridge. You need to find a bridge they can understand."

"Like what?" Jill shook her head. "Advertising? City life? The corporate ladder? I'm not sure I have anything."

"Maybe like having a sister," Thom replied. "Some things are universal, and complicated sibling relationships span cultures. My brother is studying some Greek gods who are brothers. We still have a whole lot we can identify with when it comes to the ancient Greeks and Romans because sibling relationships haven't changed all that much."

They ate in silence for a couple of minutes,

and Jill stole a glance up to see Thom watching her eat, his head cocked to one side.

"That's a very good point," she said at last. "But I'm not sure I can publicly gripe about my relationship with my sister."

"You might be able to privately gripe about it with one cousin, though."

He was insightful, and Jill gave him an approving look. "You're kind of wise, Thom."

"When it comes to other people's problems," he replied. "Not my own. I talked to my brother last night."

"How did that go?" she asked.

"Not great." He turned his attention back to his plate. "But I got the assurance that he'll give me a forwarding address." She heard the mild irony in his tone.

"So you didn't get through to him?" she asked.

Thom shook his head. "It's not about just getting the news of his move secondhand. When I say I want his respect, he can't see where he hasn't given it. And maybe he's right—he's technically been respectful enough. Maybe what I want is for him to honestly like me as a person. That's a bigger ask, though."

"Nothing is easy," Jill said softly.

"Doesn't seem to be." He shrugged. "Sorry to be the depressing one."

"Don't worry about that," she said. "It's nice to have someone who gets what I'm going through. When I talked to Elsa yesterday afternoon, she was actually worried about protecting you."

Thom swallowed his bite. "What? You're joking."

"Nope. She thinks that I'm so inexperienced with relationships that I'll somehow break you by accident, and you've been through enough. She was quite concerned about it, especially when I told her that we weren't a very serious item."

"Ah. Because of Natasha." He nodded.

Jill took another bite. When she swallowed, she added, "But at the very least, there was no pity. I mean, concern over you, but no pity."

Thom laughed softly. "So that kiss...do I need to apologize for it, or did it do the trick?"

She felt her face warm at the memory of his lips on hers, his casual way of kissing her that had sent her stomach for a tumble.

"It did the trick," she admitted.

"Good." His voice was low, warm, and she felt those goose bumps again.

"What did Sean say about it?" she asked.

"Were you warned off of me, the dangerous city girl?"

"Oh, definitely," he replied. "But for the first time in a long time, he hasn't given me that sad, sympathetic smile like I'm someone's widower grandfather."

"I know that look!" Jill laughed. "It feels good to be free of the pity, just for a little while, doesn't it?"

Thom leaned back in the chair, his grin downright boyish. "It really does. I'm glad you thought of this arranged date to the wedding."

"We could keep being each other's fake dates to things for a while," she said.

"I've got a better idea." He shot her a teasing smile. "When you visit, after we've told them it's over and we burned too brightly, we can arrange to bump into each other and act like we're about to reconnect. It'll send them into fits trying to stop it. It might be fun."

Carrying this on, having a friend here in Danke, wasn't a terrible idea. This would help them both keep their dignity, and it would be the most fun she'd had in a long time, so long as they both stayed single.

"This is more fun than I thought I'd be having on this trip," she admitted. "I just might take you up on that."

Jill scooped up his plate, stacked it on top of her own and brought them to the sink outside. Thom's chair scraped as he pushed it back, and he came to the door.

"My sister also has a bridesmaid giving her grief," Jill said, rinsing the plates and cutlery with a jug of water that had already formed a little crust of ice on top. Her name is Mae."

"Mae Swinson?"

Jill turned then. "Yeah. Why?"

"I probably shouldn't say," Thom said, and he winced.

"Well, now you'll have to tell me," she said, and she stepped back inside, closing the door firmly behind her, and then heading for the woodstove to warm back up again. "What's going on with Mae?"

"She's got a wild crush on Sean, that's what. I mean, I don't know if Sean even noticed since he was completely smitten with Elsa, but Mae has been fawning over him for years."

"Oh…" She'd been wondering if that was the case. Mae had been asked to be a part of Sean's wedding, and she'd agreed. Maybe she hadn't wanted to do it, but there was no graceful way out. And she'd now be front and center to watch Sean take his vows with another woman. "So that's why she's being difficult."

"Difficult how?" he asked.

"She's insisting upon wearing really inappropriate shoes with the dress," Jill said. "And my sister is doing her best to talk her into wearing regular dress shoes, but she won't."

"What will you do?" he asked.

"Right now?" Jill shrugged. "Nothing. I suggested my sister talk to her, figure out what's going on. Who knows? Maybe they'll get to the bottom of it without me."

"You're the family toughie," he said.

"I am." She smiled faintly. "What are you in your family? The nice guy? The wise one? The relationship advice guy?"

"Actually, I might be the nice one," he admitted. "I'm definitely not the wise one—they've got me pinned as the decent guy without being hampered by too much brilliance."

"Lucky." She chuckled and looked up at him. "I don't see it, though."

He reached out and moved a tendril away from her cheek, his rough finger brushing her face as gently as a butterfly wing. "Yeah, I don't see the terrifying ice queen in you, either. Although if you two followed Disney patterns, she'd be ice queen, wouldn't she?"

Her heart skipped a beat, and she dropped her gaze.

"I suppose." She forced a breathy laugh.

And suddenly Jill realized how close they were standing to each other, and just how tall and strong he was. Not that she felt cornered... more that she felt safe standing close to him like this, the warmth from the stove curling comfortingly around them. He smelled good—not like wood shavings yet, but something musky and manly.

"It's nice to have someone to talk to," Thom said quietly.

"It is." It had been a long time since she'd had a man in her life. "You're making this whole experience downright bearable."

"I'm glad." His voice was so soft it was almost a whisper, and suddenly, that kitchen, empty of cupboards and in all sorts of disarray, seemed to melt away. Before she could stop herself she took a step closer to him.

He caught her hand in his, and his grip was so warm and gentle that she felt a lump in her throat. Thom was a little too good-looking for this... If only he was awkward or balding or smelled bad—something! He was a sweet guy, and he didn't seem to realize the power he held.

"Can I tell you something?" she asked.

"Sure."

"You probably shouldn't kiss me again," she said quietly. If he was thinking of doing it again... If he was considering it now...

"Why not?" His voice rumbled deep and soft.

"Because I'm not used to pretending." She looked up at him, wondering if he'd understand. "Everyone thinks I'm tough, but I really have a very thin skin. Elsa might be right that I don't have a lot of experience. I don't date all that often, Thom. I'm not used to this. I can't just...kiss a man and not start feeling something, even if it's entirely misplaced."

It was her heart that was at risk right now.

"What are you feeling?" he asked.

A jumbled mess of longing, hope, softness, her carefully built walls coming down brick by brick...

She wouldn't tell him that. "Thom...you can't just kiss a woman and look at her like that and not spark something."

"Look at you like what?" he asked.

"Like I'm your whole world." Like something real between them might actually be possible. "You're a very good actor. I'm not so good at this."

Thom paused for a moment, licked his lips thoughtfully, then shrugged.

"So no more kissing you," he said quietly.

"It would be for the best," she agreed. "I mean, it was very effective yesterday, and it was even very nice, but you wouldn't want me to go falling for you, now, would you?"

"That would be terrible." His eyes glittered with humor, though. "But I can respect your wishes. No more kisses. I'll just…" He looked down at her hand in his, and ran his thumb over the top of her fingers. "I'll hold your hand. When the occasion calls for it, of course. Would that be okay?"

That was innocent enough. But why did even this seem charged with emotion she didn't want to face?

"I could probably survive that," she said.

If she couldn't handle him touching her fingers, she really did have problems. But if he kissed her again, Jill was liable to get her emotions involved, and her sister had made a good point. She and Thom wanted different lives, and they were both old enough to know better than to start hoping for something that would never work. Hearts were more fragile than young people realized. They healed, of course, but the scars never faded completely.

"I'd better get to work," he said, releasing her fingers.

"Right." She was standing in the middle of his work area, and she pulled her hands against her stomach. "I'll let you do that. I'll get started on those dishes."

Jill stepped outside into the brisk winter air, and she opened the big stove and added another piece of wood to the glowing embers inside. Eli came over from the woodpile with an armful of split wood, and he dumped it into the box just at the bottom of the stairs. He was spry for a man his age, but she noticed that he favored one arm, and his hands were knobby and looked like the cold was making his joints worse.

"Thank you for doing that," Jill said. "You're good to my aunt."

"Just doing what neighbors do," Eli said. "I'd best head back to my own farm now. Tell Belinda I hope she feels better soon. I'll miss her coffee."

Eli didn't wait for her reply, and as Jill watched him amble back in the direction of his own property, she wondered if Aunt Belinda would break this man's heart.

He was more than a neighbor, and when the old man turned and looked solemnly in the direction of that upstairs window, Jill knew beyond a doubt that Eli was in love. He'd let his heart get involved where there wasn't any hope. He should be old enough to know better than that.

Here was hoping she'd avoid the same mistake.

CHAPTER NINE

LATER THAT MORNING Jill fielded a few work calls. It was all apology for disturbing her, but did she know where to find the Esperson file, or whether or not they were leaning toward one campaign or the other, because the client was jumpy. This was the regular ebb and flow in an advertising agency, but the constant flurry of busyness was jarringly different from the pace out here.

Somehow, those files, campaigns, the flow of creative sales pitches—as much as she loved it all, and as much as she fed off it when she was in Pittsburgh—felt strange out here in quiet Amish Country.

"Do you have your computer with you?" her colleague asked. "Could you just take a quick look at this pitch? I know you're on vacation, but I'm trying to save this whole campaign!"

Jill shut her eyes. "I don't have Wi-Fi, but we can talk it through. Okay…so you're selling yoga gear aimed at a female buyer, and you want to show her wearing those yoga clothes doing other things besides yoga."

"Exactly. We need a broader buying base, obviously."

"What do you have so far?"

She looked up to see Thom watching her. He gave her a faint smile and turned away again, presumably to give her some privacy. She listened to her colleague's ideas.

"Why not connect the yoga gear with a slower life, instead of a faster one?" Jill said. "Why not show an ability to relax connected to the clothing—steaming tea, a book laying open…wait, make it upside down, holding someone's place. Show rain trickling down a window, and maybe a warm blanket wrapped around her shoulders while wearing the yoga clothes. That will appeal to every woman, not just the exercise buffs. It's about comfort, relaxation and deep thoughts."

"This is good. And a tag line?"

"Something like… Slow down in Rose Wear. Or, hear yourself think again in Rose Wear. It's an intoxicating thought, being able to change your clothes and your ability to relax all at once. A mini vacation you can wear."

"You're golden! Thank you. I'm going to bring this to the team."

"Good luck." She hung up and looked over to see Thom watching her again.

"You've been answering emails for an hour," he said. "Do they ever give you an actual rest?"

"It's part of the job," she said. "I don't mind. I love what I do."

"You just saved them there, didn't you?"

"I had an idea. We'll see what the team does with it," she replied.

"You do realize that yoga outfits have nothing to do with peace of mind," he said.

"Well…the idea is to connect the item with something less tangible that the person wants. You're selling a feeling."

"How do you do that?" he asked. "Where do your ideas come from?"

"It's the fun of advertising! I don't know. It just comes to me. All right, let's use your business as an example."

"Mine?" He looked a little uncomfortable now.

"If you were to hire me to put together a full ad campaign, I'd take a bunch of pictures of you with a tool belt and dirty hands. But your hair would be perfect, and you'd be looking into the camera as if you were looking directly into your client's soul."

He laughed then and shook his head.

"Oh, there's more!" Jill said, not to be derailed. "I wouldn't be selling your carpentry so much as I'd be selling peace of mind. You're the kind of man whose handshake means something. No more fear of lazy contractors or being taken advantage of. No, with you, they could come home to a gorgeously refinished kitchen, a smiling carpenter with a heart of gold and a life of happy family memories to be made. It's the kind of kitchen that will draw love to it."

"You're good," he said.

"And it's all true. No lies. No exaggeration. No misleading. It's all one hundred percent true. You are the kind of man who people can trust with their family memories. That's who you are at heart. I may not know you terribly well, but I can see that fact plainly."

"Yeah?"

"Yeah. I'm just finding a visual way to show the customer what they get when they hire you."

Thom didn't answer, but his gaze softened, and a smile tickled his lips.

"Harder to judge me when I'm doing it for you, isn't it?" she asked.

Thom nodded. "I'm flattered you see me that way."

"Am I wrong?"

"It's the best side of me, maybe," he said.

"It's the side I see."

He reached out and ran a hand down her forearm, then his fingers dropped away. "I can see why they can't seem to survive without you over there."

Jill's arm tingled where he'd touched her. "I hope it stays that way."

"That's why you keep working, even on vacation?" he asked.

She was silent for a moment. "This is a career based on reading people's deepest desires. If I were to advertise the perfect job to someone like me, I'd show a job so connected to who I am that without me, the entire business would go down. Is it reasonable? Not at all, but it would certainly fill my fantasies."

"To be more than needed," he said. "To be absolutely necessary."

"Yep." Somehow spelling it out tugged at a place in her heart she seldom looked at—the part she avoided with all those long work hours. "So maybe I'm living in my own fantasies that they can't go on without me. Or maybe I don't want them to figure out that they can."

Jill turned as Aunt Belinda shuffled in, slippers on her feet and a box of tissues tucked under one arm. She was dressed, though, and her hair was pulled neatly under her *kapp*.

"Aunty, go rest," Jill said, putting the phone down on the table.

"I could say the same to you," Belinda replied. "But I did get some sleep, and I'm feeling better. Today is laundry day."

"Can't tomorrow be laundry day?" Jill asked.

"No, it cannot." Belinda looked downright affronted.

"Okay, well…let me do it," Jill said.

"You don't know how," Belinda replied. "And I don't mean to offend, but I don't think you have the upper body strength, my dear." Then Belinda looked at Thom for confirmation.

Thom's gaze flicked over Jill, head to toe, then shoulder to shoulder. "I doubt she does."

He turned back to his work again, and Jill burst out laughing. They were ganging up on her, but she could see the teasing in Thom's eye when he glanced her way again.

"It's laundry! Come on, let me at least help you, Aunty. If nothing else, it'll be good for me, right?"

Belinda grudgingly agreed, and she nodded

toward the door that led down to the basement. "The wringer washer is downstairs. We'll start on sheets first, and if you could be so kind as to hang them on the line, it'll be very welcome."

"Of course," Jill said. "It also gives me an excellent excuse to put my phone away."

Maybe Jill wasn't absolutely necessary here in her aunt's B&B, either, but she could be useful.

The next few hours were used in doing the laundry, and her aunt hadn't been joking when she said it used a lot of upper body strength. The clothes had to be fed through the wringer washer, dropped back into the icy-cold water, then lifted up and fed through again and again until the water was dirty and the items were clean. The sheets were the heaviest.

Jill carried each clean load up in a hamper and then hung everything one by one with wooden pins onto the squeaking clothesline. It was called freeze drying—letting the cold turn the water in the fabric into ice crystals that could be shaken off before the items were brought inside to finish drying on lines in the basement.

Jill's fingers were red and numb by the time she was done, and her arms and shoulders ached. The front of her shirt was wet, as well as the tops of her thighs. But at least her aunt got a bit of a rest while Jill worked.

When she came back inside with the empty hamper from the last load, Thom shot her a smile. She headed over to the woodstove and held her numbed hands out to the welcome heat.

"That was harder than I thought," Jill said, and she rubbed her hands together.

"Your phone was ringing," Thom said.

"Oh—" She glanced over to the table where she'd left it and picked it up. The missed calls weren't from work, though. She frowned, looking at the number, and then checked her texts.

"It looks like Sean was calling me. Must be wedding related." She called the number back, and Sean picked up on the first ring.

"Hi, Jill," he said. "We've got a bit of a situation over here."

"What's up?" she asked.

"Elsa had a little sit-down with Mae, and things got ugly. Elsa kicked her out of the wedding party. So now Elsa is sobbing in the other room, and my mother has told me I'm to fix this immediately, and I have no idea what just happened!"

Jill sighed and rubbed a hand over her eyes. "I have some idea…"

"Elsa said you told her to talk it out with Mae, but even Mae won't tell me what happened there. She just said good luck being married to Elsa." Sean sighed. "Look, I know things have been tense with you and Elsa lately, and she told me that you're tired of being the family muscle, but we really need your help."

Jill looked up to see Belinda and Thom both watching.

"Where are you now?" Jill asked.

"We're home," Sean said.

"Where is Mae?" Jill asked.

"No idea."

"Could you call her and ask her to come back?" Jill asked. "I'm sure she'll do it for you."

"I can try," Sean replied.

"Hold on…" Jill pressed the phone against her stomach. "Does anyone have the number for a taxi service? I need to go help my sister. She had a big confrontation with one of the bridesmaids."

"Oh, my word…" Belinda shook her head and tutted softly. "Poor Elsa. If she were Amish, I'd march down there myself and straighten this out."

"I'm the next best thing," Jill said grimly.

She'd been trying to stand back and let her sister take care of things, but it didn't look like that worked terribly well. Jill and Elsa's parents were arriving soon, and when they did, there had better be a wedding with smiling bridesmaids going forward. And Mae, it seemed, needed to be a part of this, even if just to tattoo it in the woman's mind that Sean was well and truly off the market.

"Miss Belinda, if you don't mind me working a bit later tonight, I can drive Jill now," Thom suggested.

"Yes, of course," Belinda said. "Thank you, Thom. You really are a lifesaver."

Jill put the phone back to her ear. "I'm on my way. Just get Mae back to your place, and we'll all sit down."

"Thank you." Sean sounded relieved.

Jill hung up the call and looked down at her own wet clothing. "I'd better get changed."

THOM PICKED UP his tools and got his work area tidied up while Jill changed upstairs. When she came back down, she was wearing black woolen dress pants, a pair of patent leather black boots and a formfitting jewel-green sweater underneath a black woolen coat. She'd twisted her hair up, and done her makeup in no time at all. Coming down the stairs, her heels tapping against the hardwood and her eyes flinty, she was downright intimidating. He didn't envy Mae's position right now.

"Wow," he murmured.

"She's something, isn't she?" Belinda said, casting him a proud smile.

Jill pulled some black leather gloves from the pocket of her coat and cinched the belt at her waist. It was like looking at a different woman.

"This should do the trick. You've got to look the part if you want to boss people around." Then she grinned, and it was the same Jill.

He chuckled. "That will definitely do. Let's go."

Thom pulled a pair of work gloves, a couple pieces of mail and a screwdriver off the passenger-side seat and tossed them in the back to make room for her. Jill hopped up into the truck, then put on her seat belt. A waft of floral scent greeted him as he slammed his own door.

"So this is the Jill your family loves and fears in equal measure, huh?" he said, turning the key. The engine rumbled to life.

"Sure is." Jill chuckled. "I've always liked dressing up and looking sharp, if I can. It helps in my job, too. When I can walk into a conference room and look like I belong at the head of the table, I get people's respect."

"So what's the plan here?" he asked, pulling onto the road.

"If what you say about Mae's crush on Sean is right," she said, and she cast him a smile, "and I do believe you, then I think sitting down with Mae and having a short but direct chat about accepting that he's marrying Elsa and not making a fool of herself will probably do the trick. If she acts up, people will talk about her for years, and it won't change the fact that Sean and Elsa will be a married couple. She's better off putting on a brave face and getting through the day, and if she can't do that, coming down with a conveniently terrible cold and wishing everyone well."

"It makes sense," he replied. "You kind of like this, don't you?"

"I do *not* like this," she retorted. "I'm good at this, though. It's management."

"And everyone relies upon you to do it for the family," he said.

"They do." She leaned her head back against the headrest.

He could see why. Jill was impressive—the kind of person you wanted in your corner. Her family probably bragged about her when she wasn't around, although that was the kind of gossip that never did get back to a person.

Thom had been to Sean and Elsa's apartment, above a picturesque little strip mall of Amish shops, a few times. He got them there quickly and parked along the street.

They headed through the side door that led up to the apartments on the second floor, and Jill knocked. The door opened almost immediately, and Sean ushered them inside.

The apartment was neat, with wedding-related items spread over the kitchen table—pieces of cloth, ribbon, little name tags. Never having gotten this close to wedded bliss, himself, Thom didn't know the particulars, but he was confident that Elsa had it in hand.

Speaking of which… He looked around, but Elsa was nowhere to be seen. Mae was sitting straight-backed on a chair in the living room, though. She wore a pair of leggings, an oversize sweater and a pair of suede UGG boots.

"Hello," Jill said, and she pulled off her gloves and undid the belt on her long coat. It swung open, revealing the bright sweater beneath. Dang. She knew how to make an entrance. She wiped the soles of her boots on the welcome mat and strode inside.

Thom followed her in and cast Sean a sympathetic look.

"I'm her ride," Thom said in explanation.

"Yeah, no problem," Sean said. "Thanks."

Jill headed over to Mae, taking off her coat and folding it over the back of a chair before taking a seat in front of the other woman. She leaned forward, and the women talked too quietly to be overheard.

"Are you doing okay?" Thom asked.

"Wedding pressure," Sean said and he shook his head. "I didn't want this massive wedding, you know. I asked her to do a destination wedding with me. Go to Hawaii or something, come back married. But she wanted a big wedding, and I love her, so I went along with it. But it's becoming an absolute circus."

"Where's Elsa?" he asked.

"Out talking with one of her other bridesmaids." Sean shook his head. "You know, if we'd done it my way, we'd still have friends."

Thom chuckled. "I know you aren't trying to be funny right now, but I think this is par for the course for weddings. Things feel really big that aren't that big of a deal."

"This mess is a pretty big deal," Sean replied.

Thom looked across the room to where the women were talking. Mae's expression had turned alarmed, then sullen. Jill was getting to the good part, it seemed.

Thom shrugged. "This will shake out. A few days from now you'll be a married man and the whole circus will be behind you while you walk some sandy beaches with your bride. It'll be okay. Just keep it in perspective."

The door opened and Elsa stepped inside. She looked surprised to see Thom, and then her gaze swung over to Jill and Mae. She clenched her jaw and marched over to where the men stood together.

"Hi, Thom," she said. "Can I just steal my fiancé for a minute?"

She hooked Sean's arm with hers and tugged him toward the kitchen. Their voices were low, but they carried.

"What is she doing here?" Elsa hissed.

"I called your sister. She asked me to bring Mae back over so she could smooth it over for you."

"Maybe I don't want it smoothed over!"

"Look, sweetie, everyone is really worked up right now—"

"I am not worked up! I'm angry! I'm not some illogical schoolgirl having a meltdown. I'm a grown woman with a problem, Sean!"

Thom attempted to move away from the kitchen to hear a little less of that argument, but it only brought him closer to Jill and Mae. They seemed to finish their conversation, though, and Mae looked less angry, a little sad.

"I know I've been difficult," Mae said to Jill, standing up. "But you're right. Thank you for being straight with me. I'll wear the shoes. I don't know why I got so hung up on it. It was childish of me."

"And dance with a few cute guys at the wedding," Jill said. "You'll look fantastic—don't waste a minute of that."

Mae nodded and a smile tickled her lips. "I'm going to go apologize to Elsa."

"Thanks, Mae," Jill said, and she squeezed her arm. "Weddings can be crazy. This will all blow over."

That was pretty similar to Thom's advice to Sean. But just then Elsa and Sean came out of the kitchen and they were still talking, their heads close, but their voices were loud enough to be heard.

"I didn't want this wedding, Elsa. You wanted this!"

"You don't want a wedding?"

"Don't make it like that. I wanted a wedding, not this huge extravaganza! We can still run off somewhere! Let's go to a judge and be done with it!"

"Two years of my work down the drain?" Elsa's eyes filled with tears. "No one can be bothered to have a real, honest-to-goodness wedding for my sake? This isn't worth it for me?"

"It's falling apart!" Sean said.

"No, Mae is falling apart. That's all that matters to you?"

"I never said that, but I didn't want all this fighting!"

"You know what?" Elsa's voice shook. "Fine. Call off the wedding. But I'm not doing it. You call people. Tell them it's over. All two hundred and seventy of them. They can make other plans for the weekend. But I am not running off to a judge. I'll save you the trouble— the wedding is off."

"Elsa—"

"All I wanted was a proper wedding, Sean!" Tears trickled down Elsa's cheeks, and she marched back to the door and disappeared outside, the door banging shut behind her.

Everyone stood in stunned silence, and Sean rubbed his hand over his eyes. His shoulders slumped.

"Uh, maybe you could all leave," Sean said woodenly.

"Of course," Thom said, eyeing the door. He was more than happy to oblige.

Mae looked at Sean, her face softening into a look of agonized compassion, but then she glanced at Jill and headed for the door. That was the right choice, in Thom's opinion. Jumping on Sean's heartbreak right now would be unfair, and would lose her friends if she was the cause of Sean and Elsa's breakup.

"For what it's worth, Mae is going to apologize to Elsa and cooperate for the wedding," Jill said.

"Thank you," Sean said, and his voice sounded tight. "But I don't think there's going to be a wedding."

"Go after her!" Jill said. "You know how she can be. She's just worked up right now. She'll calm down, and Mae will apologize, the other bridesmaids will see how silly it all was and the wedding can go on. I know my sister."

"I don't know." Sean shook his head. "I know your sister, too. I think this big day was more important to her than the groom."

"You love each other," Jill said pleadingly.

"I'll talk to her. But not right now." But Sean's voice was still thick with emotion. "Look, I know I called you over, and I asked you to fix this, but right now I just need some space."

Jill nodded and looked toward Thom helplessly.

"Let us know if we can do anything," Thom said, and when Sean nodded silently, they headed out the door. It shut solidly behind them, and a lock slid into place.

"Oh, wow…" Jill murmured.

"I didn't see that coming," Thom agreed.

They headed down the stairs and out onto the sidewalk. The evening was growing dark, and Thom realized it was close to suppertime. For a moment they just stood there in the cold February air.

"You want to grab a burger?" Thom asked.

"Yeah…"

They got back into the truck and Thom started the engine. Some food would make this evening a little easier. Had they just witnessed the permanent breakup of a really great couple? He sincerely hoped not. Thom might not have had much luck in love, but they needed someone to give hope to the rest of the lonely hearts out there.

CHAPTER TEN

THE BURGER BARN was a family owned joint that had the best burgers in Pennsylvania. Big fat beef patties, piles of condiments, crisp bacon, melted cheese and fluffy, crusty buns that were baked on site. The fries that came in copious portions on the side of every burger were simple home-cut potatoes deep-fried with lots of salt. For the heart-health conscious, this was a restaurant to avoid. But for someone in need of some edible comfort, this was the place to go.

Jill knew this restaurant from her visits to her great-aunt over the years, so when Thom pulled into the familiar parking lot, she felt a wave of comfort at the sight of it. It looked like it had gotten a face-lift since her last visit—the parking lot was paved, the siding that used to be shabby white had been painted a brilliant red, and a red-and-white-striped awning had been added over the front door. She approved. It looked good.

She looked back down at her cell phone. She'd sent her sister three texts and called her a few times.

"Her phone is turned off," Jill said.

"Maybe she's talking to Sean," Thom suggested.

"Yeah. I hope so." But she had a sinking feeling all was not going to be so easily fixed this time around. If it was just Elsa running off upset, that was one thing. But she'd seen Sean's face. He was deeply hurt, too.

"Have you been here before?" Thom asked as he pulled into a parking space. There was parking for buggies as well as cars, and there were three buggies with horses still hitched up already in the lot.

"I come every visit," she said. She looked down at her phone again, silently wishing her sister to answer her.

"Comfort food at its finest. Unless you wanted to go back to your aunt's place?"

She shook her head. "I'm not ready to explain myself yet. I feel responsible for what happened tonight."

"Don't. Sean asked you to fix things with Mae. You did that." He opened his door. "Let's go order. This will all look better with a side of fries, I'm sure."

Jill smiled faintly and followed his lead. He was probably right about things seeming better with a burger in front of her. And maybe it was just that old role of the family fixer she always played, but she hadn't been able to fix this one.

They sat in a corner booth, and an Amish teenage girl took their order. They both asked for burgers and fries, and when the waitress retreated, Jill leaned back with a sigh.

"I wish my sister would answer me," she said.

"You know what I've learned over the years?" Thom said. "If people want to be together, they figure it out. If they don't…they don't. And the people who are in the middle when they're trying to figure it out get relegated to the periphery of their lives once they do. So whether you've got their best interests as a couple at heart or not, it's better to give them some space. Let them sort it out and come back to you with their good news."

"That sounds like experience talking," she said.

"My brother."

"Oh?" She leaned forward.

"I was doing some work on some old cabinets in their kitchen when they had this massive fight. This was almost five years ago. There was a student who'd declared her love for my brother, and his wife wasn't convinced it was all the girl's fault, you know? Call it a gut feeling."

"Yikes." Jill winced.

"Yeah. Well, I was right there, and the kids were preschool age at the time. I played referee. I shouldn't have. Looking back on it, I should have slipped out and given them privacy."

"They obviously sorted it out, though," she said. "They're still together."

"Yeah. Basically, he admitted that he'd been flattered by the girl's attention. But he hadn't crossed any lines. He swore he'd be more careful in the future, and his wife unpacked her bags again and decided to stay."

"And after that?" Jill asked.

"Well, before that my brother just thought I was undereducated and should do something else with my life. After that he pulled back more. I mean, I understood. He had to sort things out with his wife. He was embarrassed, too. It just complicated things. I wanted to help—and I did! I mean, they sorted it out. But it only hurt my relationship with him."

"It's ironic," she said.

"Yeah. He never asked me to help him with house renovations again. And neither did Janelle."

"They both pulled back." She could see the warning there. She and Elsa had their own tensions. "This is why family frustrates me. When I complete a task at work, my work is acknowledged and we all move on. You do exactly what everyone asks from you with family, and you wrestle with the fallout for the next ten years."

The waitress came back with their food, and for the next few minutes they tucked into their meals. Jill's burger had extra pickles and mayo, and she dipped a crisp fry into a little tub of mayo on the side. It was the kind of meal that filled the hole inside your heart for a little while when an actual solution wasn't available.

"So it went okay with Mae?" he asked.

"Yup. I also pointed out that she should get over any feelings for the groom. He was getting married, and she'd better find a nice guy at the wedding to dance with." Jill sighed. "I don't think she realized her feelings for Sean were so obvious. She figured it was her secret, and the fact that other people knew sobered her up."

Jill looked at her phone again. Still nothing.

"I know you want to," Thom said, "but you can't fix this one, Jill."

"You know, I fought getting involved from the start! My sister hinted that she wanted me to be a bridesmaid, and I told her that work was too demanding, and I'd only let her down. Besides, I felt too old to be a bridesmaid again. I asked if I could just be a regular guest and wish her well from the pews." She took another bite of her burger and swallowed before she continued. "She was fine with that. In fact, she didn't really want me in the bridal party— I wouldn't have been a fun bridesmaid, and I think we both knew that two years of wedding prep as a bridesmaid would have ruined what was left of our relationship." She sighed. "Anyway, when I got here, my mom was begging me to get involved in the situation with Mae. I wouldn't do it. I was so tired of being the one who marches in and bosses everyone around."

"You're good at it, though," he said past a bite of food.

"Maybe," she agreed. "But I get sick of it. This idea that Elsa is too fragile to handle real life gets very old." She put her cell phone into her coat pocket, out of sight. "And here I am, desperate to rescue her again. She's got a great little gig going, doesn't she?"

"You care," Thom said. "I see something here that you don't. You love your sister and you want her to be happy, whether that means her taking responsibility for her own life, or you helping her out. You care."

The restaurant door opened and an Amish man came inside. It took Jill a moment to recognize him from the skating pond a few nights earlier. A waitress brought him to a small table near their booth, and he and Thom exchanged a nod.

"Hi, Mark. How are you?" Thom said.

"I'm actually glad I saw you," Mark said. "Do you have a minute?"

"Yeah…" Thom looked at Jill and when she quickly nodded, he added, "Yeah, of course. Come have a seat."

Mark pulled a chair up and sat down. "I've been thinking about it, and the idea of Nellie King with some other man is just…unbearable. I can't sit back and let her marry some farmer twice her age. Not when I—" Mark's gaze flickered uncomfortably toward Jill.

"Love her?" she supplied softly.

"*Yah*. Well, I'm not a farmer. But maybe I could learn how. Maybe her father would still leave her the land if we got some help and someone taught me," Mark said. "Because no one would be as good a husband to her as I would. I don't have much money, but I've got a good job, and I've got time on my side."

"Good for you," Thom said. "Go tell her that."

"No, I can't just do that. I mean…she's got a matchmaker working for her, and the last time I saw her, Nellie's eyes just slid off me. She doesn't know how I feel. But if Belinda would say something on my behalf…"

"Then talk to Belinda?" Thom said.

"I was hoping you would," Mark said hesitantly. "Or maybe you?" He finally included Jill in his glance.

"Mark, is it?" she said.

"Yah."

"Mark, I'm terrible at this," she said. "I just watched my sister and her fiancé break up, so I'm not exactly playing my A game here, you know? If you love Nellie, then do something about it."

"I am. Right now."

"I mean, between the two of you," Jill said. "I'll never be able to speak as eloquently for you as you could for yourself. What do you want me to say—he's no farmer, but he likes her? Nellie is a beautiful woman with land coming to her, Mark. There will be other men who will develop feelings, too."

"So you won't mention it to Belinda?" Mark asked.

"No," she said. "Thom and I aren't your best option. We can talk to her, and my aunt might make a decision of her own and never mention you to Nellie. Who knows? My aunt sees things the way she sees things, and I really don't have as much influence as you might think. You need to go down there and tell her yourself. Put yourself forward. Say how you feel about Nellie. I think it will matter."

"I agree with Jill," Thom said. "As a man, you've got to march up there and do it yourself. If you want to be Nellie's husband, then you'd better prove you're man enough for marriage now. And a married man speaks his piece."

"Yah, yah..." Mark nodded a couple of times. "Okay. Thank you. I'd better get a few things arranged first, though. But you're right. If I'm saying I'm ready for marriage, then I'd better have the basics lined up."

Jill smiled. "Good luck."

"We don't believe in luck," Mark said earnestly. "But I'll do my best."

When the waitress came back to take Mark's order, he had already left the restaurant, food forgotten.

"What do you think he's arranging?" Jill asked.

"Money." Thom popped a fry into his mouth.

"That's it?"

"Maybe a new buggy or something. But it comes down to cold hard cash. Doesn't it always?" He picked up another fry.

"You're a surprisingly cynical man," she chuckled.

"I'm not cynical," Thom said. "It's just how the world works. If he wants to get married, he's going to have to show her people that he's ready to support a family. He'll have to have some savings, be able to present himself as a mature man, not just a boy in the community."

"That's fair," she said.

"That said, he's got a good job, and he loves her." Thom shrugged. "I hope she sees the potential in him."

Jill wiped her fingers on a napkin. "Yesterday I would have gone to Belinda for him."

"What changed?" he asked. "Elsa and Sean?"

She nodded. "I'm a little less confident in my own ability to manage other people's lives."

Thom smiled. "They'll be okay. Every last one of them."

But would there be a wedding? Or would

this be nothing more than a really awkward visit with a whole lot of extended family already on their way?

As THEY DROVE back toward the bed-and-breakfast, the truck's headlights cut through the darkness. The night was overcast, and fat, slushy snowflakes rushed into the windshield. His wipers swept them aside, only for them to be replaced.

Thom's heart felt heavy tonight. Sean was a good friend, and he'd been prepared to feel mildly jealous of the guy's happiness…not this. For two years Sean and Elsa had been the image of engaged bliss. To have it all fall apart—he couldn't imagine how Sean felt right now.

The first few acres of land they passed on Butternut Drive belonged to Eli Lapp, and Thom let his gaze flow over the snow-covered fields. Were things any simpler out here with the Amish? People seemed to think so—the Amish represented getting back to the basics. But what was more universal than falling in love, getting married and starting families? It was the love part that was complicated anywhere you went.

Thom glanced over at Jill in the passenger seat. She was dressed in that power outfit of hers, but he could see the cracks in her armor now. She looked tired, sad. Before he returned his gaze to the road, he saw the stooped figure of a man standing in the field. He was struggling with a heavy load in the blowing wet snow. Thom slowed down.

"Is that Eli?" he asked.

Jill peered through the gloom. "Yeah, it looks like. He's got…what is that?"

"He could probably use a hand," Thom said, and he pulled to the side of the road. He left his hazard lights on and hopped out of the truck. Wet snowflakes blasted him in the face as he jogged around the side of the vehicle and stood in the glow of his headlights.

"Eli?" he called.

"Hi there," Eli called back. "I found a dog out here—he's nearly frozen through."

"Well, come on—get in the truck, and we'll drive you back up to your house," Thom shouted.

Thom jumped over the trench between the field and the road. He could see that the dog looked scared and cold. It looked like a mostly black mutt with no collar, but it was hard to tell with all the snow that was matting its fur.

Eli's black hat was covered in a layer of wet snow, too. When Thom reached for the animal to give old Eli a hand, the dog leaned toward him as if sensing Thom was there to help.

The dog was shaking, but they all moved a little faster now that Eli could walk without the burden. When they reached the truck, Jill pushed her door open and held her arms out for the animal. Both Thom and Eli stopped, looked at each other.

"You'll get dirty," Thom said.

"Probably," she replied curtly. "Come on. Hand him to me so we can all get out of here."

Thom hoisted the dog up to her, and he saw one of those muddy, wet feet leave a streak down her pristine black coat. She pulled the dog into her arms, then scooted to the middle of the seat. Eli climbed up next to her, and Thom shut the door, headed around to the driver's side and hopped in.

Jill right next to him felt good. She was warm. He stepped on the gas and they headed forward the last few yards before the drive that led to Eli's little farmhouse.

The driveway was potholed and Thom winced as they bounced over a particularly deep one. The dog in Jill's lap poked a nose toward his face, and he felt a warm, velvet lick.

He reached up and gave the dog a rub behind the ears.

He pulled up to a stop beside the little farmhouse. It was a solid enough building with a strong roof, and a finger of smoke rose from the chimney, visible through the falling snow.

"Let me give you a hand," Thom said.

"Oh, no…the house isn't really presentable for a woman," Eli said.

"I don't count," Jill said. "I'm not Amish."

Eli considered that for a moment, then shrugged. "True enough."

Thom wasn't sure how she'd managed that so smoothly, but he was glad for it. He got out of the truck first, and then Jill handed the dog over to him. She followed him out the driver's side door. The older man led the way to the side door of the house, and Thom followed, slipping a couple of times in the new, wet snow with the wriggling dog in his grasp.

Inside, a woodstove glowed cheerily in one corner, but everything else was dim. There was the distinct smell of poultry in the house, and the soft *cluck cluck cluck* of a chicken greeted him. Then Eli lit a lamp, and the dim room came into view.

What used to be a dining room had become a chicken house. Wire cages covered the tabletop, a fat chicken roosting happily in each cage. The room was surprisingly neat all the same, and the cages had been set up so that the bottoms could easily be pulled out and cleaned. There were some old sheets covering kitchen chairs, and the floor looked like it had been swept recently, although maybe not washed. Was this really how the old man lived?

"Let's get him by the stove," Eli said, and Thom followed the old man over to the woodstove. Eli disappeared into another room and came back with a worn, torn quilt and laid it on the ground. Thom put the dog down on the blanket, and Eli squatted down next to him and felt the animal's limbs.

"Nothing broken," Eli said. "Just cold. Good thing I found him."

Thom looked around the room once more and saw Jill peering into the wire cage.

"There's an egg in there," Jill said.

"Oh, good!" Eli replied. "That'll be breakfast."

"Eli, do you mind if I ask why you have chickens in your house?" Thom asked.

"It gets cold," Eli said. "I lost a good layer to the cold, so I brought them inside. They lay better when they're warm."

"Maybe you need a new chicken house," Thom said.

"Well, you get to be my age, and you're running the farm, and you're tired and you see a short cut. I took the short cut, young man."

"I'm a carpenter by trade," Thom said.

"Yah, yah..."

"I could build you a new chicken coop," Thom added, connecting the dots for him.

Eli brightened momentarily, then shook his head. "No, I'm fine. I like this arrangement better than you'd think. I have company in here now, you see?"

The sound of hooves on the wood floor echoed from the other room, and a low moo followed.

"Is there a cow in here?" Thom asked, looking around.

"A calf. There's about a thousand pound difference between a cow and a calf," Eli replied.

Sure enough, a leggy calf appeared in the doorway. He let out another moo and came over to Eli, nuzzling at his hands.

"He's ready for his bottle," Eli said. "Would you grab it from the ice box? I've got one prepared."

Thom looked at Jill and she shrugged. There

was a bottle for the calf right where Eli had said, and Thom held it out for the eager animal.

"Your aunt hates this," Eli said, rising to his feet and waggling a knobby finger at Jill. "Hates it something fierce."

"It's…a unique choice," Jill replied. Thom smiled.

"I get lonely, honestly," Eli said. "I get back inside from chores, and just stare at a ticking clock. That's no way to pass the time, is it?"

"I imagine Aunt Belinda has the same problem," Jill said.

"No, she's got friends," Eli said, and he leaned down to pet the dog's head affectionately. "I'll get this guy some meat."

No friends. Thom frowned. The poor old man made a nuisance of himself to Belinda because he was lonesome, and he brought animals inside so he'd have some company.

Eli ambled past Thom and into the kitchen. The calf butted at the bottle, and drained the last of the milk down to bubbles, then clopped off toward the side door.

"He's house trained…mostly," Eli called. "Let him out."

Thom opened the side door. The calf went out into the snow and returned a couple of minutes later, hooves clomping across the floor as he went over to where the dog lay on the blanket and sniffed at him.

"Mostly house trained?" Jill said.

"Well, there are accidents from time to time, but accidents with an animal that size are quite the event. He's doing pretty well, though. I'll get him back into the barn once he's a bit older."

"Will he want to go?" Jill asked.

"Hmm." Eli raised his eyebrows. "I hope so."

"Eli, how much wood do you have around here?" Thom asked.

"Firewood? Plenty."

"No, wood for building," Thom said.

Eli cocked his head to one side, considering. "I've got some out in the barn. Some two-by-fours, some plywood… Not as much as you'd think, though."

"I'm going to finish up Belinda's kitchen, and after that maybe you'll give me a hand with firming up your coop outside," Thom said. "Free of charge."

"I can't ask for you to work for free—" Eli shook his head.

"Hey, it's between friends. No charge. You can help me out sometime to even the score if you want."

"Oh…" Eli's chin trembled. "All right, then."

Thom had already pushed things as far as he dared before insulting the old man's dignity, and he angled his head toward the door.

"We'd better head out. I'll be by in a few days, then."

"Will do." Eli smiled. "That's nice. Thank you. Here—"

Eli pottered over to the chicken cage, opened the door and thrust his hand underneath the bird. It fluttered up in surprise, and Eli pulled out the egg—large and brown. He brought it over to Thom with a good-natured smile.

"For your breakfast," Eli said, and added after a pause, "You might want to rinse that off."

"Thanks," Thom said, accepting it solemnly. "I'll see you."

Thom and Jill headed back out into the cold evening, and when they got to the truck, he handed the egg to Jill.

"Can you hold that for me?" he asked.

She accepted it mutely, and they both got into the truck again. He started the engine and pulled a U-turn.

"You are a very decent guy, Thom," Jill said.

Thom smiled faintly and refused to look toward her. "Don't drop my egg. That's quality organic food."

Jill chuckled. "Be bashful all you want. You are downright decent."

Somehow, he liked hearing that from Jill. Her opinion mattered in a place deep down in his heart that he hadn't looked at in a very long time. That was dangerous for his own equilibrium, but it was true.

Shoot. What was with him falling for the wrong woman again and again?

CHAPTER ELEVEN

JILL FOUND HER aunt in the sitting room next to a kerosene lamp. She had a pile of knitting on her lap and a tattered piece of paper next to her that she kept pushing her glasses up her nose to see properly. Belinda looked up.

"Oh, I have some dinner on top of the stove for you, dear. I already ate and cleaned up. I wasn't sure when you'd be back, so I hope you don't mind."

"No, no, I should have come back earlier, but—" She paused. "Aunty, I just got back from Eli's place."

"Eli's?" Belinda lowered her knitting. "He had dinner with me. He just left a little while ago."

"He must have been on his way home, then," Jill said. "Because he found a half-frozen dog out in the field, and we helped him get it into his house."

"Another animal in there…" Belinda shook her head. "Is the dog all right?"

"He found it in time," Jill replied. "It's curled up by the woodstove right now. It'll be okay, I think."

"That's good."

"It's not the dog that worries me, though," Jill said.

"His house..." Belinda nodded. "I know. I've stopped visiting him over there because it frustrates me so much. How many chickens on his dining table now?"

"Three," she said.

"There used to be five."

"Wow." Jill came into the room and sank into the couch opposite her aunt. "There's also a bottle calf that he has house trained."

"He was very proud of that." Belinda shook her head. "I'm sorry about him. Trust me. I have tried to talk sense into that man. He just won't improve things."

"Aunt Belinda, I heard him telling Thom why he does it," Jill said. "Thom seems to have a way of getting other men to open up."

"And?" Belinda asked.

"He's lonely. He isn't alone in the house if there are animals there," she replied.

Belinda sighed and lowered her knitting. She was silent for a moment.

"He didn't do this sort of things so often

when his brother was alive," Belinda said at last. "Their house was a mess, their manners were appalling, but there was a lot less livestock in the house back then." Belinda didn't say anything for a beat, and then she shook her head sadly. "I do what I can as his neighbor, Jill. I have him over for dinner. I teach him to mend his own clothes. I check in on him when I don't see him out and about doing chores. And he's…he's my friend. Well and truly. But if he wants a wife of his own, then he has to do the work on himself. I can't do that for him."

"That's fair," Jill agreed, and she let her gaze move over her aunt's neat sitting room. The wood in the room from the floor to the side table all shone with a fresh polishing. Even Belinda's woven basket of knitting supplies looked neatly organized—balls of wool all wound up tightly, and knitting needles arranged in a quilted holder that kept them all together, bundled up like a quiver of arrows. The tidiness was decidedly peaceful.

"Do you get lonely, Aunt Belinda?" Jill asked.

"Yah…" Belinda's knitting needles clicked as she started up her work once more. "I do. That's when I flag down Eli and offer him dinner. Or sometimes I get into my buggy and

I drive out to visit a friend or my son. Also, there's the guests who come to stay here at my bed-and-breakfast. That's why I started it up after your great-uncle passed. There will always be lonely times, but there will always be something we can do about it, too."

"I like that perspective," Jill said.

"Did you sort things out for your sister?" Belinda asked. "How is that…what do you call your *newehockers*?"

"We call them bridesmaids."

"*Yah.* How is that bridesmaid? Did you get it all sorted out?"

"Well…" Jill pulled out her phone and looked for messages. Still nothing from her sister. "I did sort the bridesmaid out, actually. She said she'd apologize to Elsa and stop being difficult. I'm not sure if it matters anymore, though, because while I was sorting out the bridesmaid, Elsa and Sean were having a completely different argument and broke up."

Belinda's knitting needles stopped moving. "Broke up?"

"Yes." Jill sighed. "I didn't see that one coming. Sean is frustrated with all the drama and wanted to just go get married without all the fuss. Elsa is invested in the wedding she's been putting together for the last two years. They broke up and Elsa left."

"And Sean?" Belinda asked.

"He's…tired." Jill shook her head. "I told him to go after her. He said he needed space."

"Not a good sign," Belinda agreed. "This is why Amish weddings work better. They are put together by a community, and they don't cost an arm and a leg, either. We all work together to get a couple married. For the most part, the bride and groom just show up appropriately attired."

"That does sound nice," Jill said.

"What did you do?" Belinda asked.

"Sean asked us to leave," she said. "And Elsa wasn't answering her cell phone. So there wasn't much I could do. Besides, I was talking to Thom about it, and he pointed out that the person who's caught in the middle of a couple's argument is often pushed out of their lives after they're back together again. You can't win."

"Marriage isn't about winning or losing." Belinda's knitting needles started up again.

"I know."

"But you're right. Sometimes all you can do is sit back and let the couple sort themselves out. Once they're married, they'll require privacy to deal with any issues that arise, and sometimes it's better to let them do that before the wedding, too." Belinda leaned closer to her tattered piece of paper, inspected her knitting, looked back at the paper and then continued knitting. "All the same, if this doesn't sort itself out, you bring those two to me, and I'll see what I can do."

"That's true—this is your wheelhouse," Jill said.

"My what?"

"Your specialty, your line of work," Jill said.

"*Yah*, that it is. But speaking of my…wheelhouse," Belinda said with a small smile that made her blue eyes glitter, "I have a young farmer coming to see me tomorrow about our Nellie. He's from a neighboring community, and he seems very promising. I thought you might like to sit in on the interview."

"How come you keep including me in this, Aunty?" Jill asked.

Belinda looked up, looking mildly surprised. "I thought you'd like it."

"I do. Don't get me wrong," Jill replied. "But I'm not Amish. The Amish people don't seem entirely comfortable to have me there, either. And my opinion won't matter one bit to them— I'm an outsider."

"All very true," her aunt agreed. "But you're

my niece, and since you're visiting me, they'll put up with it. Besides, it helps me. If they're just a little bit off balance, they reveal things. Like our Morris Smucker, who isn't in want of a new wife so much as still desperately in love with his late wife. I'm not sure that would have come to light as easily without you there to put him off balance a bit."

"You're clever," Jill said with a smile.

"I try to be." Belinda returned her smile. "Now, would you like to be a part of this next interview?"

"Yes, I'd love to."

"Good. I appreciate it, dear."

Jill went up to bed a little while later, and lying under the warm quilts and watching snowflakes drift past her window, she dialed her sister's number once more.

This time Elsa picked up.

"Hi." There were tears in Elsa's voice.

"Elsa…what happened?" Jill asked. "Did you and Sean make up yet?"

"No." Her voice sounded choked. "The wedding is off."

"Did you talk to him at least?" Jill pressed.

"Yeah, I went home and we talked and talked and nothing really seemed to change. He's sick of the wedding plans, and my friends, and how the wedding just seems to keep getting bigger. He doesn't get that that's how weddings work—that's how families work! His family isn't like ours… They're small and mind their own business pretty well."

"Not like ours at all," Jill said ruefully.

"Yeah, well… I come with a family, and friends and hopes and dreams of my own." Elsa sighed. "He says he'd marry me still if we elope."

"Will you do it?" Jill asked.

"No! I want the big church wedding. I want my father to walk me down the aisle, and my mother to help me with my veil. I want the proper wedding I've always dreamed of."

"Isn't it better to just marry him?" Jill asked.

"Does he really want to marry me?" Elsa asked. "He seems to be changing his mind. And I'm telling you, everything was just fine until Mae started making a scene."

"Do you think Mae is involved in this?" Jill asked cautiously.

"She's got a thing for my fiancé!" Elsa said. "You know?"

"Yes, I know! And I trusted Sean's love for me. But when the pressure hits, all of a sudden he starts saying the very things Mae's been saying for a while now. That weddings are big and expensive and ridiculous, and that if you really loved someone, you'd just get married in some little ceremony somewhere…implying I don't really love Sean half enough."

"She's been stirring the pot," Jill said, her own irritation starting to simmer.

"Yes, she has."

"Why did you even choose her as a bridesmaid, then?" Jill asked.

"Because I thought that if she had to watch us get married, it might drive it home for her that he's getting married, and she needs to move on." Elsa's voice shook.

"I talked to her," Jill said, "and she'll be finding you to apologize soon. Elsa, I know you don't want to hear this, but what if you did what Sean wanted? What if you just abandoned this whole wedding and ran off to Vegas or something to make it legal?"

"Because I believe a lifelong vow deserves the pomp and celebration that comes with a great big, floofy wedding," Elsa said. "And that's who I am. That's who he said he wanted to marry. If he's changed his mind about that… it's better to just face it, don't you think?"

"Maybe it is," Jill said softly. "Oh, sweetie. I'm really sorry."

"Will you help me tell people the wedding is off?" Elsa asked, sniffling.

"No," Jill said.

"Why not? I can't do this alone!"

"Because I still have some hope for you two," Jill replied. "I want you and Sean to come over to Aunt Belinda's place tomorrow evening. Talk to Aunt Belinda together. If you can't sort it out, I'll help you do all the footwork of canceling things."

"And if Sean won't come?" Elsa's voice shook.

"I think he'll come," Jill said gently. "Have a little faith in him."

And if he refused, Jill was marching down there and dragging him by the ear. Those two had planned a massive wedding and invited everyone in from out of town to celebrate. At the very least, Sean could come have a rational conversation with their Amish great-aunt. And if things didn't shake out then, Jill would do as her sister asked and help to cancel the whole affair.

Thom crouched in front of Belinda's new kitchen counter and used his electric drill to drive a screw into the hardwood below. It took a lot of muscle to drive even a wood screw into solid poplar. As the screw finally tightened down flat, he released the drill. The framework was done, as was the new counter. A large double sink was installed in the center, just under the window. That was the last one—he didn't want to make too much noise while Belinda was interviewing another match for Nellie.

A young Amish farmer sat at the kitchen table, and out of respect for Jill, he was speaking in English, which meant that Thom could understand, too. His name was Freeman Gaetz. There was a hat line around his dark blond hair from where the band had pressed his hair down. The women had been chatting with him casually enough—fetching coffee, getting him some shoo fly pie, asking after his relatives, some of whom Belinda seemed to know.

Thom wouldn't normally be taking such personal interest in someone else's business, but this one did feel more personal. This was a potential husband for Nellie King, and if she did find some appropriate farmer, that would mean that Mark Yoder would be out of luck, and he found that he was solidly in Mark's corner.

Thom shouldn't care this much. It wasn't his life…but still, his ears pricked up when Belinda asked her first serious question.

"And what about your farming experience?"

Belinda asked. "You don't have a farm of your own, I understand."

"No, my *daet* is leaving the family farm to my older brother. We all know it, and it's okay. So I've been working with a roofing company." He paused. "But if I did have a farm, I've got ideas of how I'd keep things running. I built my *daet's* windmill, and I can do it again with my eyes shut. I'm good with cattle, too, and I have a good sense when it comes to crops. My brother said we could work the family farm together when the time comes, but honestly, he wants the benefit of my experience without giving me half the land."

"These things happen…" Belinda murmured. "And your relationship with your family?"

"We're all close," Freeman replied. "I don't mean to imply I don't get along with my oldest brother, but a man needs to make his own way. Of course, I'll help my brother where I can—I'll go help him at harvest time and with the calving season, but I've got to build something of my own, too, if I'm to leave something to my own *kinner*."

"There was a girl you were courting…" Belinda said softly.

"Yah. Yah." Freeman started to fidget then, and Thom picked up the shelf for the inside of

the cupboard. He brushed the wood dust off and slid it into place. It fit perfectly onto the rubber-topped metal tags that were waiting to support it.

"I did care for her an awful lot," Freeman said. "But she didn't feel the same way. What can I say? She's marrying someone else this fall."

"And if she changed her mind?" Jill asked.

Freeman looked startled that Jill had spoken.

"She won't," he said.

"But if she did," Jill pressed. "If she came to you tomorrow and said she'd made a mistake and wanted to be your wife, what would you do?"

"I'd say no." The response was quick, calm, firm.

"Why?" Belinda asked.

"Because I don't want to be with a woman who can jump from one man to the next like that. She wouldn't have the character I'm looking for," he replied.

A good answer, Thom had to admit.

"Could I ask a few questions about the young lady?" Freeman asked.

"Yah. Yah," Belinda said. "Go ahead."

"How many brothers and sisters in her family?" he asked.

"They're four all together. All girls, and all married now except for Nellie."

"And what is her relationship with her sisters like?" Freeman asked. "Do they argue much?"

"No, they are all very supportive of each other."

"And if Nellie gets this farm, would the others be upset?"

"No, she's the oldest," Belinda replied. "It should go to her. Her father's health is in decline, and her sisters all married before she did, two of them even had a double wedding one fall."

"How many men have been interested in this farm?" he asked.

"A few," Belinda said. "I'm not at liberty to say how many."

"How many has she gone out riding with?" he asked.

"None that I know of," Belinda replied. "She's left the sifting in my hands."

"And are there any you think might be good for her?" Freeman asked.

"None I'm leaning toward yet," Belinda said. "You're trying to suss out her character."

"*Yah*, I am," he replied. It was smart. Marrying a woman and finding out later if she was a flirt would be a bitter thing to discover.

"She's not a flirt," Belinda said, following Thom's line of thought. "She's very shy, actually. She's convinced she's not beautiful, but I disagree with her. I think she got that impression because somehow she was passed over."

"Is she honest?" Freeman asked. "Does she tell little untruths sometimes?"

"No, she tells the truth," Belinda said.

"Is she kind?" he pressed. "Does she have a sharp tongue? Does she say what she thinks whether it hurts someone or not?"

"She's very kind," Belinda replied. "And as for a sharp tongue, I've never seen it from her. But I might want to give you a little advice, young man. Any woman can be pressed to a limit where she'll speak sharply if her husband doesn't treat her gently. If you want a gentle woman, then you'd better treat her with the sensitivity of a newborn lamb. Women do not stay gentle when being poked and prodded by an irritable husband. That's some free advice for you to use anywhere you like."

Freeman nodded. "I'm sorry. I didn't mean to sound too judgmental, but this is a careful decision. I'm looking for a woman to spend my life with, and these are the things that matter to me."

"You are asking the right questions," Belinda said, softening her tone.

"What about appearances?" Jill asked. "What would you hope your wife would look like?"

"Well... I hope she'd be pretty," Freeman said. "And I hope that she'd be shorter than me. I'm not an overly tall man, but that would be nice."

"She is shorter than you," Jill said, and there was a smile in her voice.

The conversation moved along, and Thom turned his attention to attaching hinges to the cabinet doors. This business of arranging marriages was uncomfortably clinical. Boxes ticked, requirements met and the two of them hadn't even laid eyes on each other yet. What if Freeman didn't feel anything special when he looked at Nellie? What if Nellie found out too late that another man was deeply in love with her?

Not my business, Thom silently remonstrated with himself. If this was the Amish way of things, then who was he to argue? It wasn't his relationship being arranged by a matchmaker, his future in the balance. Nor was this exactly a woman being sold off for a piece of land, either. Miss Belinda was obviously putting in a great deal of work to find a decent man for Nellie.

But still, trusting a lifetime to someone who simply ticked the right boxes seemed dangerous to him. There had better be more to it than that.

By the time Freeman left, Thom put the cabinet doors onto two lower cabinets, and he'd tightened the simple brass knobs into place. He stood back to look at his handiwork, and Belinda walked up next to him.

"It looks good, Thom," she said. "Really good."

"I'm glad you like it," he replied.

She crossed her arms and inspected the cabinets for a moment, her brow creased. Thom followed her gaze.

"Is there any problem?" he asked.

"No, no," Belinda said, shaking her head. "It does look good, Thom. I'm sorry, I was thinking about Freeman Gaetz."

The older woman pressed her lips together, then looked over at Jill. "What do you think, Jill?"

"He seems…very nice."

"And concerned about the right things," Belinda added. "He didn't once ask about the size of the farm, or anything like that. He wanted to know about her character." Belinda looked up at Thom. "Any thoughts?"

"I'm not the right person to ask," he said.

"You're a man," Jill said. "Did you notice any warning signs we might be missing?"

He wished he could say yes, but there wasn't anything.

"He seems like a really decent guy," Thom said. "I'm sure he's very nice, but is that enough to make a lifelong partnership work?"

"Marriages have been successful starting with less," Belinda said distractedly.

"But today? I mean, sure, fifty or a hundred years ago, there might have been enough outside pressures to keep a couple together. But it's different now," Thom said. "You're asking two people to not only get married, but to stay married for their entire lives no matter how the marriage turns out. That's a huge request."

"They'd meet each other first," Belinda said, shaking her head as if he was being silly. "This isn't the final decision. They'd have to meet each other and see if they both felt that the marriage should be pursued."

But what about Mark Yoder? She should know how he felt before she made any lifelong decisions.

"I like him," Jill said. "He's good-looking, has a good reputation back home and even answered my question about his ex-girlfriend very well." She fixed Thom with a serious look. "If Nellie wants to inherit her family farm and she needs a farmer to do that, then I think Freeman seems like a good match."

"And if there were a man in the community who loved her?" Thom asked, fixing Jill with a pointed look.

"Then he'd better step forward to tell her that," Jill replied, equally pointedly. "Should she put her entire life on hold for the possibility that this other man will say something? And when he does, what if she doesn't feel the same way?"

Thom hadn't actually considered that. Mark was going to have to make his move if he wanted a chance with Nellie, but no matter what, it was her choice.

"I like Freeman, too," Belinda said. "I think he'd do nicely."

Belinda went to the mudroom and they heard the door open, sending a cold swirl of air through the kitchen.

"Freeman!" Belinda called. "Come here a minute!"

Jill came over to where Thom stood. The door shut behind Belinda, and her boots could be heard on the step.

"You really think Mark is the one for Nellie?" Jill asked.

"You think Freeman is?" he asked.

"I don't think it matters what either of us thinks," Jill replied. "This is up to Nellie. She's got a farm and a choice in front of her."

"Yeah." He sighed. "But marriage can be a whole lot harder than people think it'll be. You'd never know the kinds of things my brother and his wife were tackling behind closed doors. People put their best faces forward, but marriage is for a lifetime, and if you aren't with the one person you can't live without, it seems like it would be too much work."

Jill shrugged. "Nellie came to Aunt Belinda. This is what she was asking for—an arrangement."

"Yeah." Thom shouldn't be taking this so personally. "I'm just going to admit it. That Freeman fellow seems like a great guy, but I'm rooting for Mark, anyway. I saw how he feels about her, and I think that's worth fighting for."

"But does *he* think it's worth fighting for?" Jill asked. "That's the question, isn't it?"

The side door opened again and shut, and after a moment Belinda reappeared in the kitchen, wearing her slippers once more.

"Well, that takes care of that," Belinda said.

"I've asked Freeman to come back tomorrow morning to meet Nellie. We'll put them at the kitchen table together and see how they feel."

"Easy as that?" Thom asked.

"Easy?" Belinda rolled her eyes. "There is nothing easy about any of this. But it's a start. I'm convinced he's a decent person. That's the bulk of my job—sorting out the good ones from the pretenders. Now Nellie will have to see what she thinks of him."

Nellie was meeting a very serious contender tomorrow...

"Miss Belinda, I'm going to need to bring an extra guy in with me tomorrow to hang the top cabinets. It's a tough job, and I can't do that part alone. I hope you're okay with that."

"Of course, dear," the old woman said. "I fully understand."

This was Mark's chance—and Thom was going to go against all of his better instincts about interfering in other people's lives, and he was going to get the younger man to help him hang cabinets. Maybe Mark should see the competition he was up against.

CHAPTER TWELVE

LATER THAT EVENING Jill stood at the fence, stroking Eeyore's nose. The light from the house shone warmly golden on the snowy ground behind her, and she could smell her aunt's cooking on the outdoor porch—some sort of noodle casserole and a roasting chicken. Eeyore nudged her so solidly that she had to take a step back, and she smiled.

"You like the attention, don't you?" she said, and she gave the sides of his jaw a thorough scratch.

She'd come outside for some time to herself and to enjoy the brisk evening air. Funny—standing outside in the damp cold of a February evening with a donkey was the best stress reducer she'd found yet.

Jill pulled out her phone. She saw a few group emails, but work seemed to be carrying on without her just fine. She wasn't sure if that was a good thing or not.

The donkey nudged her again and she continued petting him. His big brown eyes had long lashes, and he nickered softly as she scratched him. Was this what life was like out here in the country—where a donkey's affection could feel like it was beating back all those worries that normally crept through her mind?

Just for one week—or even one day!—she wished someone else could be the strong, reliant one for a change. Let Elsa come to her rescue. She smiled at that thought—because she knew she'd just micromanage her sister through the entire process.

At the sound of a car's engine, she turned to see a blue sedan come up the drive. That would be Sean and Elsa.

They parked but didn't get out of the car right away. She could make out the murmur of their voices from inside the vehicle. After a couple of minutes the doors opened and they walked toward the side door with a foot and a half of space between them as if they were a prim and proper Amish couple.

Neither Sean nor Elsa had seen her, and she didn't mind the invisibility for a while. She deeply hoped this chat with Aunt Belinda would help them. Annoying though Elsa had been with wedding plans, Jill had never seen her sister quite so happy as she was with Sean.

The side door opened and Thom came outside with his tool bag in one hand just before Elsa and Sean reached it.

"Hi," Thom said. "Let me get the door for you."

Thom held the screen, and Sean and Elsa went inside. For a moment he stood on the step looking thoughtful, then he started down. His gaze swung over to where she stood and he gave her a nod.

She watched as he headed for his truck. Had that been a farewell? But he tossed his tool bag into the passenger side, then angled his steps back in her direction. She smiled as he leaned against the rail and reached out to give the donkey's neck a pat.

"Do you think she'll succeed?" Thom asked.

Jill looked over her shoulder toward the house. She saw Aunt Belinda pass the window, a pot of tea in her hands. Sean and Elsa were probably at the table, their broken hearts strung out between them.

"I really hope so," she said softly.

Thom nodded. "Yeah, me, too. If anyone can do it, it's Miss Belinda."

Jill's phone pinged, and she looked down at an incoming message from her mother.

Hi Jill!! I haven't heard from your sister, but just letting you know we'll be in town tomorrow! Can't wait to see you girls! Love you!!!

She tipped the phone so Thom could see the message. "My mom is excited. You can tell by the number of exclamation points."

Thom smiled. "You going to tell her what's going on?"

"Nope." She pocketed her phone again. "It's not my news to tell, and I'm still hoping that a miracle will happen in there. Besides, Mom would freak out. She'd call Elsa repeatedly. And our aunts, and then they'd freak out. Mayhem would ensue."

Thom pulled out his wallet and he took a small picture out of it and passed it over to her. It was a school photo of a boy with glasses and a blue sweatshirt. It had the laser effect in the background that was popular about twenty-five years ago.

"Is that you?" she asked.

He shook his head. "My mom sent me a Valentine's Day care package. She figured I could use some extra affection this year, I guess. She sent me some of her homemade cookies, and some chocolate bars, a package of socks…and that photo. It's my brother."

"No other pictures?" she asked.

Thom shook his head, and he took the photo back and stuck it back in his wallet. "Nope."

"Is she trying to tell you something?" Jill asked.

"Of course." He smiled faintly. "She's reminding me who my family is. She always said that brothers had to look out for each other, but I don't know what she expects me to do with Mike right now."

"You tried talking to him," Jill said.

"I did."

Jill nodded. "It sounds like Mike doesn't want the family support right now."

"I agree." He shrugged. "The opposite of your problem, huh?"

"It was easier when we were kids and when the mean girls picked on my sister, I could make them feel about two inches tall with withering glances. Problem solved. Not so easy anymore."

"This picture's from grade eight," Thom said.

"A special time?" she asked.

"A tough time. My brother got meningitis and was sick for most of a school year."

She slipped her hand into the crook of his arm and leaned her head against his shoulder. He slid his hand over hers.

"That's really serious."

"He almost died. It shook us all up a lot. I overheard my parents talking about it, and it terrified me. I didn't want to lose my brother. Mike was scared, too. They tried to hide how bad it was from him, but he could feel it. He told me once while he was in the hospital that another boy on the pediatric ward had passed away, and he was afraid he'd be next."

"That's incredibly traumatic," Jill murmured.

"Yeah...and then he got better. I don't know if he knew how scared I was for him."

They were silent for a moment. Their breath hung in the air and Eeyore wandered off a few paces.

"Did it make you two closer—him being sick?" Jill asked.

"Yeah. It did. The next year we were in the same grade because my brother had to repeat the year, and we hung out a lot. His friends kind of moved on without him, and it was tough for Mike. But we were finally equals."

"So what changed?"

"Mike wasn't satisfied with that. He worked his tail off to finish eighth grade faster, and then started on ninth grade work. By the time I was in tenth grade, he'd worked his way back to a year ahead of me. And that changed him. He was more aloof. He figured he didn't need people."

"That's not a great solution," she said.

"It only got worse as the years plodded on. Intelligence was everything. Academic accomplishment gave him his sense of self. He saw it as proof of his intelligence, and those who took different paths—like me—were beneath him all of a sudden. He figured he was smarter than everyone. I guess he felt safer if he was superior."

"I'm sorry."

"Yeah… Funny how life turns out, huh? But I know him better than that. I know that under all that snobbery is the boy who was terrified of dying. At the end of the day, I'm his brother and I know him better than he thinks."

Jill looked back toward the house, thinking she knew her sister better than Elsa thought, too. Thom squeezed her hand. The door behind them opened and Sean and Elsa came back outside. They were holding hands this time, and leaning toward each other. That was a good sign—a very good sign. Elsa looked over and waved, and the couple paused. Jill slid her hand out of Thom's grip and headed across the snowy ground toward her sister.

"Is the wedding on?" Jill asked when she reached her.

"Yeah, it's on," Elsa said, and she looked up at Sean with a misty smile.

Sean leaned over and kissed her forehead.

"Good. I'm glad. Go on home," Jill said, waving them on. "I'm just glad it's sorted out."

"See you." Elsa shot Jill a smile, and then mouthed the words *thank you*. Then they headed off to their car again.

When the car had headed back up the drive, Jill went over to Thom.

"Crisis averted," she said quietly.

"And you didn't have to do the heavy lifting with it, either." He met her gaze in the moonlight with a small smile. Thom touched her chin with the pad of his thumb, his dark gaze catching hers. But then he let his hand drop.

"Your aunt is watching," he said with a rueful smile. Belinda stood on the doorstep, bundled in her shawl and slippers.

"I know." Jill chuckled.

"Good night, Jill." Her name sounded warm and protected on his lips. Thom turned and headed toward his truck again, and called over his shoulder. "See you in the morning."

Jill let out a slow breath, feeling a flutter of

hope in her stomach. She had to stop this. But Thom was very, very easy to fall for.

Jill headed back to the house and walked inside with Belinda.

"What did you say to them?" Jill asked.

"I just reminded them that they loved each other," Belinda said. "It was simple enough."

"I did that," Jill said. "It didn't seem to work for me."

Belinda shrugged. "I guess I did it better."

Jill burst out laughing. "Aunt Belinda, you probably did! I'm glad. Thank you for fixing the situation."

"Dear, sometimes it takes an old woman," Belinda said. "We have a certain authority that comes with wrinkles and white hair. I also reminded them both that the wedding was just one day, whether you've planned that day for two years or not. Whether the chaos of the day will be stressful or not. It's the day after the wedding that really counts—when they spend the first full day as husband and wife, and start the journey together."

"That's beautiful," Jill said.

"Then your sister saw you and Thom standing out there together, talking, and she said she remembered when she and Sean were like that." Belinda smiled mischievously. "And

Sean went over and looked at you two, and he looked down at Elsa and that was it. They were back together."

"Because of us?" Jill asked. "But we aren't an actual couple."

"No?" Belinda said.

"Aunt Belinda, you let them believe a lie."

"Are you so very sure you aren't a couple, my dear?" Belinda asked, raising her brows. "That time together outside—that wasn't part of a ruse."

No, it hadn't been. It had been comforting and sweet, and… Jill would dearly miss that man when she went back to Pittsburgh. In fact, the thought of saying goodbye now left her throat tight. She hadn't expected to feel this way, to get so deeply attached to him. This was dangerous ground.

"I thought you were going to introduce me to a podiatrist at the wedding?" Jill said.

"I still am, if you want to meet him," Belinda replied. "But I'm going to feel bad for Thom if you settled down in Amish Country for Dr. G and not him."

"I'm not settling in Amish Country for either of them," Jill replied. "Aunty, my life is in Pittsburgh. I don't want to be a podiatrist's wife… and as for Thom…"

A life with Thom would be undeniably sweet, but they were far too different.

"All I know is that I saw you out that window, too, Jill, and I remember feeling just like that with my Ernie."

Belinda turned toward the woodstove. She bent down and poked another piece of wood into the fire. Jill's phone pinged, and she looked down to see a new email. She opened it to find another question from work. She paused, her fingers poised to answer, and then she turned her phone off and slipped it back into her pocket.

"Why don't you tell me about Uncle Ernie?" Jill said. "And I'll make us some tea."

Some things were more important, like time with her great-aunt and stories from years past. And it would get her mind off that gentle man she'd been leaning against out there in the winter evening.

THE NEXT MORNING Thom picked up Mark Yoder on his way to Butternut Bed and Breakfast. Mark was waiting by the mailbox at the end of the drive with a lunch bag over his shoulder. Behind him Thom could see Mark's father going into the stable, the door bouncing shut.

It was a quiet morning, and the men were getting ready to leave for their jobs.

"Morning," Thom said as Mark got in the truck.

"Morning." Mark did up his seat belt. "Thanks for bringing me in to work with you today."

"Your boss was okay with you taking the day off?" Thom asked.

"I used a vacation day, so he was fine with it." Mark let out a slow breath. "You said that Nellie will be at Belinda's place today?"

"Yep," Thom said. "That's the plan, at least. Are you going to make your move?"

"I think I will," Mark said, nodding. "*Yah*, I think so. I should, right?"

"It's your life—your future," Thom replied. "You've got to do what you think is best."

"I'm not a farmer, though."

Thom glanced over at the young man. He was still arguing with himself. And maybe he wouldn't have the courage to tell her how he felt, but at least he'd have the chance. Mark wouldn't be able to blame anyone but himself if Nellie married another man without him at least saying his piece.

"So how long have you known you wanted to marry her?" Thom asked.

"Oh..." Mark's face colored. "I don't know.

Forever? I thought before I'd never be able to because she was two years older, and she saw me as a kid. I mean, I didn't have my growth spurt until I was seventeen, and I didn't start shaving until around then, too, so I guess that's why. But I've caught up."

Thom chuckled. "Yeah, everyone does eventually, right?"

Mark pressed his lips together. "So how many farmers are lining up for her?"

"I don't know," Thom replied honestly. "But the last guy to come by had both Miss Belinda and Jill pretty impressed."

"What did he have that I don't?" Mark asked.

"Farming experience. That's about it."

Mark nodded and turned toward the window. The rest of the drive to Butternut B&B was a quiet one, and when they arrived they spent the first half hour unloading the cabinets from the back of the truck and moving them inside. Like before when Thom had unloaded supplies, Belinda insisted that they leave their boots on, and stood by with a mop, wiping up puddles of melting snow behind them. It still made him feel bad.

"I don't mind a bit," she kept saying. "That's what mops are for. You just carry on."

Thom noticed that Jill wasn't downstairs yet,

and when she did come down dressed in a pair of jeans and with an Amish shawl wrapped around her, Thom and Mark already had the cupboards lined up on one side of the kitchen.

"Hi," Thom said, looking up.

Jill came over, tugging her shawl a little tighter. "It's coming together."

"Yeah."

He met her gaze. He didn't want to talk about hanging cabinets, but they weren't alone now. Things had changed between them, and he could feel it in the warmth of the kitchen— the way they migrated toward each other, the temptation to touch her, the way she looked up at him.

"So everything is sorted out with your sister?" he asked, lowering his voice.

"They're back together. All is well." Jill smiled faintly. "According to my aunt, the thing that brought them back together was—" her cheeks pinked "—us."

Them? Well, probably just Jill. She was the eloquent one.

"Did you say something particularly wise to Elsa?" he asked.

"No, they were watching us out the window."

Mark walked past, heading back outside with an armful of moving blankets that Thom had used to protect the wooden cabinets in the back of his truck, and Jill fell silent. But Thom's mind was sifting through the night before. They hadn't kissed, though most of the time he'd stood out there with her, he'd been thinking about it.

"What did we do?" he whispered, stepping closer to keep their words as private as possible. She was so close, he could have easily taken her hand. He wouldn't, though.

"We reminded them of what it felt like when they fell for each other," she said, and the color in her cheeks deepened.

"Did we look like...we were falling for each other?" he murmured.

"Apparently."

He felt his own face heat just a bit, and he glanced over his shoulder as Mark came back inside.

"Silly, I know," Jill added, "but I don't dare set my sister straight just yet."

"Yeah." He could see why. But the truth was, Thom *was* falling for her. If she was the kind of woman who wanted to make a life out here, he'd be moving this relationship forward. "I'd better get to work."

She smiled. "You probably should."

"When do Nellie and Freeman get here?" he asked.

"Aunt Belinda said about ten," she said, and her gaze flickered over to where Mark stood, munching on a muffin Belinda had given him. "Is Mark going to say anything?"

Thom shrugged. "No idea. I hope so."

The next hour passed quickly enough. Mark's help turned out to be incredibly necessary when it came to hanging the shelves and making sure they were level. Mark was strong, and between the two of them, they had two sets of cupboards anchored to the wall before the clop of hooves was heard on the drive outside.

Mark nearly dropped a cabinet when they heard the buggy approach, and Thom muttered in irritation as he helped to catch the heavy piece.

"Sorry," Mark said, but his attention was locked on the side window.

Nellie arrived first. Belinda welcomed her inside, and her shy gaze flickered over the room, landing on Mark with surprise.

"Hi," Mark said.

"Hi, Mark." She smiled. "Are you helping out?"

"*Yah.* Thom needed a hand. Just pitching in."

"That's good." She looked over at Belinda,

who gestured toward the sitting room. Mark deflated and rubbed a hand through his hair as the women left.

"Nellie!" Mark said.

The Amish woman turned back, and her cheeks had colored. She looked a little breathless. "*Yah*, Mark?"

"How...how are your parents?" he asked feebly.

"Oh. They're fine," she said, and she laughed self-consciously. "And so is my cousin...if you're meaning to ask after her."

"I'm not asking after Fannie," Mark said. "I mean... I'm glad she's fine, but—" He heaved a frustrated sigh.

"How are you doing?" she asked.

"Good. Good. I'm working hard."

"I heard you cut your thumb pretty bad."

"Healed up." He held out his hand as proof, and Nellie leaned forward for a closer look. It was almost more intimate than a touch.

Thom could see the chemistry between these two from across the room.

A buggy pulled up outside and Belinda said brightly, "Freeman is here, Nellie. Let's just have a word together before he gets inside, *yah*?"

"*Yah.*" Nellie dropped her hand, her face redder still. "I'm sorry, Mark. I have to meet him."

She seemed to be waiting for a reply, and when Mark didn't say anything else, Nellie followed Belinda into the other room. Thom eyed Mark, watching for some kind of reaction, but Mark's shoulders slumped. It was Jill who let Freeman inside.

"Hello," Jill said, her professional persona back in place. "Come inside, Freeman. Good to see you again. The ladies are waiting for you in the sitting room."

Freeman looked nervous as he glanced around the kitchen, and when his gaze landed on Mark, he gave him a nod—recognition of a fellow Amish man.

"Good morning," Freeman said.

"Morning," Thom said, turning away. There was no way he was getting himself entangled in this. Mark didn't answer him at all.

"Just this way," Jill said, and Freeman followed her into the sitting room.

For a couple of minutes Thom and Mark stood there in the quiet of the kitchen, listening to the indistinct conversation and the tick of the clock.

"She'll like him," Mark said miserably.

"There's no saying how it'll shake out," Thom replied. "Marriage is serious business."

"I know her," he said. "He'll impress her, I'm sure."

Thom's heart went out to the guy. But maybe Mark needed to see this—get it out of his system, move on to another girl.

They had managed to hang another cabinet together by the time Freeman came back out of the sitting room, Belinda in tow. Belinda and Freeman didn't pause to even look in the men's direction, but soberly went outside together. The door shut with *a thunk* behind them. Mark went to the window and looked out.

"They're talking by his buggy," he reported.

Jill and Nellie came into the dining room then, and Mark stepped away from the window. Jill gave Thom a veiled look, and he had to wonder what had happened in that room. If he knew Amish people at all, the most important stuff would have occurred between the lines. That was how they communicated.

"Do you like him?" Mark asked Nellie.

Nellie startled. "What?"

"Do you like this farmer?" Mark asked.

"I don't know if he likes me, Mark," she said, her voice sounding a little shaky.

"That's hog feed," Mark said. "He'd be a blind fool not to want to marry you."

"You're sweet." Nellie tried to force a smile

but couldn't muster it. She had her hands folded in front of her with a white-knuckle grip.

"I'm not trying to be sweet," Mark replied irritably. "I want to know if you like him."

The door opened then and Belinda came inside. She unwound her shawl from her shoulders as everyone in the room watched her, breath bated.

"That was very successful," Belinda said with a smile. "Freeman likes you a lot, Nellie. He will be coming to you with a formal proposal soon. He wants to talk about when you can come meet his family and set a date for the wedding...if you're agreeable to that."

No one moved, and Belinda's eyebrows went up. "Isn't this good news?"

"Yah!" Nellie was the first one to speak. "He really wants to marry me?"

"He really does." Belinda smiled warmly. "Now, let's discuss how you felt about him. You need to decide if you'll accept him."

Mark's face was ashen, and Thom nudged him.

"Are you only considering farmers, Nellie?" Mark asked, his voice a little too loud, echoing off the new cabinets.

Nellie blinked at him. *"Yah*, because of the farm, you see. My *daet* won't leave it to me unless I've got a husband who can run it. So I've got to look for a farmer."

Mark dropped his gaze. "*Yah.* I see."

Belinda ushered Nellie back toward the sitting room, leaving Thom, Mark and Jill alone in the kitchen.

"Mark, now is your time to tell her how you feel," Jill said softly. "She's got a proposal coming."

"She wants a farmer," he said.

"You never told her that you were offering yourself," Jill replied. "That might change things."

Jill was right, but Mark just shook his head. "I don't know."

Maybe something else was holding Mark back. Maybe his fantasies weren't quite adding up to reality, or he was noticing something he'd missed when he'd been thinking about this before. Maybe Mark knew that Nellie would be the one to beat from here on out—the woman who'd stolen his heart but who wanted more than he could give… Maybe Mark would have to lower his sights a little bit. Thom knew what that felt like, too, after meeting Jill.

Sometimes, a man's heart could be in tatters, but walking away was still the right thing to do.

CHAPTER THIRTEEN

JILL TRIED TO stay out of the way as Thom and Mark finished hanging the cupboards that evening. It was heavy work, nothing Jill could assist with as the men strained, holding up cabinets and driving screws into the studs behind. Thom was finishing the work up—he was preparing to move on to a new project, no doubt, and this time together at Belinda's bed-and-breakfast would be over. Nothing lasted forever, not even kitchen renovations.

Belinda fed them all a supper of turkey stew and crusty rolls, and then the men got back to work. They stayed late to make sure everything was perfect.

"It's so close to being done," Thom said. "I just want to finish it up, if you don't mind, Miss Belinda. You'll be back to cooking indoors tomorrow morning."

It was nearly eight o'clock and Belinda stifled a yawn behind her hand. "*Yah*, that will be nice to get back inside for the cooking. You do what you need to."

And Thom did. The kitchen looked fresh and new, the cabinets were perfectly fitted to the space and cupboard doors opened and closed on hinges that gently tugged the door shut on their own. Everything smelled of wood and varnish, and the kerosene light reflected off the new cabinetry by the time they finished at nine.

"It is very, very nice," Belinda said, her eyes shining. "Thank you so much, Thom. Here is your payment."

She handed over an envelope, and Thom thanked the older woman with a smile.

"It's my pleasure, Miss Belinda. I'm glad you like it. If you have any problems, or need anything, you let me know, okay?"

"Of course! Thank you again." Belinda beamed up at him and then started opening cupboards and peering inside. She fetched a couple of water glasses and brought them to an empty cupboard.

When Thom glanced down at Jill, she read the silent request in his eyes. He wanted to talk to her before he left, and she gave him a small nod. This was it—Thom was done working in her aunt's home. His work was impressive, but her chest felt tight and heavy. This felt too much like a goodbye.

Mark and Thom carried out the last of their tools and when Mark hopped up into the truck, Thom turned back to meet Jill on the step. The winter evening was brisk, and Jill crossed her arms over her chest. She was half-afraid that if she went inside for a coat that he'd leave.

"So this is it?" Jill said.

"For my work here, at least," he replied. He shifted his stance, blocking the wind for her. "Are you going to miss me?"

His smile was teasing, but there was something deeper in those dark eyes that caught her. She could joke back, but she didn't think she was capable of it.

"I think I will," she said softly.

He sobered and touched her chin tenderly. "Good."

"We weren't supposed to get attached, Thom," she whispered.

"We're human," he replied. "I'll miss you, too."

This wasn't the way any of this was supposed to go, but he was right. They were two people who'd found some comfort and understanding together. Maybe that was all this was, and when she went back to the city, she'd feel more like herself.

"Are we still on for the wedding?" he asked.

"We'd better be," Jill said with a forced laugh. "I still have a potential client to impress with my excellent taste." She let her smile fall. "And I don't want to give Elsa and Sean any excuse to back out."

"We've turned into regular meddlers here, haven't we?" He grinned, but she saw some melancholy in his eyes, too. He glanced over his shoulder toward his truck. "I'd better go."

She nodded.

"I'll pick you up Saturday at four. You'll hardly recognize me. I've been told I clean up pretty well."

Thom looked good in his wood-dusted blue jeans, but put that man in a well-tailored suit… The problem was, she was starting to imagine what he might look like lounging in her apartment in Pittsburgh, or walking with her along a downtown street, window-shopping.

"You sure you still want to do this? Go to the wedding? Play the happy couple?" she asked.

Thom was silent for a moment. Finally, he said, "You still have a client to land."

"I do, but…this got more complicated than we thought."

"I still want to do it," he said at last. "And it isn't just for you landing this client, or because I want to stop the matchmaking or keep people from feeling sorry for me."

"No?" she breathed.

"I want to go with you. I want to spend the evening with you. I just want... I want you there. With me. As my actual date. Nothing fake about it." He raised his gaze to meet hers. "You okay with that?"

That sounded much better than anything they should be toying with, but... "Yeah. I'd like that, too."

Thom smiled, then squeezed her fingers. "I'll see you tomorrow night."

He trotted down the steps and headed toward the truck. Mark was inside, probably watching the whole thing, although she couldn't make him out inside the dark cab. Thom opened the driver's-side door and the light came on inside, illuminating the Amish man. If she was local, she might care about the gossip, but this wasn't home. She'd be back in her cozy little apartment again in a matter of days, putting all of this behind her.

And yet somehow, as she watched Thom's truck reverse, she did care what people thought of her out here. This community was protective of Thom, and she had no intention of hurting him. Would people know that? Or would their little ruse go down in public opinion like Natasha had?

Jill turned back inside, and when she came back into the kitchen, Belinda's tiredness had disappeared, and she was busy putting dishes back into cupboards. Jill noticed Thom's drill sitting to the side—he'd forgotten it.

"Your parents arrive tomorrow," Belinda said over her shoulder. "And we'll be able to cook inside again. This has all worked out very nicely."

Maybe it would have worked out better if Jill hadn't involved Thom in her personal drama—if he'd just been the carpenter, and they'd had a polite conversation at the wedding and moved on. But she had a feeling that she could never have avoided connecting with him on a deeper level.

"Will you give me a hand?" Belinda asked. "It won't take us too long if we work together."

Of course she would help. This was what family did.

THE NEXT DAY Jill's parents arrived in a cab directly from the airport. Elsa and Sean were too busy with last-minute wedding preparations to go and get them themselves. The kitchen was neatly put back together, and when they came in with a bustle of bags and chatter, Jill stood back, letting them hug Aunt Belinda first.

"Oh, this kitchen!" Donna gushed. "Belinda, this is stunning!" She pulled Jill into a hug. "And thank you for dealing with the Mae situation, sweetie. You always have a way."

How much had Elsa told their mother? Jill eyed her mom for a moment, but she didn't offer any extra information about the near-breakup. For now she was content simply to let the wedding go ahead.

"Hi, Jill," her father said, giving her a squeeze. "When this whole thing is over, you and me are going fishing."

She chuckled. "When this whole thing is over, I've got work, Dad."

That was normally a comforting prospect, but she wasn't sure it would be enough to rid her heart of what had happened this past week.

"Fine—the next long weekend." Her father smiled. "Can you believe Elsa's going to be a married woman?"

"Sean is just the sweetest guy," her mother added. "She's in good hands…"

Everyone continued chatting. Leftover turkey stew was brought out, and Belinda made grilled cheese sandwiches in a cast-iron pan on the woodstove. There was laughter and gossip as snowflakes spun down past the glass outside.

A knock at the door made everyone stop, and Jill got up first.

"You all keep eating," she said. "Sit, Aunty, sit. I'll get it."

Jill went to answer the door and felt an unexpected rush of relief to see Thom standing there. He cast her a smile.

"I forgot my drill."

"Yes, you did." She stepped back and he came inside.

"Oh, Thom!" Belinda said. "We have your drill!"

Belinda had Thom's drill wrapped in a cloth shopping bag, and she brought it over as if handing him a gift instead of his own tool.

"This is the young man who redid my kitchen," Belinda said, a note of pride in her voice. "This is Thom Miller."

"Oh, very nice work," Rob said. "It's just beautiful in here."

"Thank you," Thom said. He looked over at Jill. "See you tomorrow?"

She nodded.

"Are you coming to the wedding?" Donna asked, leaning forward with a smile.

"He's a friend of Sean's," Jill said, and she paused a beat. "He's also my date."

Her parents looked surprised, their gazes flickering between her and Thom.

"Oh, so this is the mysterious date!" Donna said. "Thom, come in here and sit down!"

"No, no!" Jill laughed. "The last thing he needs is a cross-examination by you two!"

It was casual…wasn't it? It was feeling increasingly less so, though.

"Actually, I'm heading over to Eli's place to help him with a chicken coop," Thom said.

"Oh, well, then bring him this—" Belinda carried a Tupperware container of turkey stew over to Thom. "Tell him to bring back the container—no using it for feeding chickens."

Thom chuckled. "Will do, Miss Belinda. Nice meeting you, Mr. and Mrs. Wickey."

Jill followed Thom back to the mudroom away from prying eyes. He looked down at her, and for a heart-stopping moment his dark gaze locked with hers.

"I'd ask you to come help me reinforce a chicken coop, but it looks like you're busy."

"I should spend some time with my folks," she agreed. "But thanks."

"That's fair." He pulled open the door. "For the record, moms love me."

He shot her a grin, and she laughed softly as he headed back out to his truck. Her family *would* love him. That wasn't the problem.

When Jill returned to the kitchen, all eyes were on her. She felt her cheeks start to warm. She wasn't normally fazed by people's stares, but she was starting to feel vulnerable where Thom was concerned.

"What?" she said.

"He looks nice," Donna said.

"He's very nice," Jill replied. "But Mom, let's just focus on marrying off one Wickey daughter tomorrow, okay?"

Her mother chuckled, and Aunt Belinda went to the counter for a blackberry crisp that was still hot from the oven. Her father leaned forward to look out the window at the retreating vehicle.

They'd eat. They'd talk, and they'd adjust to the new family dynamics—together. And hopefully, that would help Jill to keep her feet firmly on the ground. Thom was not an option for her.

THOM PARKED HIS truck beside Eli's little farmhouse, and he looked across the narrow field to the Butternut Bed and Breakfast beyond. Smoke curled up from the chimney, and snow fell softly, veiling his view. It was muted, distanced, like a memory already. He'd miss her deeply, and he knew he wasn't going to be able to stop thinking about her. This was supposed to be fake—but tomorrow they would have one real date.

He carried the container of turkey stew with him as he headed around the side of the house, looking for signs of the old man.

"Eli!" he shouted.

A dog barked in response—an excited yapping bark that wouldn't quit. The stable door opened, and Eli's grizzled head popped out.

"Oh, Thom! In here!"

Thom put the Tupperware on the step, then headed over to the stable. The structure looked a little battered, too, and he wondered if the Amish community would pull together and get old Eli fixed up one of these days.

"Belinda sent you supper," Thom said as he went inside. "I left it on the step."

"That woman," Eli said fondly. "She sure can cook."

The dog from the other night was in the stable with Eli. He sat a few yards away from a quarter horse, who eyed him distrustfully. Obviously, a truce had not been made between the two just yet.

"Do you have time to work on that coop?" Thom asked.

"*Yah*, I can make the time. Let me finish with this stall. I'm almost done."

Thom found another shovel in a corner and he joined the old man in scooping up soiled hay. The dog came to Thom's heels, and he stopped to give it a pet.

"You'll keep him?" Thom asked.

"*Yah*. I figure I found him, he's mine."

"What's his name?"

"*Hund*," Eli replied. "It means *dog*. Not terribly original, but he answers to it."

"*Hund*," Thom said, bending down to pet the dog again. "He doesn't know how lucky he is to find a good home like yours."

"Probably not," Eli replied. "Even people take blessings for granted."

Thom wheeled the barrow out to the manure pile to dump it, and when he came back in, Eli was brushing down his quarter horse with long strokes, murmuring to the animal in Pennsylvania Dutch.

"Does the horse know English?" Thom asked.

"I've had him since he was a colt, so I'm going to say no, he doesn't," Eli replied. "But he and I have all sorts of long talks. He's a good listener."

Eli's was a lonely life, but he was compassionate with his animals, and Thom watched him until he'd finished with the brushing and gave the horse a carrot as a reward. He patted the horse's glossy side.

"Eli, how come you never married?" Thom asked.

"Everyone keeps asking that," Eli said. "Your lady friend asked the same thing."

"What did you tell her?" he asked.

"That there was a girl I was interested in, and she married another man. There were others, but for some reason or other, it never happened. Sometimes, a man ends up alone."

Thom nodded slowly. "Was the girl you were interested in Belinda?"

Eli pressed his lips into a thin line. "How appropriate would that be for me to live next to her all that time, watching her build her life with someone far better than I was? That would be shameful."

"She never knew how you felt?" Thom asked.

Eli shrugged. "What was I going to do? Ruin her happiness? She'd chosen Ernie. He was a good man, and she loved him, not me. I wished them well, and I lived my life."

"You could have married someone else," Thom said.

"I did try," Eli said quietly. "I think living next door to her made it harder. I'd stand by my house, looking across at theirs, and I'd see Belinda come outside with a child on her hip, and every other properly available woman would pale in comparison."

"Did Ernie know how you felt?" Thom asked.

"Yah." Eli's face reddened. "He told me once to keep my eyes on my side of the fence, so I guess I made my feelings clear enough. But he never told Belinda."

"And now you spend your time driving Belinda crazy?" Thom asked.

"I don't mean to drive her crazy," Eli said. "I'm just being me. That's always been my problem. I have my ways. I think the way I do. And I have my own sense of humor. No one else really seems to understand it, including Belinda. It isn't really her fault."

Eli put the brush up on a shelf and exited the stall.

"She thinks of you, though. She wanted you to have supper," Thom said.

"Yah." Eli grinned. "I'm weaseling into her heart. It starts with a woman caring if you starve to death. I can work with that."

Thom chuckled. "I imagine you can, Eli."

"The coop—" Eli led the way out of the stable and into the brisk winter air. "Thank you for helping me with it. I need to get the chickens back outside again. *Hund* here is taking up more space in the house, and he's been looking at those birds like he'd like to make a meal of 'em."

They paused outside the stable and Thom found his gaze moving in the direction of the bed-and-breakfast. What was Jill doing right now? Likely laughing with her family, enjoying her parents' company again.

"Yah, yah..." Eli said. "It's an interesting experience staring at a house that holds the woman you love, isn't it?"

"What?" Thom shook his head. "No, no, I'm..." But he couldn't quite explain himself. He cleared his throat.

"Right," Eli said with a small smile. "I know that look. But be careful. It can consume a man if it goes unchecked, and you'll find yourself with chickens in your kitchen and a calf taking over the ground floor of your home if you aren't careful."

"You could have married another woman, Eli," Thom said. For some reason he wanted to fix things for this man—maybe to prove to himself that it was possible. He had to find the escape route that Eli had chosen not to take.

Eli slowly shook his head. "And when she saw me looking at my neighbor in a way I never did for her? You think that wife would be happy with me?" He softened his tone. "I did try and court a woman. She was sweet, stalwart, strong. She could cook well. I thought it was going places, and she told me to stop calling on her."

"Did she say why?"

"She said she saw the way I laughed with Belinda, and I never laughed that way with her. She wasn't interested in competing for a man's love. She wouldn't even let me try to do better."

"Wow…" Thom murmured.

Then Eli threw up his hands. "*Hund!* That's not for you!"

The dog had managed to dump over the Tupperware, the lid was off and he was eating the cold stew off the ground in big gulps. Eli hobbled over and muttered a few things in Pennsylvania Dutch. The dog gave him no mind whatsoever and continued to eat the stew.

So Eli had been pining after Belinda all these years. He wasn't just an odd man who refused to be ordinary in an effort to marry an ordinary woman. He'd been a heartbroken man who'd not been able to summon up interest in anyone else.

Thom should take heed. Because what he was feeling with Jill was strangely powerful, even in this short period of time, and he had a feeling that he wasn't going to be able to forget her that easily.

It was sad to see a man spend his entire life pining, and Thom didn't want that to be him. He'd better remember why she wasn't right for him and stop his own tumble after her, because being on the outside looking in would be a special kind of heartache he didn't want to endure.

He'd find a good woman who wanted the life he did. And that wasn't Jill, no matter how much he might long for it to be different. Eli's warning had hit home.

CHAPTER FOURTEEN

JILL SMOOTHED ON some lipstick and looked at herself in the full-length mirror in the upstairs bedroom of Butternut Bed and Breakfast. Her little black dress was perfect—slim fitting, flattering and designed to sit with dignity in the background. She glanced out the window at the snowy yard, crisscrossed with boot tracks from morning chores. She and Aunt Belinda had been up early getting all the animal care done and giving Eeyore and the horse some extra attention.

But her mind wasn't on the animals, or even on her sister's wedding. Not exactly… She was remembering Thom's words… *I want you there. With me. As my actual date. Nothing fake about it.*

At least the pressure of lying to her family about having a date was off her shoulders. This *was* a date. But what did that even mean? She was going back home in a couple of days, and there obviously wasn't a future for them. And yet...there was *something* between them that she couldn't deny.

Was she leading him on? Was she courting heartbreak? How foolish was this? Because Thom wasn't just some stand-in guy, after all. He was special...and she was starting to wonder if he might be willing to visit her in Pittsburgh. Maybe she'd get him to a farmers' market, or take him to a film festival. Maybe he'd enjoy strolling with her through the arts district, munching on a scone from a great little bakery she knew.

There was a tap on her bedroom door and her mother bustled in.

"You've got the mirror," Donna said. "Sweetheart, I wish you'd wear more color. This isn't a funeral. It's a wedding."

Jill pushed back her thoughts and stepped into her strappy black heels.

"I'm trying to give my sister the spotlight," Jill said. She looked back at her mother, who was dressed in a mauve mother-of-the-bride ensemble. "You look great, Mom."

"Thank you... I think I'm almost as nervous as your sister. She's been texting me since six a.m. about all the details."

Jill shot her mother a smile. "I'm glad. This is her day. Let her enjoy every last minute of it."

Jill picked up her string of pearls, and her mother wordlessly took them from her hands and did up the clasp for Jill behind her neck.

"What about that carpenter?" Donna asked. "Belinda adores him."

"He's a great guy," Jill replied.

"Is it serious?"

"No. No. But he's really nice. And I really care for him."

"Hmm." Her mother nodded.

"Can we focus on Elsa and Sean?" Jill asked with a forced laugh. "I've got a date to the wedding, so I'm obviously not just crawling out from under a rock. There's nothing to worry about on my end. I promise."

"I never worry about you," Donna said, picking a stray hair off Jill's shoulder. "You're my levelheaded child."

Never, indeed. But it was good to know that today was going to go smoothly, and Jill would have Thom there as a perfect distraction from family wedding intensity.

"Are we all going together in the cab?" her mother asked.

As if on cue, Jill heard the rumble of an engine outside, so she went to the window. Thom had just arrived in his pickup truck.

"No, I'm going with Thom," Jill said. "We'll meet you there."

Jill's father appeared in the bedroom door in a black suit. He held a tie in one hand.

"You two look lovely," Rob said. "Is this where the mirror is?"

"Yup," Jill said, and she gave her father's arm a squeeze on her way past him. "My ride is here. I'll see you both at the church."

Jill headed down the stairs, pulling her faux mink wrap around her shoulders as she made her way down. Aunt Belinda was in the kitchen, an apron wrapped around her and her hands in dishwater.

"Aunty, the cab will be here soon!" Jill said.

"I'm almost done," Belinda said. "And I'm ready to go."

Jill would leave the rest to her mother, and she shot her aunt a smile before heading out into the chilly winter air. She shivered, the wind whipping around her legs as she picked her way over the snowy ground in her high heels. Thom hopped out of the truck and offered her his arm. He was in a suit—charcoal gray with a black tie. He met her gaze, and she felt goose bumps run up her arms that had nothing to do with the February chill.

"You do put together nicely," she said.

"I couldn't embarrass you now, could I?" He pulled open the passenger-side door for her. "You look beautiful."

He gave her a strong boost up into the warm cab, heat pumping onto her chilled legs. The door slammed shut and she exhaled a soft breath. He'd said he wanted this to be a real date… What did that mean, exactly?

Thom got in and put on his seat belt.

"All right," he said. "Let's go make sure those two get married."

The wedding was being held at the red brick church with the tall white steeple on the far end of town. They weren't the first to arrive, and Jill spotted the rented limo that would have carried the bride and groom to the church, although Jill didn't see Elsa or the wedding party anywhere.

The extended Wickey family had traveled for the event, and there were a few Amish relatives clustered together whom Jill didn't know. They must have taken a cab to get out to the wedding, because there weren't any buggies in the parking lot. The first few minutes were spent in greeting her relatives and introducing Thom. Having Thom there meant that the more invasive questions remained unasked—which had been part of the plan. But as she stopped to chat with one of her aunts, she noticed that Thom had a good many people greeting him, too, and not because of his connection to her. He knew people at this wedding—they knew him.

Kent Osborne was chatting with some people from Sean's side of the wedding. He wore a smart, tan-colored suit, and his wife at his side positively glistened with jewelry. When Kent spotted Jill he sent a smile and wave her way that included Thom.

"Jill," Kent said, shaking her hand first, then Thom's. "Meet my wife, Meghan..."

There were the usual introductions, handshakes and pleasant comments.

"Just to let you know," Kent said, turning his attention to Jill. "I've taken a look at that proposal, and I have to say, it's impressive."

"I'm glad to hear it," she replied.

"I hope you aren't intimidated by her brain," Kent told Thom with a grin.

"Not at all. I enjoy being impressed by her," Thom said, and he slipped a hand around her waist.

Shoot. Did he have to be this smooth? But the effect seemed to work on Kent, because the older man grinned and nodded.

"I don't want to mix business with your family wedding," Kent said to Jill. "But I've been looking for the right people to take on this campaign, and I feel like you're the kind of people we're looking for. We'll talk back in the city, okay? I'll make an appointment at your office."

"Perfect." Jill smiled. "I look forward to it."

Thom gave her waist a subtle squeeze.

"Nice meeting you, too, Meghan," Jill said, and shook his wife's hand, as well.

The older couple moved off, and Jill felt a wave of relief. This had been the plan. Leila James would be thrilled to hear this. And Jill's standing in the firm would be boosted. She'd be the candidate of choice the next time a spot above her opened up.

"Mission successful?" Thom murmured.

"So far, so good," she whispered back. "Thank you for this, Thom. You're good at the boyfriend act."

"I'm good at being a boyfriend, period." He met her gaze, then winked. "For the record."

"Noted." She chuckled, but her heart gave a little stutter.

Aunt Belinda and Jill's parents arrived shortly after. The ambiance was cheerful and excited as both families prepared to see Sean and Elsa married. A few minutes later Aunt Belinda came up to Jill and Thom with a portly, shorter man at her side. He had a well-trimmed beard and a nicely cut suit.

"Jill, dear," Belinda said. "I wanted to introduce you to Dr. Evan Gregorson. I think I might have mentioned him."

Jill tried to keep a straight face as she met her aunt's sparkling blue gaze.

"I think you might have, Aunty," Jill said soberly. "Evan, is it? Nice to meet you."

They shook hands, and Belinda slipped away then.

"This is Thom Miller," Jill said.

"Hi." Thom reached out to shake Evan's hand and if Jill wasn't mistaken, Thom's grip looked a little stronger than it needed to be.

"Yes, I think we've met? Did you do some work on my office?" Evan asked.

"I did. Nice to see you again."

"Likewise." Evan turned to Jill. "Belinda mentioned that you're her great-niece."

"Yes," Jill replied. "I'm just in town for the wedding. I'm from Pittsburgh."

"It's a great city," Evan said. "I go to Pittsburgh for seminars and that sort of thing on a pretty regular basis." Evan looked hesitantly toward Thom, and Thom put an arm over Jill's shoulder. She almost laughed.

"It's nice to meet you, Evan," Jill said. "We

should probably go find our seats before the ceremony starts."

"Absolutely. Nice to meet you," Evan replied.

"You were posturing with him," Jill whispered as they made their way up the aisle.

"Are you interested in Dr. G?" Thom whispered back.

"No."

"Because if you are, I could step back," he said, but the way he was walking next to her, his hand on the small of her back, didn't match his words.

Jill rolled her eyes and slid into the seats reserved for the immediate family at the front.

Her mother was already seated there, as well as Aunt Belinda. Dad would be waiting to walk Elsa down the aisle. Jill leaned over to squeeze her mother's hand.

"Is Elsa ready?" Jill whispered.

Her mother nodded. "The pictures are done, and she's just sitting with the bridesmaids, waiting."

Just then, a bridesmaid swept up and bent down next to Jill and Thom. It was Alison, one of her sister's best friends. Jill started to smile, but then saw the worried look on the young woman's face.

"Have you seen Sean?" Alison whispered.

Jill shook her head. "No, why?"

"The photographer wants to take a few shots with him and his brothers before the ceremony," she replied. "We can't find him!"

"But he arrived at the church, right?" Jill asked.

"Yes, Elsa and Sean arrived together. Then Elsa got into her dress here at the church, and Sean…has made himself scarce."

"What's happening?" Jill's mother whispered, scooting over so that she could hear.

"They can't find Sean," Jill whispered back, and her mother's face paled.

Jill looked over at Thom, and he shrugged and said, "Let's go look."

Even if this was the only real date they had, Jill was glad that Thom was with her. There was something very solid and reassuring about him in the midst of family stress, and she reached out and took his hand. He twined his fingers through hers and stood up, tugging her to her feet.

"We'll go look," she repeated to Alison, and she shot her mother a reassuring look. "He's got to be somewhere. Don't worry."

As they headed back down the aisle, hand in hand, Jill spotted Evan Gregorson sitting in a pew a few rows back. Behind him, the Osbornes were seated, Kent with his arm around his wife, looking at the order of service together. Evan looked up, and so did Meghan. Jill smiled at each of them as they carried on past. With Thom at her side, his hand holding hers, and the warmth from his arm emanating against her, she felt safe, warm, protected.

Let her enjoy this for a little while. It was a rare enough experience in her life, and it would likely be a long time before she got to enjoy this again.

THOM HAD NOTICED how Evan watched him and Jill, his attention sliding down to their handholding. Yeah, let him gawk. If Jill gave Dr. G a chance later, fine. But if she moved to Danke for the podiatrist and not him, that was going to hurt.

At least neither he nor Jill had been given any pity today. He was glad to see that her family was watching them in mild surprise and approval instead of some misplaced sympathy, as if being single was terminal.

Jill's hand felt good in his, though, as they slipped back down the aisle together. He shouldn't have twined their fingers like this—not because it didn't fit the image of "dating" that they were putting out there for the day, but because his heart seemed to twine along with his fingers. She felt so good tucked in next to him, her high heels tapping against the church's hardwood floor.

"Let's check the basement," Jill said, "then work our way up…and then outside. There's got to be a bunch of Sunday school rooms down there that might have a brooding groom inside them."

Thom smiled wryly. "Good point."

They headed down the stairs and into the basement. There were a few women down there lined up outside a bathroom, and they slipped past. It was probably best not to announce that the groom was temporarily missing. That was how rumors started.

The doors were all unlocked, and they peeked into each one without success. Jill led them back upstairs and through a swinging door that opened onto the sanctuary again, as well as an outside door. Jill pushed that one open, and she shivered in a blast of cold air. Thom looked over her shoulder and there Sean was, standing not too far away from the church, his hands in his pockets, some snow clinging to his hair, and Mae standing close to him.

Thom and Jill exchanged a look. Very likely, her family would expect her to march out there and make it right, but this situation was delicate.

"Let me talk to him," Thom said quietly.

Jill nodded, and he slipped past her, out onto the paved parking lot.

"Sean!" Thom called.

His friend turned, and he looked a little flustered. Mae's face pinked, then blanched when she saw Jill. She scurried away. Yeah, she'd better watch her step when it came to Jill's sister's wedding.

"Everything okay?" Thom asked as he reached him.

"Yeah…yeah." Sean frowned in Mae's direction thoughtfully.

"Are you getting married today?" Thom asked quietly, getting right to the question that really mattered.

"Of course," Sean said. "Why would you ask that?"

"All right." Thom rubbed his hands over his face. "I'm going to tell you straight what no one else seems to want to tell you. Mae has feelings for you. She has had for years. And if you're going to unload some prewedding jitters with someone, it shouldn't be her."

Sean shook his head. "We're good friends. That's all."

"That's all it is on your side," Thom replied. "Everyone else knows it, man. I'm just telling you what everyone knows, and you don't want to see. Your wedding starts in what—" he glanced at his watch "—fifteen minutes, and the photographer is looking for you to do a few last-minute pictures. And you're outside have a tête-à-tête with one of your best female friends. Elsa is the bride, and as such, she's under a tremendous amount of stress right now. She knows exactly how Mae feels about you, and if she saw this it would really upset her."

"She's just stressed out with the wedding," Sean said.

"No, I mean you'd break her heart." Thom caught his friend's eye. "You're getting married. You're choosing Elsa, and this friendship with Mae is going to have to change if you want a wife. Period."

Sean looked in Mae's direction, and Thom did, too. The young woman was staring at Sean with misery in her eyes. She had her arms wrapped around herself, her cream-colored shawl doing little to warm her in this cold. Jill stood next to her, her fur wrap settled over her shoulders elegantly, looking generally annoyed.

"Oh, my God…" Sean murmured.

That look on Mae's face was hard to mistake. What had she been saying to Sean out here before his wedding? What little seeds of doubt had she been planting?

"Yeah, you see it now?" Thom asked. "Now, you've been head over heels in love with Elsa and you haven't noticed any other woman fawning after you. That's to your credit up until now. But now that you have seen it with Mae, you have no more excuses."

"Right. Wow." Sean sucked in a breath. "Should I go talk to her? Tell her I'm marrying Elsa and that's that?"

"No," Thom said. "You don't have time to make a big scene with your fiancée's bridesmaid! You should get yourself back to your dressing room with your brothers, get some really nice photos of those final touches of getting ready and go take lifelong vows with your bride. Mae knows what's happening here. She's very clear on that. Jill will take care of her. Elsa is your priority from here on out. Go make this a day that Elsa looks back on with the fondest of memories for the rest of her life."

"You're right," Sean said. "Look, man, thanks for just—saying it."

"No problem." Sean started back toward the church, and Thom raised his voice slightly to be heard. "And congratulations, man. I'm happy for you."

Sean grinned and headed straight for the door. Mae moved as if to say something to him, but he didn't pause, just hurried inside.

The women followed him into the warm church and when Thom got inside, he overheard Jill's soft words.

"You're beautiful, young and have a whole life ahead of you," Jill was saying. "Remember my advice? Find some cute guy at the wedding and dance with him. Pining is a waste of time. Okay?"

Mae nodded, and she slipped away, tears in her eyes.

"I feel a little bad for her," Jill said softly. "But only a little. She's going to feel incredibly foolish about all of this a year from now."

"Yeah, she probably will," he agreed. "Let's go find our seats, and when Sean and Elsa are legally married, you owe me a dance."

Jill looked up at him, a surprised smile on her lips. The soft scent of her perfume wrapped around him like a ghostly embrace, and his heart nearly stuttered to a stop. Dang. She'd have to stop doing that, or he'd lose the last shred of self-control he had and fall headlong in love with her.

THE WEDDING WAS BEAUTIFUL, and Jill sat next to Thom with a lump in her throat as she watched her sister walk down the aisle, her hand in the crook of their father's arm. Dad came back to sit with the rest of the family after giving Elsa away, and he probably shed more tears than Donna and Belinda combined.

Elsa glowed—there was no other way to describe her. She was absolutely transcendent in her flowing white gown with a gauzy veil that let just the sparkle of her diamond earrings flash through. Jill's little sister—married to the man she loved. Seeing this day was worth all the discomfort of being the single older sister.

Thom was a warm, reassuring presence through the ceremony, and she angled her knees against his leg as Elsa and Sean said the vows they'd prepared and signed the paperwork with the minister.

Then came the recessional, and they all went outside to cheer and throw birdseed, and it was over.

A couple of hours' worth of photos would happen next, which Jill needed to be present for, and she and Thom agreed to meet at the reception after.

Danke's largest hotel was small by city standards, and the ballroom was rather cozy, but Elsa had put together a lovely combination of fairy lights, evergreen boughs and crystals that hung like glittering icicles from the greenery. The Valentine's Day theme was evident with a cupid ice sculpture and red rose centerpieces at every table.

Much later that evening, after all the toasts and speeches were completed, after the first dance between the bride and groom, and all the teary hugs and congratulations were over, Jill and Thom sat together at an empty table. All the other family members had spread around the room visiting, leaving just the two of them with wadded napkins and empty wineglasses. Evan was seated with two other couples whom he seemed to know, and she'd noticed that he'd chatted with them throughout the evening. The Osbornes left after a polite amount of time, and

Kent came over to say goodbye before he had. A sign that all was going to move forward professionally the way she'd hoped.

Aunt Belinda and most of the older folks had left around the same time the Osbornes did, including her parents. Jill might have left then, too, if it hadn't been for Thom. Staying just a little bit longer seemed right with him at her side.

"So what do you think?" Thom asked, reaching over and squeezing her hand. "Did we survive this wedding with dignity?"

"I think we did," she said. "Thank you for doing this for me, Thom. It couldn't have come together any better. All of it."

"They're an inspiration, aren't they?" His gaze moved to the front of the room where Elsa and Sean were dancing with eyes only for each other.

"Yeah...in spite of it all, I think they'll last," Jill said.

"I agree." He looked back over at Jill. "So... you owe me a dance."

"I'm not much of a dancer," she said.

"That's okay. I'll make up for it," he replied. "Besides, this is what couples do, you know."

There were a few couples on the dance floor.

Mae sat at the head table alone, leaning on her elbows. She'd been a good sport, after all, and even gave a lovely toast to the bride and groom.

"Dance with me," Thom said, his voice low, and with every ounce of her being, she longed to say yes. But if she got out onto that dance floor with him, she was going to let go of the last sliver of emotional reserve she had. Weddings were emotional enough without her developing impossible feelings for a handsome guy in Danke. This fake relationship would have to come to a very real end.

"Would you do me a favor?" she asked, and she had to swallow a lump down in her throat.

"Sure. Anything."

"Ask Mae to dance."

Thom blinked at her. "What?"

"She's alone over there. Tonight is the worst night of her adult life, I'm willing to bet, and she did right by my sister, after all." Jill nodded toward the slim woman with sad eyes. "Ask her to dance. It's the decent thing to do."

"You really want that?" he asked.

She nodded. "Yes, please."

"Okay." Thom scraped his chair back and

stood. He caught her eye just once, then saun-
tered across the ballroom to the head table.

It would be better for Thom and Mae to
dance. It might even be good for the both of
them. They wanted a life in Danke; they were
both available...and hate it as she would to see
Thom dance with another woman, it was probably good for Jill, too.

Whatever Thom said, this wasn't a real date.
This was an arrangement. It was better to face
that cold fact. She sucked in a shaky breath.
She should go home...she'd put enough time
into this reception, hadn't she?

Thom wound his way through the chatting
people, and she watched Mae's surprised expression. Then the younger woman nodded and
stood up, taking Thom's hand. The song playing was a slow one—Jill's goodwill had im-
peccable timing, it would seem—and he pulled
her into his arms and started to dance.

He was a good dancer, and Mae looked de-
lighted.

This had better count for some amazing
karma or something, because this hurt more
than she thought it would.

She gathered up her purse and faux mink
wrap and was about to slip out when she saw

Thom dance Mae over to Evan's table. Thom stopped, leaned down, said something and Evan stood up and took Thom's place. Mae and Evan both seemed a bit baffled, but there was a smile on Dr. G's face that showed exactly how he felt about this turn of events.

Thom ambled back over to her.

"You were going to run out on me?" he asked, gesturing to her purse and wrap. "Seriously?"

"I thought—"

"I saw the way he's been watching her all evening," Thom said. "Trust me. I just did them a favor. If they end up married next summer, I want credit." He held out a hand to her. "I was serious about that dance."

"I'm not a good dancer," she admitted, her face warming.

"It's a slow dance," he said. "You can't mess it up. We'll just slow it down farther." He beckoned, his hand still held out to her. "Come on."

Jill put her fingers in his, and he tugged her to her feet with an impish grin. He led her onto the dance floor and pulled her into his arms. Her hand rested on a muscular shoulder, and he held her other hand gently in his, cupped over his chest. She could feel the tremble of his heartbeat so close to her fingertips.

"See?" he said softly. "Not so bad, is it?"

"Not so bad," she murmured.

He held her close, definitely leading, and she settled in against him. He made it seem easy, which was credit to him and she knew it.

"Were you really going to throw me at Mae and leave?" he asked.

"I thought I'd do you a favor," she said, and for some reason her voice caught.

"Hey—I'm with the woman I want to be with tonight, okay?" he said. "I meant it when I said this is a real date. Even if it's only for tonight. When I take a woman out, she gets the best of me...and I don't go dancing with other women."

She didn't know what to say. He was looking down at her with those dark, smoldering eyes, and it was like every thought had drained from her head. This was the kind of evening she was too afraid to dream of for herself, because dreaming of something only made it hurt more when it couldn't be hers.

"Okay?" he prompted.

"Okay."

The music changed to a heartrending ballad, and perhaps it was the champagne, or the long day, or the emotion of it all, but she felt herself blinking back tears.

"Are you okay?" He slowed down farther, stopped, still holding her close against him.

"Yeah... No."

"Is it me?"

"It's all of this," she said. "It's too impossibly perfect. The ideal Valentine's Day that no one's going to be able to top now. You stole it."

"Stole it?" A smile touched his lips. "Are you saying I just set the bar that every other guy after me is going to have to compete with?"

"I think you did," she whispered. And she hated and loved it at the same time. A night like this one wasn't going to be easy to beat...

"Good." He released her fingers and touched her chin, tipping her face up, and then lowered his lips over hers.

She hadn't expected him to kiss her right here in the open, but she didn't pull back. The music swirled around them as they kissed. His breath tickled her face, and his lips tasted ever so faintly of wedding cake.

When he pulled back, he kept her against him, and she tipped her cheek against his shoulder as they continued to dance. Somehow, she didn't want to go home anymore. She didn't want to go back to reality, or to work, or even the crisp, clean sheets at Aunt Belinda's bed-and-breakfast, because then she'd have to face her own loneliness. It was better to stay in his arms and forget that there was any reality waiting for her at all…

For a little while longer.

CHAPTER FIFTEEN

SNOW HAD STARTED to fall again as Jill climbed into Thom's passenger seat. The flakes through the golden glow of streetlights settling on the vehicles around them. This Valentine's Day had been better than she'd anticipated. She'd thought that she'd have her sister's wedding, some family chitchat and then an early evening at Aunt Belinda's place. Instead, she'd spent the evening in Thom's arms, dancing to anything the DJ played.

Her legs were cold, and she tugged her faux fur wrap a little closer around her as she waited for the cab to warm up while Thom brushed fluffy snow off the windshield. Soon, he got into the truck, too, and he reached over and took her hand.

"I should have warmed the truck up for you," he said.

"It's okay."

She wouldn't have wanted to sit in the hotel lobby waiting, susceptible to more family chatting—though this time she was no longer nervous about receiving pity. Now it was a new fear—the questions about her tall, handsome date whom she had absolutely no future with.

Thom released her hand and put the truck into gear. Jill looked over at the handsome man next to her. His truck still smelled faintly of cut wood, and somehow that was comforting. A nice suit didn't change everything.

"So what do you think?" he asked. "Did we succeed in stamping out the pity tonight?"

"I think we did." She chuckled. "Thank you, Thom."

"Hey, it was my pleasure." He shot her a warm smile. "I like dancing with you."

"I'm a terrible dancer," she said.

"All I need is for you to sway with me," he said. "And you did just fine."

She felt her face warm, and she hated it. In the boardroom, she had ice in her veins—nothing fazed her and nothing made her blush. But here in a truck with Thom Miller, she couldn't find her composure.

"What about you?" she said. "You won't have the pity of your community, either. Maybe they'll stop talking about your ex."

"Instead, they'll be talking about you." He smiled over at her. "Thank you for that."

Deal done. Mission accomplished. They'd gotten to know each other so that it wouldn't be a lie, and here she was in the passenger side of his rumbling pickup truck, feeling illogically heartbroken that it was over.

"You okay?" Thom asked.

"Yeah… I'm fine. Just tired, I guess."

They drove in silence for a few miles, out of town and onto the narrow highway that led to the Butternut Bed and Breakfast. The falling snow that splattered against the windshield was whipped away by the wipers.

"So what's next?" Thom asked as he slowed for Butternut Drive.

"I guess I go home and get back to work," she said. "Kent will make an appointment at the office. So that's a good thing."

"What about us?" he asked. "Any plans to come back out and visit? Maybe a little springtime weekend getaway?"

That was too tempting. If she came out to see him, whatever was forming between them would grow roots, and when they were ripped out, it would only hurt more.

"Uh—" She swallowed. "No, probably not."

"Oh." He looked over at her, then made the turn onto Butternut. "Look, if I went too far tonight—"

"It's not that." She shook her head. "Tonight was really wonderful. I'll never forget it, and it absolutely will be the bar no man can reach from now on."

"So why not come visit?" he asked softly. "It's beautiful out here in the spring. Even when it rains. I'll schedule in some time off."

He was going to think she didn't feel anything at all, and she didn't want that, either. "Thom, I can't come see you. Not for quite a while. This has been—" she looked over at him as he slowed in front of her aunt's drive "—it's been really great, and I've loved it, probably more than I should. But I'm getting my priorities all jumbled up."

"Meaning?" His expression was somber as he pulled to a stop in front of the dark house. For a moment they sat in silence, the engine rumbling comfortingly beneath them.

"Meaning, I don't want to end up like Mae, pining after a man I have no business being with." She swallowed. The last time she'd felt like this, she'd found out her boyfriend was married. She knew how to cut things off when she needed to…so why wasn't this easier? "Thom, you're a really incredible man, and we have an easy connection. If I come back and visit you, my emotions are going to get involved, and—"

"Only then?" Thom asked, his voice low, and she looked back at him to find that dark gaze locked on her face. "You don't feel anything now?"

"Yes, I feel something now!" Why was he pushing this? "That's the problem! Would you let me have some dignity here? I feel foolish enough as it is!"

"Why?" he demanded. "You feel something. What's so wrong with that?"

"Because we want different lives, Thom! We aren't kids. We can't just follow a feeling. You have a life you love here where you are deeply respected, and you have a real place in this community. That matters. You know what you want. And I have the same thing back in Pittsburgh. We aren't just starting out. We have fully fleshed-out lives!"

"Yeah, yeah…" He caught her hand in his warm, calloused grasp. "But forget the logic right now. I want to know what you feel for me."

His dark eyes were pinned on her, and his thumb stroked the top of her hand gently. She could melt into a moment like this…just like the dancing, but with just their hands clasped.

She could forget everything around her all for the gentle touch of his fingers on hers.

"I feel—" She felt her eyes mist. "I feel like if I keep going down this path, I'm heading for heartbreak."

"Because your heart's involved," he said softly.

"For crying out loud, Thom!" She pressed her lips together. "Yes, my heart's involved! I've already fallen for you, okay? And I need some space away from you to get myself sorted out!"

Thom didn't answer, and she looked toward the house, the windows dark except for a soft glow in the kitchen. Was her aunt up? She should go inside before she said anything else she'd regret, but Thom hadn't let go of her hand, and she couldn't bring herself to pull it back.

"For whatever it's worth," Thom said softly, "I've fallen for you, too. I meant it when I said that was a real date. This isn't playacting for me anymore."

"That's not helpful," she whispered.

"Why not?" he asked. "You want me to make it easier for you to walk away?"

"I kind of do!" She leaned against the headrest. "This is the kind of thing that makes sense when you're twenty-one…not now."

"Well, all I can give you is the truth," Thom said. "I've felt something with you that I've never felt before, and I don't want to just let it go. I want to see you again."

"Thom…"

"I do. I want you to come back and spend time with me. I want to take you for long walks, and curl up with you in front of my fireplace. I want to take you skating again, and take you out for dinner, or one of those amazing burgers. I want to see you, Jill. I want to hold your hand, and kiss you, and—"

"Thom!" Her voice felt choked with emotion. "Stop playing with this!"

"I'm not playing!" he shot back. "I'm in love with you!"

Jill blinked. "What?"

"I'm—" He shut his eyes. "I didn't mean to say that."

"You love me?" she whispered.

"I know it makes me seem like an idiot," he said softly. "I know it. This is fast. I've recently gotten out of a serious relationship. I look pathetic."

Was it so pathetic to feel something organic and real for each other? Wasn't this what people longed for—this kind of connection that just dropped on them one day when they least expected it?

"No!" She reached out and put her hand against his chest. His heart was hammering against her fingertips. "You're not pathetic." She sucked in a wavering breath. "If you are, then so am I. I'm in love with you, too."

Now it was out. Maybe they were both fools. She couldn't let him imagine that she thought he was anything but noble and sweet and good. But that didn't make him the right man for her, either.

"You love me, too?" Thom said, almost afraid he'd misheard her.

Jill's hair was a little disheveled now from an evening of dancing and then the cold winter wind. Her makeup was muted, her lipstick long gone. The impressive woman dressed to kill was now relaxed into a softer version of herself, and he couldn't help the way his entire chest felt tugged toward her.

Her eyes shining with unshed tears, Jill said, "This turned out to be something real, and I don't think either of us expected that."

Thom certainly hadn't. He'd been doing a favor for his client's niece and fending off well-meaning pity for himself—nothing more. At first. But that had changed, and he felt a surge of relief that it wasn't only he who was wading through these engulfing feelings.

"Then why are you pushing me away?" he asked.

"Because our feelings for each other don't change anything that matters! Your life is here—your *soul* is here. You grow wide and deep, remember? You've got something in Danke that doesn't come along every day. I know that. And I've got one thing I'm good at…and I get to do it in Pittsburgh. I'm not some young woman just starting out. I've worked for something—achieved something! So have you."

He did grow deep. He was most stable with the wide-open spaces around him where his roots could spread out, give him balance and an unshakable strength. And Jill…she soared overhead. They were from different worlds.

"I know exactly what you're saying, but that doesn't erase what I feel," he said.

"Me, neither." She licked her lips. "I know you wouldn't consider moving for Natasha, and I'm sure it's too much for me to ask you to consider it for me, but…you might like the city, Thom."

"I've visited," he said quietly. "My brother lives there, remember?"

She nodded. How Thom wished he could tell her that he'd do it—he'd pull up those roots of his and go where she was comfortable and happy. But Thom knew himself, too, and those city sidewalks, the looming buildings, the crush of traffic…

"I fall for the wrong women," he said, his throat tight.

"I've fallen for the wrong men before, too," she said. "But you're a good one. You're honest, and kind and really, really decent. It'll make it harder for me to forget you."

Thom pulled her fingers up to his lips and pressed a kiss against them. "We could be friends."

"Could we?"

He pushed her hair away from her face and bent down, catching her lips with his. She leaned into his embrace, then broke off the kiss with a ragged breath.

"Friends don't do that, Thom…"

He shut his eyes against the goodbye he knew was coming. "I know."

But somehow, after dancing with her tonight, his heart had closed around her. It was far too fast. But it had happened before he even realized it, and it was too late to pull himself back.

Was this what he really wanted—to fall in love with another woman who couldn't see herself living the life he longed for? Did he want to be the one who sacrificed everything he'd worked for? But this wasn't just any relationship—this would be for Jill...

It was tempting—deeply, deeply tempting—the thought of pulling her into his arms every night and having her close. It would soothe that jagged, aching part of his heart, but it would cause other problems. He wasn't thinking straight. Thom had been down this road before, albeit not with someone who made him feel this tangle of emotion so powerfully or so quickly... Still, he knew how it ended.

"I don't think just being friends will work," he said, and getting the words out was like pulling out a piece of himself. But he had to be honest. "I'm not going to be able to respect that line."

"Me, neither." She squeezed his hand tightly.

"So what do we do?" he asked.

Jill was silent for a miserable minute. She looked down at their hands, their fingers entwined as seemed to happen without Thom ever thinking about it.

"We go back to our lives," she said hollowly. "You…enjoy this community, and help Eli with his coop and meet someone wonderful."

"And you?" he asked.

"I'll…go back to the city, back to my job, my apartment," she said quietly. "And I'll put some real effort into meeting someone, too. Maybe I'll sign up with Kent Osborne's dating app."

"Very logical," he murmured. Very specific. He didn't want to think about either of them moving on.

"Yes, but that's the only way to do this!" she said, and irritation flashed in her gaze. "We've both had painful breakups. We know how to get over these things. You just keep marching forward. It gets easier." She let out a shaky breath. "Eventually."

"Eventually." He let go of her hand and she pulled it into her lap.

The soft light grew behind the closed kitchen curtain. Suddenly, the fabric pulled back and Belinda's pale face appeared, lit with a hand-held lamp.

"Thom, I'm not just brushing you aside. But I'm going to do my best to stop loving you. Okay?"

"Yeah." He felt tears rising up inside him, and he blocked them off with effort. "Yeah... You should do that."

Thom wanted to say more than that—to say that there was some stupid, stubborn part of him that hoped she'd choose a life here in Amish Country. A life with him. He wanted to say that whatever guy managed to earn her heart would be lucky, and he'd loathe the guy on principle. But he didn't.

Jill pushed open the truck door, and the dome light illuminated their miserable faces.

"How much longer are you here for?" he asked.

"A couple more days," she replied.

He should stay away, then. He should give her her space.

The side door to the house opened and Belinda appeared, wrapped in a thick white bathrobe. Her hair was covered in a blue handkerchief, but she had her glasses on.

"Goodbye, Thom." Jill slipped down, and the door banged shut behind her.

He opened his door, ready to at least get Jill safely to the step in her high heels, but then, the Amish woman's gaze moved from Jill to Thom. Her mouth opened in a silent "oh" and Belinda put a hand over her heart, her eyes flooding with sympathy. Yeah, so much for hiding it. But then Belinda was a matchmaker, so maybe she had a better insight than most.

Belinda put an arm around Jill's shoulders as she came into the house, and the door shut solidly after them.

Thom pulled his door shut, leaving him in darkness. The light in the kitchen glowed comfortingly, but the curtains remained closed, and his heart felt like it had crumpled inside him.

He put the truck into Reverse, turned around and drove back up to Butternut Drive.

He'd fallen in love with the wrong woman again, and this time he didn't think he'd recover easily. This time the feelings came from the most honest places in their hearts. There was no hiding, no deception. And even with all of it laid out before them, there was no solution.

When Thom got home, he headed inside the house and leaned against the counter in his darkened kitchen. He pulled out his cell phone and glanced down at it. He had a text message from his brother: Call me when you get this. In the morning is fine.

He wasn't in the mood for this, but it was better than just sitting here alone in heartbreak on Valentine's night. It was almost 12:30, but the text had been sent ten minutes ago. So he grudgingly hit his brother's number. Mike picked up on the second ring.

"Hi," Mike said.

"Hey...shouldn't you be in bed?" Thom asked.

"Janelle and I just got back from dinner and a movie," Mike said. "I didn't know if you'd be up or not."

"Yeah, I'm up," Thom replied. "So...what's going on?"

"Well, you dominated our conversation this Valentine's Day, thank you very much," Mike said wryly. "Janelle figures I did you wrong."

"How so?" Thom asked, and he rubbed a hand over his tired eyes.

"She says I owe you a proper explanation," Mike replied. "Why we're moving and all that."

"Okay. So why are you moving?" Thom didn't have the energy to watch his tone.

"I'm doing it for Janelle," Mike said. "You remember that student of mine who caused all that drama for me, saying she was in love with me and all that?"

"Yeah."

"Well, she's back, and she's taken two of my classes. When I announced I was leaving Pennsylvania, it was a message to her. I haven't done anything wrong, but this woman is causing a lot of stress for my wife, and when I was offered a better position in Georgia…well, we decided to do it."

"You're doing it for your marriage," Thom said. "That's a good reason."

"Yeah, I think so, too," Mike said. "It's just embarrassing. This is my reputation at stake. I'm sure this will be enough for the message to get through, but if this student shows up in Georgia, I can get a restraining order against her."

"Right…" Thom exhaled a slow breath. "So am I going to see you before you go?"

"If you want."

"I'm having a pretty rough night tonight," Thom said. "So I'm just going to say this straight. Tiptoeing around hasn't helped, anyway. What happened between us? We used to be close, and now we're just about strangers. I find out you're moving from a buddy on the street. And while it hurt, it didn't actually surprise me."

"I don't know…we're just different people."

"We're also family," Thom said. "Is this because I was there when Janelle almost left you? Is this a pride thing? I saw you at a tough moment, so you won't look me in the face again?"

"No."

"Then what is it?" Thom demanded.

"I don't need my little brother to be my friend!" Mike shot back. "Remember when you were my only friend in school when I went back after being sick?"

"I guess."

"I swore I'd never let that happen again."

"Don't you have friends? At work or in your neighborhood?" Thom's heart thudded in his ears, his mind spinning with this new information.

"A few. But…not like you do in Danke. With that whole community accepting you."

"I don't remember being your *only* friend," Thom said. "But I remember us being best friends that year."

His brother was silent.

"Look, at this age friends are great additions to our lives," Thom went on. "But they come and go. They're there for a while. They move on with their lives. The people who are solid for a lifetime—most of the time, that's family. I don't see the shame in that, Mike. I really don't."

"Well, I saw it as failure. I don't need my little brother's pity."

"You never had my pity," Thom replied, a

lump in his throat. Pity was the very thing he'd been trying to avoid, too. "That was the best year of my childhood. I thought I was going to lose my brother—and then you got better. You have no idea what that meant to me."

"Well, it's different being the one who got better, and whose life was on hold for a year. I guess that feeling of everything passing me by stuck with me. When Janelle and I got married, we eloped," Mike said. "We considered a wedding, but she had like eight friends who'd have to be bridesmaids, and I had...you."

An imbalance. Thom went deep and wide... he had a community, people, a support network. And his brother had gone high, and the higher he'd gotten, the more his support network had fallen away.

"I guess I understand that," Thom admitted.

"I still felt like I haven't caught up to what my life should have been," Mike said. "I'm just saying it isn't really about you. I was trying to sort out my own stuff."

Thom picked up the school photo his mother had sent him from the counter and looked down at his brother's adolescent face. They'd had different lives, different hopes, different paths...but Mike was still his brother.

"Hey, this isn't all on me," Mike said. "It's not like you wanted any help from me, either. I kept trying to give you a hand for years."

"A hand?" Thom barked out a laugh. "It sounded pretty condescending when you offered your advice about how my life in Danke could be fixed to match your expectations."

"You're smart, Thom. You could have gone to college, but—"

"It's not about brains. I could have gone to college, but I wanted to work in carpentry. That's it."

"Well…" His brother paused. "I'm sorry about that. I was trying to find common ground, and to be your older brother. I'm supposed to help you, not the other way around."

But if there was one part of Thom's life that Mike would have truly approved of, it would have been Jill. Mike would have seen what Thom saw—a once-in-a-lifetime kind of woman. Was Thom being a fool by refusing to change to be with a woman like her?

"What if there was something you could help me with?" Thom said slowly, the idea not even fully formed yet.

"Like what?"

"I'm not sure, but I might want to start up

another branch of my carpentry business," Thom said. "But it would be tough starting in Pittsburgh. I don't have connections there, besides you."

"Yeah, I have a lot of colleagues looking for quality contractors," Mike said. "An honest, reliable contractor is like gold these days. I could introduce you. You'd be booked up through the next calendar year. Why? You're actually considering moving?"

"I'm not sure yet," Thom said.

"Is everything okay?" Mike asked.

"I'm not sure about that, either," Thom admitted.

Uprooting a life and starting up a new business in a brand-new city wasn't easy...or quick. Would he still be the guy Jill loved in Pittsburgh, or would it change things? This would be a massive risk for his life, his livelihood and what he had with Jill. He hadn't been willing to do this for any other woman, but Jill was a cut above.

"Well, if you're looking to hang your shingle in Pittsburgh, I could help you with that," Mike said. "I could recommend you to a lot of people before I move, at the very least."

"You want a hand moving?" It was the

only thing Thom could think of to offer, but he wanted to give his brother something, too.

"I'm hiring a company," his brother replied.

"Right." Of course. He felt that old sweep of frustration.

"But if you wanted to come for dinner one of these days, it would be great to see you again," Mike said, his tone softening. "I know the kids would be really happy to see you, too. I've missed having a brother."

So had Thom.

"Sure. That would be great."

"Okay, then…" There was silence for a moment, and Thom could hear the distant voice of his brother's wife in the background.

"Go have a nice evening with Janelle," Thom said.

"Thanks. You have a good night, too."

Thom hung up and looked at his phone thoughtfully. Maybe it was time to start helping each other again…and asking for help, too. Thom probably needed to change in that respect as much as Mike did. They were awfully alike in their determination to be self-reliant.

When Thom sat down with his brother, he'd tell him about Jill—tell his brother the honest truth about how much love could hurt, and how much he wished he could give Jill everything she wanted.

Honesty could heal wounds.

And maybe, it could make new beginnings… Maybe.

CHAPTER SIXTEEN

THE NEXT MORNING when Jill woke up, light was already streaming past the bedroom curtains. She'd overslept, and she felt hollowed out after a night of crying. She shouldn't feel this heartbroken—at least that was what she kept trying to tell herself—but she did.

Her phone pinged—she'd missed a couple of texts from work. That must be what had woken her, and she checked the messages. One coworker was telling her about some office gossip. Leila James was ready to retire.

Leila was a partner and creative director at the agency…and that would leave a spot open for a new partner to move up and take her place. If the rumor was true, that would be an exciting step up—the very step up she'd been preparing for.

This was the sort of thing she needed to focus on—next steps in her career. But somehow, this morning it just didn't thrill her the way it normally did. Out here in Amish Country with the wide-open fields, the blowing snow, the wood-stoves pumping heat into the house…there were different priorities, and the corporate ladder felt very far away.

But at least Valentine's Day was over, and she could get past all the romantic hopes and go straight to the discounted chocolate. She'd need it this year.

Jill got dressed into a pair of jeans and a cozy cream sweater. She pulled on socks and slippers, and then checked herself in the mirror. Her eyes looked tired and red from crying, and her cheeks were pale. Her hair was limp, and she pulled it back into a ponytail. She had no one to impress today.

When she got downstairs, her aunt wasn't alone. Nellie sat at the kitchen table, and she had her hands folded tightly in front of her.

"Oh, Jill, dear, you're up," Belinda said. "How are you feeling this morning? Is it better in the light of day?"

Last night her aunt had stayed up with her for another hour, talking over her feelings for Thom. But even with an hour of Amish wisdom, she couldn't see a way to make it work.

"Not really," she admitted. "But time will help."

Nellie looked over at her in surprise. "Did you turn down a proposal?"

"What?" Jill shook her head and leaned against the new countertop. "No, that's not really how it works for us. But I did fall in love with a man I can't be with. And I'm…sad."

Nellie nodded sympathetically. "I'm sorry about that."

"Thanks."

Belinda came to the table with a plate of carrot muffins, and she put it down in the center.

"Our Nellie has a choice to make," Belinda said.

"Freeman's proposal," Jill said softly. Would there be a wedding for this well-meaning young woman? Jill hoped so.

"Not only Freeman's proposal," Nellie said. "Mark Yoder came to my place last night, and he took me out for a drive in his buggy. He said he wanted to talk to me seriously about something. I thought he'd ask my advice about a girl, but…" Her face reddened.

"He wants to marry you," Jill surmised.

"*Yah*. He said he's loved me for ages, and I just never saw him that way. He's two years younger than me."

"That doesn't add up to much when you're an adult," Belinda said.

"I know…but he was always just a boy to me, you know? He was skinny and short for such a long time. And I have to admit, we've been getting to know each other over the last year, and I have started to notice he was awfully kind. The problem was me being older than him. That's kind of a big deal for us. The girl is normally younger. I didn't think he'd see me like that…"

"Tell her the rest," Belinda said with a smile.

"Well," Nellie said, "he said he loved me, and he said he knows he's not a farmer, but he's got a good job. Then he kissed me."

"And how was the kiss?" Jill asked with a small smile. This was a detail that mattered in these sorts of decisions.

"It was… Oh, it was wonderful. I suppose I realized with that kiss that Mark has well and truly grown up. And that maybe he's not so much younger than me, after all. That was a grown man's kiss, and I don't mind admitting that I melted."

Good for Mark. Jill was glad he'd finally gotten the courage to tell Nellie how he felt. And it sounded like he did more than tell her in words, too.

"And he proposed?" Jill asked. "In so many words?"

"*Yah.* He said I know him rather well now, and that I can see what kind of man he is. If I chose him, he'd marry me as soon as I'd let him, and he'd love me the way he figures I should be loved—with his whole heart."

"Wow…" Jill put a hand over her chest. "And?"

"And now she has to choose," Belinda said. "Mark, Freeman, or neither of them."

"If I marry Freeman, I get the farm," Nellie said. "And he's so handsome, and he seems very decent."

"And Mark?" Jill asked.

Nellie's cheeks flamed again. "If I marry Mark, the farm goes to my sister. But…but he loves me. He really does… Freeman doesn't even know me. But Mark—if you could see the way he looked at me…and we talked for hours. It was different than other times we've talked. This time it was…talk with a real purpose. We discussed the kind of life we could have together, and the children we could raise, and he said he'd take me riding every Sunday, even after we're married. He said he'd never forget what I gave up for him, if I chose him."

"He really loves you," Jill said softly.

Nellie nodded. *"Yah."*

"And how do you feel about him?" Belinda prompted.

"I think I love him, too," Nellie said. "But my *daet* wants me to marry Freeman. He and *Mamm* have their hearts set on it. They met him, and they say he's the kind of man they want for me."

"Did you tell them about Mark?" Belinda asked.

She shook her head. "I didn't say anything… I wanted to keep that private."

Jill stood up and went to the window. The snow was drifting down, and she could see Eli tramping along the fence line with *Hund* in tow. Belinda and Nellie fell back into Pennsylvania Dutch as they discussed Nellie's options. A good and decent farmer who would make her a rather rich woman when she inherited the family farm, or a poorer plumber who just loved her.

Romance wasn't simple. Nellie had to choose the lifestyle she wanted versus the man she wanted to live her years with. And that was exactly what Jill was doing this morning— weighing the lifestyle she thrived in against the man she'd fallen in love with. Thom had shown her exactly the way she'd been longing to be loved, but the career and the life she'd built were a lot to give up.

Thom wanted a life here in the tiny community of Danke where all of Jill's expertise and years of climbing in her career would amount to very little. She'd worked so hard, proven herself and some exciting opportunities at her job were starting to open up. She'd worked for this!

But like Nellie, Jill had been offered a man's heart.

She pulled out her cell phone and looked down at the screen. She'd told Thom that she'd do her best to forget him, and her own words stabbed at her now. How could she possibly forget him?

She typed him a text: How are you doing this morning?

Because she wasn't doing all that well, and she didn't know what she wanted to hear… maybe she just wanted to connect with him a little bit more.

Missing you, he answered.

She smiled sadly.

I'm missing you, too.

This was foolish, no doubt. She shouldn't play with emotions this strong, especially since she knew she couldn't just cast aside everything she'd worked for.

"Jill?" Belinda said.

Jill turned around to find her great-aunt and Nellie looking at her expectantly.

"Sorry, I didn't hear what you said," Jill said.

"I was wondering if you could message Thom for us," Belinda said. "Nellie needs to talk to Mark, and we thought Thom might be able to track him down faster than we can."

"Have you made up your mind?" Jill asked Nellie.

"I love him," Nellie said, tears in her eyes. "I know I won't get the farm, but marriage isn't about land, anyway. It's about a home, and a kitchen and two people who love each other. I don't need acres and acres for that. Kitchens aren't that big."

Jill smiled at the image. "You'd give up the farm for Mark?"

Nellie nodded. "*Yah*, if he still wants to marry me, that is."

"Would you message Thom for us?" Belinda asked. "Or would that be too awkward?"

"It's fine," Jill said, and she sent him the message.

Thom didn't reply right away. Her phone

pinged again with another message from work this time.

"Jill, dear," Belinda said.

"Yes?" She turned, blinking back a mist of tears.

"Was that Thom?"

"No," she said. "This one is from a colleague at work. A senior partner at our advertising firm just confirmed that she's taking early retirement for her husband's health."

"Oh…" Belinda frowned. "Meaning, you might be moving up in your job?"

"Yes, that's the hope." But her enthusiasm had waned. She gave a short explanation about Leila's situation. Now it seemed that Leila had made an official announcement about her retirement.

"Rather quick, isn't it?" Belinda shook her head. "One day she's running things, and the next day they'll be slotting someone in as her replacement."

"Well, someone has to do the work," Jill said. "It's an important role. One I'd be good at."

"I don't doubt it," Belinda replied. "And I imagine they'll give it to you. I'm just speaking as an older woman, myself. It must be eye opening for Leila how quickly she'll be replaced and everything will keep rolling forward. As a woman of a certain age, that would sting."

It was true, though. Leila would be replaced within a week, and the firm would roll on. That was part of holding down a job—making sure her contribution kept her employed. And Jill loved it—her career made her feel alive most days.

Jill had been wanting to climb so that she wouldn't be replaceable, but ultimately they all were. There was one place a person was never replaceable, and that was with family. But still, she longed to use her skills, to be acknowledged for them, to earn a good income with her experience...

Did Jill really have to choose?

Maybe a better question was: Would she really put a job ahead of the man she loved?

She turned back to the window and looked out at the blowing snow. Danke was a well-kept secret out here in rural Pennsylvania. And with internet these days, remote work might be a possibility...

Everyone was replaceable, and so was she. So why not make a few of her own rules? Maybe she could find a way to have everything she longed for, starting with a life built with Thom Miller.

THOM SAT IN the Burger Barn, food in front of him, but his gaze was on a little Amish family in a booth across from him. The woman in her white *kapp* was wiping a toddler's face with a napkin. Her husband sat across from her with two little kids next to him. His hat was off, and Thom could see it balanced on his knee under the table. The wife said something, and the husband smiled.

It was that smile that caught Thom's attention. Regardless of culture or language, love looked the same, and that man was in love.

The waitress came to check if he needed anything, and Thom thanked her then looked back down at a meal that would normally be salve on a tough day. But he didn't think it would help. It was the day after Valentine's Day—this was supposed to be easier now. And with any other woman, it would be.

But Jill was special in every possible way.

He didn't even notice Eli had come into the restaurant until the old man slid into the seat opposite him.

"Eli," Thom said in surprise. "How are you?"

"Oh, not too bad," he replied. "I ordered some food to go. I wanted to bring something to Belinda. Is Jill still there?"

"Yep." He dropped his gaze to the food in front of him. "She's leaving town tomorrow."

"Hmm." Eli nodded. "And why aren't you over there, too? If I know Belinda at all, she'd feed you."

"Jill and I aren't… We're…" How to explain what happened this past week?

"Are you so determined to let her go?" Eli asked, squinting at him.

"I have to," Thom said. "Look, Eli. I've done this before. I've been with a woman whose heart was in the city. And she eventually just left. There's love, and then there's the pragmatics that make love work in an actual relationship. You need both."

"I wouldn't really know about all that," Eli said. "I'm just an old bachelor."

"A bachelor ordering food for a woman he loves," Thom said.

Eli tapped the side of his nose. "I've got a long game in mind."

"Oh, yeah?" Thom asked with a tired smile. "How's it going to work?"

"I've got to show her what life would be like with me," Eli said. "So far she figures she'd be trying to civilize a wild goat. And I can understand why she thinks it. But I have to show her that with me, her life will be better, easier. That my love will be good for her."

Thom was silent, watching the emotions flicker across the old man's face.

"She's watched me be a real bother for many years," Eli went on. "She's seen me angry and belligerent. She's seen me stubborn. She's seen me foolish. And I can't deny any of that, so it will take time to convince her that I'm also capable of being faithful, loving and strong for her. I might be old, but I'm still a man."

"Good for you," Thom said quietly.

"Belinda is a strong woman," Eli said. "And showing her everything I see—including the possibilities for us together—will take time. That's just a fact."

Thom looked down at the food on his plate, but his mind was spinning.

"You have to have a vision, Thom," Eli said, tapping his temple. "You have to see the picture of what you want in your own head before you can show it to her. And I have a vision."

Every time he thought of a woman by his side, he thought of Jill. No one else would do. She'd said that he'd set the bar for her next romance, but she'd done worse for him. She'd made it so that he couldn't imagine being with anyone else…a whole lot like old Eli here, who was in love with Belinda and determined to play the long game.

"We Amish have a saying," Eli said. "We say that life and marriage are long."

"Okay…" Thom pulled himself out of his thoughts.

"I don't know much about marriage," Eli said. "But I know about a long life. It's felt longer still without the woman I love. I figure I've got the time to convince her. And I'm holding out. There isn't anyone else I want, anyway. Never was."

Life and marriage were both long…with any luck. And if Thom wanted a beautiful long life with Jill, it might mean stepping out of his comfort zone, accepting his brother's help, doing the tough thing and starting a business in the city…and letting Jill shine. Who knew? Maybe they could move back to Danke when kids came into the picture.

Life was long, right?

"I love her," Thom said quietly, more to himself than to Eli.

"Then what are you going to do about it?" Eli asked. "Because me? I'm gonna win over

Belinda one of these days. Mark my words. I'll marry her."

Thom chuckled. "I believe you, Eli. You want this meal? I'm going to head out."

"Oh, don't mind if I do…" Eli looked hungrily down at the plate that Thom slid in front of him.

Thom pulled out a couple of bills to pay and left them on the table, then he gave Eli a nod, and he slid out of the booth.

A long game didn't mean giving up everything he loved. But it did mean a bit of waiting for all of it to come together. A life with Jill was the part he couldn't wait on. He headed out to the truck, and when he glanced down at his phone, he noticed a missed text from Jill.

Nellie has decided on Mark. He proposed to her last night and she wants to say yes. Wondering if you could pass the message along that she wants to see him?

So Mark was getting his chance with Nellie… Good for him. Love was getting a win out here in Amish Country, and if Thom had any luck at all, he'd get his chance at a life with Jill, too.

I'll see if I can find him, Thom texted. I'll bring him for dinner, if I can. And I need to talk to you, too, Jill.

Because he loved her, and he'd just decided now that he had a long game to play.

CHAPTER SEVENTEEN

JILL STOOD AT the fence with a pocketful of carrots for the horse and the donkey. She broke a carrot in half and offered half to each animal.

As they chewed noisily, her aunt's words spun through her head, as did Nellie's decision. Nellie was choosing love, and she'd watch her sister and her sister's husband run that farm. She'd never be a farmer's wife. She wouldn't have a full paid off farm to leave to her children. She'd never be the woman she'd imagined that she'd be. Ever.

She'd be a plumber's wife—and a happy one, at that.

Eeyore nudged at her pocket, and she pulled out another carrot, snapping it in half. Eeyore gobbled up his half, and the horse took the other. Inside the house Nellie and Belinda were talking over tea.

Belinda wanted to be sure that Nellie knew what she was doing. Deep down Jill was pretty sure that Belinda wanted Nellie to choose Freeman—he was the farmer she'd found for her, after all. With Freeman came the land, but Nellie was certain. Mark was her choice.

Thom's truck came up the drive. Mark hopped out first, looking so pale he might faint.

"You okay?" Jill called to him.

"Is… Is Nellie inside?" he asked.

"Yes, go on in," Jill replied.

Mark nodded quickly and headed toward the door. Aunt Belinda would get the engagement for Nellie; it just wouldn't be the one she was angling for. Thom got out of the truck more slowly, and once Mark was inside the house, he came over to where she stood.

Eeyore stretched his neck and grabbed the last carrot from Jill's pocket, and she smiled at the silly donkey.

"Hi," she said, looking up at Thom.

"Hi…" He bent down and caught her lips with his. For a moment she stood there, the winter breeze whipping around them, his lips on hers. Then he pulled back. "Okay, so I tried to rehearse this in my head on the way over, but Mark just would not stop talking."

Jill smiled ruefully. "He's about to get his girl in there."

"Lucky guy." Thom grinned.

"Okay, so…just say it."

"I love you," he said.

"You texted me that." She met his gaze, and he rolled his eyes.

"Yeah. I did. But I mean it. I love you, and Eli has a strange amount of Amish marriage wisdom for a confirmed bachelor, but he said that life and marriage are long. And it got me to thinking…"

"About marriage?" Her voice sounded strange in her own ears.

"Yeah, about marriage." He caught her hand. "I want a life out here in Danke, but you've got your whole career in Pittsburgh. The thing is we have a lot of time to explore our options. And if you want to live in Pittsburgh to start, I'm okay with that."

"Long distance?" she asked with a frown.

"Together." Thom tugged her closer and put his hands on her cheeks, looking down into her face. "Here's what I'm thinking—we get married, and then we figure it out as we go. Maybe we start out in the city and when we have kids we come back here. Who knows? All I'm saying is, I want a life with you, Jill. I want the long haul with you. I want to belong to each other."

"You'd move for me?" she whispered.

"Yeah."

"You wouldn't do it for anyone else, though…"

"No, I wouldn't," he replied. "But I'd do it for you."

Tears misted her eyes. "Because I was thinking, too. And if you want to live out here, there might be a way for me to make that work. I could work remotely, and go into the city for specific meetings with clients. I talked to Leila about the possibility, and she thought it would be doable. I mean, she's leaving, but she said the other partners really want me, so… Maybe I could schedule them on Mondays or something. Maybe I could start up my own business. Or… I don't know. I just want a life with you, too, Thom. I want to go skating with you, and take walks with you, and…and… I don't know, stand in the kitchen and make toast with you!"

"Toast sounds great." His eyes misted, and he blinked.

"I thought so, too." The thought of doing daily minutia with this man sounded just about perfect. "So what do we do?"

"Well…" He licked his lips. "I'm thinking we admit that this is real, and we take it from there. No fake dating. Solid plans together."

"Real ones?" she asked.

"Like I said, I couldn't exactly rehearse it with Mark talking the entire time, second-guessing if Nellie would even want him," he said with a low laugh. "But yes, I want a future with you. I want to get married. But if it's all the same to you, can we skip the two years of wedding planning and just do something small?"

"Yes!" Jill said, and he slid his arms around her.

He lowered his lips over hers and kissed her slowly. When she pulled back, he said, "I'm going to hold you to that when the time comes. Let's go figure out how this is going to work."

The door opened to the house, and Nellie stood beaming out at them, her hands clasped in front of her. Mark stood behind, a hand on her shoulder—quite a bit of PDA for an Amish couple.

"Do you have news?" Jill asked.

"Yah!" Nellie said. "We're getting married! But it's a big secret for our community until they read the banns just before the wedding, so you have to be sworn to secrecy. I just had to tell someone!"

Jill grinned back at the young woman, then looked up at Thom, her eyes wet with tears. They'd figure it out from there...but an image in her mind had started to form of Mr. and Mrs. Miller, and she was seeing Pennsylvania farmland surrounding them, and Amish neighbors and Aunt Belinda's sound advice. It also had a good Wi-Fi connection, Zoom calls and many, many more ad campaigns for her future clients.

"Thom, let's start out here in Danke," she said.

"You mean that?" he asked, frowning.

"Yes, I do."

"If you change your mind, that's okay, too," he said. "Just don't bail on me. I don't think I could take it."

Jill laughed softly. "I'm not bailing on us, Thom. That's a promise."

Because she had a feeling that out here, she wouldn't be quite so easily replaced...not in Thom's heart, and not with her family, either.

They had a long, long time building a life together and settling into each other's arms, and she couldn't wait to start.

EPILOGUE

TRUE TO THEIR AGREEMENT, Jill and Thom planned a small and simple wedding out in Amish Country in May when the snow was gone, and buds were forming on the trees. They hadn't needed much time to sort out the details of their future. They rented a local barn that was often used as a wedding venue, and the ceremony and reception were both to be held there. Elsa and their mother had almost fully taken over the details, and Jill didn't mind a bit. They had good taste, and she was busy enough getting her job transitioned over to work from Danke.

There were also some Amish cousins who'd volunteered to give a hand in wedding preparations, and Jill had been surprised and touched. Aunt Belinda had been doing some work behind the scenes. They said she was family, and they knew a thing or two about weddings. So those family connections were starting, too, and Jill couldn't help but feel grateful for every single one of them.

Elsa would be Jill's maid of honor, and Mike was going to stand with Thom. Just one on each side—the ones who were closest to them. This was going to be a wedding boiled down to the essentials.

The night before the wedding, Jill and Thom were invited over to Aunt Belinda's house for pie. Belinda had a night free from her paying guests, which was rare these days, because while Jill hadn't done an official advertising campaign for her aunt, her tales of the peace and tranquility that this Amish community had to offer had flown around her colleagues and friends in Pittsburgh, and Butternut Bed and Breakfast was booked solid for the next few months. Ironically enough, the Amish way of doing business with word of mouth worked, just as Belinda said it would.

When Jill and Thom arrived, Aunt Belinda bustled them inside with smiles and hugs. She settled them down with cups of tea and large pieces of cherry pie, fresh from the oven.

"I had to give you your wedding quilt!" Aunt Belinda said. "This is a very important Amish tradition. A bride normally works on her own wedding quilt for months before her wedding, stitching it with the help of her sisters and friends. But I know it's a little different for you, dear, so I thought you might appreciate a quilt stitched by me…and a few of your aunts and cousins pitched in to finish it on time."

Belinda pulled out a package wrapped in paper, and Jill swallowed her bite of pie and accepted it with a smile of thanks.

"Aunty, this is really wonderful," Jill said, and she opened the paper up to reveal an intricately stitched quilt done in the wedding ring pattern. Belinda had used greens and pinks for a fresh spring look for the quilt, and the tiny white stitches were almost invisible. Jill ran her fingers over the intricate workmanship.

"Thank you so much, Aunt Belinda," Thom said. He'd immediately jumped from Miss Belinda to Aunt Belinda the minute their engagement was announced, and it suited both of them just fine.

"You're very welcome," Belinda said with a smile. "Now, this quilt is going to come with some good old Amish marriage advice, too. After you're married, you need to sort things out on your own, and I wouldn't dream of meddling between a married couple. But now, the night before your wedding, I can tell you what I know."

"Please do," Jill said earnestly.

"I was hoping you'd say that." Belinda's expression sobered. "I want you to memorize how you feel for each other tonight. I want you to go through your wedding tomorrow, and remember how much you're willing to sacrifice for each other, just to have a life together. Because marriage isn't easy. It comes with a great amount of giving, and loving and learning how to put another person first. The level of selflessness that a good marriage requires doesn't come naturally to anyone—Amish or English. But if you can remember how much you were willing to give on this night before your wedding, it will make everything else easier as you move forward in your marriage."

"That's good advice," Thom said, and he reached over and squeezed Jill's hand. "Because I'd just about move heaven and earth for her."

And he had. Thom had been working hard to put together an office in the spare bedroom of his house for Jill so she could work remotely.

Belinda's cheeks pinked a little bit, and she looked away as Thom leaned over and gave Jill a peck on the lips.

"Marriage is long," Belinda said, pretending she hadn't seen. "You'll go through so many things together—joys, disappointments, children, grandchildren, great-grandchildren...

You'll age together, grow a little bit fat together and you'll become deeper, better versions of yourselves together, too. Marriage is long. And when there are hard times, and you get frustrated with each other, I want you to remember that. There is so much more ahead of you that is worth fighting for."

Jill looked over at Thom—his mop of curly hair, his dark eyes, his strong hands—and she felt how her heart had filled with love for this man.

"We'll remember that," Jill said.

"Good. That's my advice." Belinda nodded toward their plates of pie. "Now, eat up. You think you'll eat tomorrow, but you probably won't get much into you."

In that moment, as they ate their pie and drank tea, and Jill could feel Thom's knee pressed affectionately against hers under the table, she did just as Aunt Belinda had advised, and she tucked this memory away into her heart for safekeeping.

Because she loved Thom with every atom of her being, and she couldn't wait to start a life with him. She knew just how precious love like this was... She would be a little more patient, a little more giving and she'd never take this man for granted.

That was her silent promise to herself.

Tomorrow she'd give a different kind of vow in front of their closest friends and family. And with her "I do" would come her entire future. She couldn't wait to see what life had in store for them.

* * * * *

Don't miss the next book in Patricia Johns's
The Butternut Amish B&B miniseries,
coming July 2023 from
Harlequin Heartwarming.

Get 4 FREE REWARDS!

We'll send you 2 FREE Books plus 2 FREE Mystery Gifts.

FREE Value Over **$20**

Both the **Love Inspired®** and **Love Inspired® Suspense** series feature compelling novels filled with inspirational romance, faith, forgiveness and hope.

Get 4 FREE REWARDS!

We'll send you 2 FREE Books plus 2 FREE Mystery Gifts.

FREE Value Over **$20**

Both the **Harlequin® Special Edition** and **Harlequin® Heartwarming™** series series feature compelling novels filled with stories of love and strength where the bonds of friendship, family and community unite.

YES! Please send me 2 FREE novels from the Harlequin Special Edition or Harlequin Heartwarming series and my 2 FREE gifts (gifts are worth about $10 retail). After receiving them, if I don't wish to receive any more books, I can return the shipping statement marked "cancel." If I don't cancel, I will receive 6 brand-new Harlequin Special Edition books every month and be billed just $5.49 each in the U.S. or $6.24 each in Canada, a savings of at least 12% off the cover price, or 4 brand-new Harlequin Heartwarming Larger-Print books every month and be billed just $6.24 each in the U.S. or $6.74 each in Canada, a savings of at least 19% off the cover price. It's quite a bargain! Shipping and handling is just 50¢ per book in the U.S. and $1.25 per book in Canada.* I understand that accepting the 2 free books and gifts places me under no obligation to buy anything. I can always return a shipment and cancel at any time by calling the number below. The free books and gifts are mine to keep no matter what I decide.

Choose one: ☐ **Harlequin Special Edition**
(235/335 HDN GRJV)
☐ **Harlequin Heartwarming Larger-Print**
(161/361 HDN GRJV)

Name (please print)

Address   Apt. #

City   State/Province   Zip/Postal Code

Email: Please check this box ☐ if you would like to receive newsletters and promotional emails from Harlequin Enterprises ULC and its affiliates. You can unsubscribe anytime.

Mail to the **Harlequin Reader Service:**
IN U.S.A.: P.O. Box 1341, Buffalo, NY 14240-8531
IN CANADA: P.O. Box 603, Fort Erie, Ontario L2A 5X3

Want to try 2 free books from another series! Call 1-800-873-8635 or visit www.ReaderService.com.

*Terms and prices subject to change without notice. Prices do not include sales taxes, which will be charged (if applicable) based on your state or country of residence. Canadian residents will be charged applicable taxes. Offer not valid in Quebec. This offer is limited to one order per household. Books received may not be as shown. Not valid for current subscribers to the Harlequin Special Edition or Harlequin Heartwarming series. All orders subject to approval. Credit or debit balances in a customer's account(s) may be offset by any other outstanding balance owed by or to the customer. Please allow 4 to 6 weeks for delivery. Offer available while quantities last.

Your Privacy—Your information is being collected by Harlequin Enterprises ULC, operating as Harlequin Reader Service. For a complete summary of the information we collect, how we use this information and to whom it is disclosed, please visit our privacy notice located at corporate.harlequin.com/privacy-notice. From time to time we may also exchange your personal information with reputable third parties. If you wish to opt out of this sharing of your personal information, please visit readerservice.com/consumerschoice or call 1-800-873-8635. **Notice to California Residents**—Under California law, you have specific rights to control and access your data. For more information on these rights and how to exercise them, visit corporate.harlequin.com/california-privacy.

HSEHW22R3

COUNTRY LEGACY COLLECTION

19 FREE BOOKS IN ALL!

EMMETT
Diana Palmer

COURTED BY THE COWBOY

THE RANCHER AND THE BABY
Marie Ferrarella

Cowboys, adventure and romance await you in this new collection! Enjoy superb reading all year long with books by bestselling authors like Diana Palmer, Sasha Summers and Marie Ferrarella!

#467 HER SURPRISE COWBOY GROOM
Wishing Well Springs • by Cathy McDavid

Laurel's career ambitions keep her safe; after almost losing her business, she is cautious about letting Max and his adorable twin daughters into her life. Until she is faced with the choice to grow her business...or her family.

#468 A FAMILY FOR THE RODEO COWBOY
The Montana Carters • by Jen Gilroy

Former rodeo cowboy Cole Carter returns to his family's Montana ranch to start over. The first step: organize a cowboy challenge with animal physiotherapist and single mom Mel McNeil. But the real challenge is holding on to his heart...

#469 CAUGHT BY THE COWGIRL
Rodeo Stars of Violet Ridge • by Tanya Agler

All Kelsea wants from former rodeo cowboy Will is for him to put wind turbines on his ranch—and save her new sales job at EverWind. Until she begins feeling at home in the cozy Colorado town...and with Will, too...

#470 THE FIREFIGHTER'S RESCUE
Love, Oregon • by Anna Grace

Running kids' Cowboy Camp will be enough of a challenge for Dr. Maisy Martin without working with thrill-seeking firefighter Bowman Wallace! A childhood tragedy has left her wanting a stable, predictable life. But there's nothing predictable about falling in love...

HWCNM0323

HARLEQUIN
PLUS

Try the best multimedia subscription service for romance readers like you!

Read, Watch and Play.

Experience the easiest way to get the romance content you crave.

Start your **FREE TRIAL** at
<u>www.harlequinplus.com/freetrial</u>.